RAVEN MORRIS

Flirting with Thirty

THE INTERNET DATING CHRONICLES

MERJINN PRESS

PHILADELPHIA, PENNSYLVANIA

This series is dedicated to all the intrepid singles out there. All the best in your search!

CHAPTER ONE

"Hello, beautiful."

Now that was a greeting.

I sat at my desk in my home office and adjusted the monitor so I could read the tiny print above the instant message window on the internet dating site—the internet dating site I was wondering why in the hell I'd even bothered with. I didn't even *want* to date.

And, hell, I'd left my profile open since I'd checked it before my run and shower this morning. Nothing said desperate like leaving the thing open for hours.

"How are you?"

Mr. LAX7615, age thirty-three, was hot if the picture could be believed.

Thirty-three? Thirty-*three*? The guy "hello"-ing me was sixteen years younger than I was. This was *exactly* why I should never have signed on and paid money to join this site.

"???"

Geez, the guy was persistent.

My fingers hovered over the keyboard. *Don't do this, Dana Mallory Jenkins-Smith. Not a good idea.*

Probably, but I had, after all, paid my hundred and fifty bucks for six months. Might as well get something out of it and if an ego boost was my reward, well, hey, we could all use one of those.

I started typing: *"I'm wondering why a thirty-three-year-old is IM'ing a forty-nine-year-old."* I paused over the Send button then added, *"I'm old enough to be your babysitter."*

I hit Send. Poor misguided guy must have missed my age. I mean, I knew it was a decent picture of me, but sixteen years was still sixteen years and he was closer to thirty while I was knocking on fifty's door.

"I always had a thing for the babysitter."

Um… Okay. So that was how this was going to go.

"And my best friend's mom."

Oh boy. Here it comes.

The thing was, this guy didn't know what I did for a living. I wrote romance, specifically, erotic romance. I wrote the fantasies people had but didn't act on. I certainly didn't, but I didn't have any trouble writing them. And here was one just *begging* to be put to paper.

I straightened my back and flexed my fingers. Game on. *"Was your friend's name Stacey?"*

"Huh?"

Oh, geez. The age gap was showing already. *"Your friend. Was her name Stacey? You know, like the song?"*

"No. But her mom was hot."

"That must have been, um, interesting. Did your friend ever know?"

"No."

Okay, obviously the guy wasn't the most verbal. Which led me to wonder, again, why he was IM'ing a woman my age.

"But she knew."

Strike my last comment. *"The mom knew you had a crush on her?"*

"Yup."

"How?"

I waited a couple of heartbeats, then watched his answer appear on the screen.

"I took her panties."

Well there was a one-liner I hadn't seen coming.

But the response I had in line would probably surprise him, too.

My fingers again hovered over the keyboard. I so shouldn't do this. I'd only joined this site in a moment of drunken self-pity, and if I hadn't been on my tablet and they hadn't taken PayPal, I would've had to get out of bed to find my credit card and therefore, would've come to my senses. But they did, so I hadn't, and here I was with an online profile and a hot thirty-three year old flirting with me.

What the hell. A woman only lived once and since the ex had left, there hadn't been much "living," so why not say it?

My fingers, typists that they were, flew over the keys. *"With your teeth?"*

His IM screen went blank for few moments. Long enough that one of us had to restart the conversation.

I waited. We'd see if this guy had the *cojones* he thought he had to come back and finish this. Poor thing, he really had no idea who he was dealing with. Comments like this didn't embarrass me.

Well, in a book, they didn't embarrass me. But asking such a personal question for real...? I was glad this conversation was via computer.

"I'm not sure I should answer that."

Chicken. He could dish it out, but couldn't take it. Oh, well. Time to get back to work.

I typed *Bye* and was about to hit Send when his window lit up again.

"Unless you really want to know."

Houston, we have a live one.

I'd been having a bit of writer's block—or summertime sloth—and this might just be the thing I needed to kick start the creative process.

Lord knew, it was kick starting something else.

It'd been a long, lonely three years.

I sat up straighter in my chair, tossed my long brown hair that was normally up in a clip over my shoulder, and planted my feet firmly on the ground. *"Either you did and think I might be scandalized, or you didn't and don't want to admit you missed an opportunity."*

I got a good chuckle when he didn't respond in time to prevent the IM window from closing again.

He opened a new one. *"Did anyone ever do that to you?"*

The guy was good. *"What? Steal my panties or take them off with his teeth?"*

"Either."

"Steal my panties… Not that I know of. Take them off with their teeth? I'm not an old hag here. I've had my share of fun."

"So what's your favorite pair?"

"My favorite pair of panties?" Hmm… Did I have a fetish guy on the line here?

I shrugged. If he *was* a fetish guy, it'd make for good copy—as long as it didn't get out of hand. No sense encouraging the crazies, but people did meet online. Luckily, I'd been circumspect in what I put in my profile. There was nothing to give away any personal info other than the general area of where I lived if he got too interested. Not even my first name and definitely not that I write erotic romance. What could it hurt? *"I'm thinking that's on a need-to-know basis."*

"Well, then… I need to know."

"And that would be because…?"

"So I can practice."

Um… yeah, that worked. It worked very well. So well, that I was the one who let the IM window close this time.

Another window popped up. *"You still with me?"*

Hell yeah, baby, I was still with him.

Not that he needed to know. *"Sorry, got a text. Had to answer."*

Call me a mood killer, but I had to slow this down. I'd forgotten what it was like to be young and on the prowl.

Hell, I'd forgotten what it was like to be on the prowl. I may have been single for three years, but I'd been *un*single for twenty-three. And while sex, I'd been told, was like riding a bicycle, dating? Not even close. The last time I'd dated, the world wide web was a gleam in some geek's eye, and I doubt he was thinking about using it to date.

Then, again, maybe he had been.

"You're not going to tell me, are you? Your favorite panties? I'm guessing you wear boycuts."

"No woman should ever wear lingerie with the word 'boy' in them." Because unless you were built like a pre-pubescent boy with no hips and no curves, those things wouldn't stay up. And what heterosexual guy wanted a pre-pubescent boy?

"Not a thong, then?"

Butt dental floss? Hardly. *"They don't qualify as panties."*

"Then I'm going with bikinis."

After four kids? I wasn't going to disillusion the guy. It wasn't as if we'd ever meet. *"Bingo, Yahtzee."*

"Yahtzee?"

Oh geez, the age gap thing. *"Never mind."*

"So do they have ties on the side, or little elastic bands because I can't see someone who looks like you having the fabric all the way around."

Yeah, sure, why not? *"Ties."* After all, we were talking about him taking them off with his teeth—

Wait. Hold on. Holy crap. I was talking to some strange youngster about him taking off my panties with his teeth.

I shifted in my chair and had to count to ten to get my bearings back. This was only a game. *Online.* I was never going to meet this guy, so I could be whatever and whoever I wanted because he'd never know. And anyway, he was probably some *schlump* who'd used a picture of a good-looking guy as his avatar. None of our conversation was real.

Wish I'd thought of that. My picture was my real one. One of the shots I'd rejected for my author photo, thank goodness. But still, recognizable should he ever stumble onto my name.

First thing when we were finished with this conversation, I was changing that photo. Because, seriously, I wasn't actually on the site to date anyone. I'd signed up in a pity-me moment— wine had been involved—when I'd wanted to not be so lonely.

I'd since learned to steer clear of drunken pity-me moments with wine. Now I either got totally annihilated on the stuff so that I fell right to sleep when I got home, or I hung with water.

More often than not these days, I was a water baby. With my kids out and about at night and on weekends, and the ex nowhere in sight, I was the sole parent. If I had drunken nights, those would be the ones where the cops would show up to tell me my kid had been in an accident and I had to go to the hospital, or my kids would text me to come get them somewhere because their ride had stranded them and I wouldn't be able to drive. Some role-model parent I'd be.

Yes, the prick-who-left had not only stolen my marriage, my future, and my partner, he'd also taken my chance for fun and relaxation. I really liked wine.

So, dammit, if I couldn't have fun the inebriated way, at least I could amuse myself with this guy's sexy conversation. And, hell, I might even get a book out of it…

Man, if I'd known this guy was going to give such good text, I would've been copying and pasting the messages. But, unfortunately, I hadn't. And I couldn't because when the window disappeared, so did the text.

I wasn't going to let that happen again, so I started with my last line.

Ties.

"Satin or cotton?"

Well, duh, that was an easy one. Who had fantasies about cotton anything? *"Satin."*

"Thick or thin?"

I couldn't resist. *"That's what she said."*

"LOL. I deserved that."

Yes, sweetie, you certainly did.

"So?????"

Yup, guy was definitely persistent. But he hadn't met Cyber-Dana.

I gave my fingers free rein. *"Your turn. Thick or thin?"*

Oh my God, did I really just type that?

"Thick, baby. Of course."

Well, yeah. That'd be a *duh* question too. What was he going to say, shrink-aged and shriveled?

"You're really hot, you know."

Right now I certainly was. And I hadn't started menopause yet. *"Thank you."*

"No, thank you. I didn't think you'd respond."

"So why'd you IM me?"

"Because you're hot."

"It's just one picture. How do you know I didn't have it touched up?"

"Did you?"

"Well, no, but you don't know that."

"I do now."

This guy was good. I had a feeling he was a charmer in real life. Which made me wonder why he needed a dating site. Thirty-three was prime dating age these days. A couple hours at a bar looking like he did, and he'd have filled his little black book with phone numbers and Facebook pages.

"Why are you on here?" I figured if we'd gotten to the point of him removing my satin-tied bikinis with his teeth, I could ask him a few personal questions. Besides, it'd be characterization for a new book.

"Same reason as you. To find someone."

Well, no, that wasn't exactly true. I wasn't looking for anyone. I was, in fact, enjoying being single and not having to deal with relationship issues. I liked not having to consider anyone else or ask someone's opinion or make schedules work.

Except for those times when I didn't.

I flexed my fingers, then put them to work. *"I find it hard to believe that someone who looks like you and, being the age you are, couldn't find someone on one night out."*

"It's always a crapshoot. You never know if you're Mr. Right or Mr. Right Now. On this site, with the profile thing, you get to see what people want before you approach them."

"You read my profile?"

"Duh."

That made me sit back. He wasn't actually saying that he was interested in me, was he? That he liked what he saw on my profile? I'd been thinking that he saw the picture, saw that I was online, and just figured he'd have fun with an old broad. I hadn't imagined he'd actually read anything about me.

"I like what you have to say."

I immediately opened another window to bring up my profile to see what was so fascinating that a young guy would consider giving up prime family-rearing years to talk to me because, at my age, there was *no* way I was starting a new family. The one I already had was more than enough.

I scanned my profile.

Single mom looking for someone to have fun with. Movies, dinner, dancing, maybe even some travel. Just hanging out. Going to games. Watching TV. I'm fairly low-key, but clean up nice when I have to. Looking for a friend, a partner, not someone I have to take care of. Been there, done that.

Hmmm, some bitterness showing through perhaps? I'd have to edit this again.

I love the beach and the mountains, winter more than summer, eating out or ordering in, but can cook when the spirit moves me. Sharing the small victories in life and celebrating the big ones. Love my kids and my pets, though not always in that order.

I was counting on my kids never reading that. Then again, I hadn't told them I'd joined a dating site. I hadn't told anyone; Mr. LAX7615 was the only one who knew.

I scrolled down to read the last line.

Not into motorcycles, and golf can be your getaway, but I'm game for almost anything else.

Uh oh, was that the line that'd gotten to him? Me being game for almost anything else? What *else* did he think I was talking about? I'd had something along the lines of a sunrise hot air balloon ride in mind when I'd written that, not sex with a stranger. *"Um, not so sure what you think you read, but you might have misinterpreted a few things."*

"I like the beach and mountains too."

I shook my head. He was purposely being obtuse. *"Not that."*

"I can't cook, so eating out is the norm for me. The fact that you can cook is a plus in my book."

"Not that either."

"I'm sure your kids will understand when you choose the dog over them."

"Nope. Guess again."

"I'm not a golf fan either."

He was going to make me say it.

And since this was Cyber-Dana's conversation, I could. *"It's the taking care of someone thing. I'm not doing that again."*

"What makes you think you'd have to with me?"

Hmm, I thought he'd zero in on *anything else.*

Well, I certainly wasn't going to. So I picked something else. Something that actually *was* an issue. *"Our age difference. I have more life experience than you."*

"Honey, you have no idea what my life has been like. I bet I could run circles around you in that department, so let's not jump to conclusions, okay?"

I sat back again. That almost sounded… real. Adult. Mature. As if he really was interested in a relationship.

But with a woman my age? I (obviously) wasn't born yesterday.

I brought up his profile.

Life's too short to waste. I'm tired of the bars, hate getting fixed up by well-meaning friends, and approaching interesting women on the street has gotten me slapped more times than I care to admit. The single life isn't all it's cracked up to be and I'm done with it. When I find that special lady, I want to spend as much time with her as I can so I need to find her now. Someone who's secure in herself, can laugh at the crap, knows how to love and isn't afraid to do it.

It didn't sound like a fake profile.

"What do you do for a living?" I asked. He hadn't filled

out that section or the income level. Not that I needed a certain income level in my next potential partner; my writing provided very nicely for me and the kids. But I also wanted to make sure any guy I was with wasn't looking for a handout. Been there, done that. Had the T-shirt ripped right off my back in the divorce.

"I work online."

"So you play video games?"

"LOL. Good one."

I noticed he didn't correct me, and given that it was ten thirty in the morning on a Tuesday and he was online flirting with someone old enough to be his babysitter, video games didn't seem so far-fetched.

"What do you *do for a living?"*

I always dreaded this question. Not that I'm ashamed of what I do—hell, no. It pays enough that I don't have to deal with corporate bullshit. Plus, I get to work in my pajamas, which, sadly, aren't the satin teddies people like to imagine. More often than not, I'm writing the hot scenes in my books wearing a ratty T-shirt, my hair clipped haphazardly to my head, and a glass of cranberry juice next to me on the desk. Such is the life of a best-selling author.

No, the reason I dreaded this question was the reaction I typically got. First there was the, "Um… oh…" thing because erotic romance author wasn't on a list of college majors. Though after the success of *Fifty Shades*, maybe it should be.

If someone made it past the um-oh… stage, then there was the wow-that's-really-um-interesting back-pedaling, followed by the you-can-make-a-living-at-that disbelief. Once that ice had been broken, then came the comments about sex, invariably followed by the I-can-give-you-story-ideas-if-you-run-out offer.

Um… no. Thanks. What people shared with me was almost exhibitionism. I'd learned way too many details about friends, neighbors, and acquaintances that I never wanted to know in the first place. I had to remind them that I wrote *fiction*. Which meant I made it up.

"Hello?"

Except for this. This wasn't fiction and I was making sure to copy every word that came out of LAX7615's keyboard.

"Sorry. Kid texting."

See? Fiction.

"How many do you have?"

Instantly, that question shot my guard up. I didn't post anything about my kids online. My readers knew I had kids, knew that they were at least of driving age, but that was it. No gender, no ages, no names, and no number of kids. All of that was on a need-to-know basis and some woman reading my story about a couple's fantasy life didn't need to know that.

Nor did a guy with a babysitter fetish.

"More than one, less than twenty." Standard answer and they usually got it from that.

"Ah. Mystery lady. I like that."

I was getting that impression. But it still didn't explain *why* he'd IM'd me in the first place. Looks only got a woman so far.

"Sorry, didn't mean to overstep the boundaries. Since I don't have kids, I'm not as tuned in to parents' reactions with their kids' online presence. My apologies."

"Do you want kids?" There. That would open the door to the "no way in hell am I doing this again" discussion which would put this little online flirting firmly back in its place. Forty-nine-year-old women did not start second families with thirty-three-year-old hotties they met online. Not even in one of my books.

Though, maybe…

No. I was forgetting myself. My audience read me for the fantasy. Diapers, sore nipples, and late-night feedings—not to mention lack of sex—were not what made for a hot erotic fantasy.

"Not really. I have ten nieces and nephews. Done my share of diaper-changing and emergency Heimlich maneuvers for army figurines and hot dog bites. Not really my thing. I like kids when they can hold a conversation."

"At least you're honest." He'd probably break some

twenty-nine-year-old's heart when he told her kids were off the table, but that wasn't my problem.

"*I* am *honest. No sense being disingenuous. Life's too short.*"

I was sensing a pattern here and wondered if, maybe, he didn't have a lot of life left? Was he going for it because he'd gotten a diagnosis?

I wanted to ask, but an illness seemed a little heavy to bring up with a guy who was trying to get into your satin-tied bikinis.

He's not really *trying to get into them*, I had to remind myself. This was a flirtation, nothing more.

"*You have that right. Life is too short. You never know when your life is going to skew left.*" As I knew firsthand. One day my life had been going along the path I'd carved for it and the next—wham! Ex lost his mind, got a bimbo, decided to move out, and abandoned the kids and me. Talk about a left turn…

"*Exactly. Which is why I had to contact you. I want to meet you.*"

I almost swallowed my tongue at that. Meet me? Seriously? Did he actually think that after that bikini-underwear-removal comment that I was actually going to want to meet the guy? The beauty of the Internet was that you could be invisible. Me and my (not) bikini underwear were going to stay that way.

The IM window blanked out again.

And instantly a new one popped up. "*I've either surprised you or scared you.*"

Both. But the scared part wasn't in a creepy sort of way. Because for a few seconds—enough to close down the chat window—I'd considered it.

Seriously, what would it hurt? No one knew I was online dating, so no one would know if I did meet him. Though, actually, if I decided to, I would have to tell someone in case the guy turned out to be a serial killer with babysitter fetishes.

Oh my God, I wasn't actually contemplating meeting him, was I?

CHAPTER TWO

"I don't think that's a good idea." I sat back. There. I was being responsible. Smart. A grown-up. Not some teenager who thought she'd find her Prince Charming in the first good-looking guy who wanted to take off her satin-tied bikinis with his teeth.

Damn if I didn't get just a little wet at the thought of that.

"I've scared you. Honestly, I'm not some Internet predator, but I guess you can't know that."

"It's not that." Yes, it was that. It was so that. That sort of stuff showed up all the time on the news: Suburban Housewife Missing, Only Her Satin Bikinis Mark The Spot.

I rolled my eyes at the melodrama. But seriously, if I found out that my daughter was even contemplating meeting up with some guy she'd met online, I'd lock her in her room until she turned fifty.

Yet here I was, forty-nine and free.

"Then what?"

"It's just that this has been fun, but I am, if you remember, more than a few years older than you. I don't have time for games."

"Who says this is a game?"

I smiled. The guy was definitely a charmer. *"It's certainly not real."*

"Why not?"

Seriously? Didn't we just have this discussion? *"I've never had a babysitter fantasy."*

"You ought to try it sometime. They're the best kind. More experienced woman leading a kid down the path to sexual initiation. Powerful stuff."

"Did you lose your virginity to the babysitter?"

"Maybe."

"That's just wrong."

"She wasn't my *babysitter."*

Now that made me laugh. *"You're good."*

Oh, shit. I shouldn't have typed *that.*

"Honey, I'd love to show you how good."

And that made me wetter. He really was good.

Damn. If he was this good online, I could imagine what he'd be like in person.

I was imagining it. A little too clearly.

It'd been a long freaking time since I'd gotten wet. The four dates I'd been on since the divorce hadn't done it for me and those last few times with the ex before I'd found out about the bimbo… I'd thought he was hitting the age of the little blue pill. Yeah, it'd been a while.

Oh dear Lord. Was I actually thinking about meeting up with this guy and letting him remove the satin-tied bikinis (that I'd have to run out and buy) with his teeth?

Um, yes, I believe I was.

This time when the IM window disappeared, I let it. Someone had to come to their senses and if I was relying on the timing mechanism of an online dating site, well, at least I had a plan.

"Did I scare you away?"

A plan that was shot to hell when he typed back.

I took a deep breath and flexed my fingers over the keys. I had no idea what I was going to say.

Thankfully, my indecision was saved by his action.

"Look, here's who I am." He sent me a Facebook link. *"Nothing to hide. Normal, everyday guy who saw a beautiful woman and went for it. I'm not a psychopath, no serial killing in my past or future, I have a normal family, a normal life, and I'd like to share it with someone."*

All of which sounded totally normal and reasonable.

"Whose panties I'd like to remove with my teeth."

Well he might actually get the chance because I needed to go change those panties—satin-tied or otherwise—because this guy's words were doing what the ex hadn't been able to.

Make me ache.

And throb.

And get horny as hell.

Horny enough that I clicked on his link.

Scott Masters. Lived about twenty miles away. Software engineer, bicycle enthusiast, had gone to Virginia Tech, played on a rec soccer league, and had a bunch of pictures of friends and families at various holidays and functions. His political views were in line with mine, his musical tastes ran to country which I didn't mind, and with four hundred and sixty-three friends, he wasn't friending everything in satin-tied panties, but he also wasn't a total recluse. He seemed like a guy on the up-and-up.

Who wanted to go down and dirty.

I kinda wanted to let him.

"Hello?"

My fingers tripped over themselves getting to the keyboard. *"Hi."*

"You're awfully quiet."

"I was checking you out."

"Turnabout is fair play, I guess."

"LOL."

"So does that mean you might be interested?"

Okay, so here was where I had a decision to make. If I said no, Mr. Scott Masters, thirty-three-year-old hottie would end the conversation. Of that I had no doubt. It'd be pointless to try to convince someone who wasn't interested to continue a conversation, and Scott was all about life being too short.

If, on the other hand, I said yes, well, he might expect something to happen that I wasn't planning on.

Then again, I hadn't been planning to have a panty-removal conversation when I sat down at my desk this morning.

I didn't know what I wanted to do, didn't know what I wanted, but I wasn't quite ready to end this conversation. At the very least, it was good fodder for my next book.

"I might be."

"Ah, a lady of mystery. I guess I can't get your name?"

"Not yet." Lady of mystery. I liked the sound of that. And I liked being one for the moment. It bought me some breathing space with good ol' Scott.

"Well, I have to call you something."

"No you don't. We're chatting online, no names needed."

"I meant I had to call you something for myself. In my head. When I'm picturing you after we go back to work."

"You're going to picture me when you're at work?"

"Absolutely... In my bed, on your back, with my hands on your hips and those bikinis down around your knees as I finish removing them. You're aching for me, wanting me to touch you. And I will, baby. I'll spread you open and stroke your clit until you are begging me to fuck you. And I will. Two fingers at first, pumping them inside you as you call out my name. Your back arched, your tits in the air, I'll even suck on them, tonguing your nipple as I play with your sweet pussy. Do you see that image, Mystery Lady? That's what I see in my head. You. Naked. Wanting my hands on your body. And me putting them all over you."

Bingo, Yahtzee, just like that, the guy made me come. Right there, in my chair, in my ratty T-shirt and hi-cut underwear, no masturbation involved at all, the guy rolled an orgasm through me via the computer.

Holy hell. I'd never thought that was possible, but apparently, if Scott was on the other end of the keyboard, it was.

"Hello?"

Shaky fingers crawled to my keyboard. *"Give me a minute."*

"LOL."

He knew what he'd done. Or, at the very least, he had to know how turned on I was. Frankly, I didn't care. If the guy were standing in front of me, I'd plant a big ol' kiss right on him.

As the last of the waves throbbed through me, I sucked in a couple of breaths—needed to get some air going into my lungs—then used my shaky fingers to click on his picture.

If he were standing in front of me, I'd do a hell of a lot more than kiss him. Scott Masters, LAX7615, was hot. More so now that I'd sort of spoken with him. And definitely more now that he'd given me my first non-self-induced orgasm in three years.

I enlarged his photo. He really was good-looking. Just my type. Dark curly hair a tad too long, brilliant blue eyes, a nice smile, perfect nose, and lips that said they knew what they were doing. He even had dimples which weren't a must for me, but certainly wouldn't be a reason to kick him out of bed.

I'd like to take *his* underwear off with my teeth, then take him in my mouth—thick, he'd said—and slowly suck him deep. I'd circle my tongue around the rim of his cock, delve into the slit, and taste his pre-cum before swallowing him as deeply as I could.

Holy hell, the throbbing started again and it was all I could do to clench my muscles against coming again.

Wait. Why didn't I want to come again?

I unclenched. Then I clenched again. Then, wow, another orgasm rocked through me.

"Sweetheart? You still with me?"

I didn't bother to try to answer him. Because I couldn't. My body was shuddering as I tried to get my breathing under control. That image of me with my back arched, his fingers inside me… Jesus. It was enough to make me want to toss caution to the wind and go meet the guy.

"So, was that one or two?"

The bugger knew exactly what was happening to me.

"2"

Traitorous fingers.

"Good. But I'm still one up on you."

One up— *"Were you jacking off during our conversation?"*

Hell, if the guy got me off online, I could say that sort of thing to him.

"Well, yeah. You're hot, and imagining taking your panties off doesn't exactly leave me unaffected, you know? And who are you to complain? You just got off yourself."

"I didn't get myself off. You did that."

Oh, Christ. Way to admit that.

"You weren't touching yourself?"

"Of course not."

"So you were just sitting there and you came?"

"Yes."

"Holy fuck."

Well, yeah, it had kind of been a religious experience.

"What?"

"Sweetheart, you just got off without touching yourself. My words did that?"

Oh, boy. Someone was going to get a big head—and not where it'd count.

I didn't answer. Didn't have to. It was a rhetorical question after our little discussion.

"I have to meet you."

"Why? So I can have an orgasm at dinner with you sitting across from me?"

"Sure. Why not? Think how much fun that'd be."

Did nothing faze this guy? *"I don't typically come in restaurants."*

"I wasn't thinking a restaurant. I was thinking Chinese take-out in my bed."

Damn if I didn't start throbbing again. *"That would get rather messy."*

"Baby, I want to get messy with you. With you this orgasmic, we could have a really great time together."

I'd never been this orgasmic in twenty-two years of marriage, and I was attributing it to the fact that I'd been celibate for over three years. Sitting on the washing machine could probably make me come after the lack of sex I'd been dealing with.

"I don't know you well enough."

"That's easily remedied."

For him, maybe. He was young. Me? Not at all. Four dates did not a professional dater make and the last time I'd really dated, Michael Jackson had been alive and black. Well, sort of.

"I don't know, Scott. This is new to me. I'm not sure how comfortable I am meeting a guy who gave me an orgasm before he gave me his phone number."

"I'm in the same boat. I've had three and I don't even know your name. You don't see that stopping me, do you?"

But he didn't have kids to worry about. And, God forbid, what if my friends found out? Sad as it was, in my age group, there was still a stigma attached to a sexually adventurous woman.

Not that I was being all that adventurous. But taking it to that next level, going to meet him for sex? Yeah, my friends would have a collective heart attack.

And I might have one from the orgasms alone.

Come to think of it, that wouldn't be a bad way to die.

But then there'd be the press coverage and everyone would find out. Nope. Not worth the potential scandal.

"Look, I thank you for your interest, but this just isn't me. I'm not the woman you've seen here. This was a moment out of time. An aberration." And totally his fault, but when you broke up with someone, there should be a lot of "I" statements so there wasn't any finger-pointing, and, really, this *was* all about me. *I* was the one who was uncomfortable with having had a few orgasms with a complete stranger, even if it was only online. I didn't dislike it, per se, but while it was fun for the short term, anything more was just, well, not me.

"Whoa. Hold on. Okay, you don't want to meet yet; I get that. But that doesn't have to mean we stop chatting. I'm sorry

I pushed, but I'm having a great time talking to you and I think it'd be awesome to meet in person. But if you're not comfortable with that, I can wait. You might find that I'm a good guy and want *to meet me."*

"Don't hold your breath."

"Ah, but I can. For a really long time. In ways women have enjoyed."

Damn it, but he got me wet again. These panties were toast. *"So you use your teeth to remove the satin underwear of every woman you meet online?"*

"You'd be the first."

"I find that hard to believe."

"You'd find something hard if you were at my place right now."

Jesus. It was hot in here. And considering I had the A/C cranking, that was saying something.

I glanced at the ceramic clock on the wall opposite my desk. Almost eleven. I was missing some prime writing time before the kids got up and started with the bickering. My teenagers. could suck the life right out of me, which was why I dragged my butt out of bed every summer morning at five thirty to get a full day's worth of uninterrupted writing in before they started in on me. I had about a half hour left before the zombies awoke.

And that meant this conversation had an end time. So I figured, what the hell. Might as well get as much material for the book as I could. *"Are you always this uninhibited?"*

"Meet me and find out."

Jeez, let it go already. *"I thought we already established that I'm not comfortable with that."*

"A guy can dream."

This was getting a little too real. What'd started out as something fun and momentary had now morphed to a twenty-minute conversation. And only some of it was usable in the book that was now picking at my brain. I mean, my heroine wouldn't exactly be turning this guy away. Not in erotic romance. She'd be all for meeting him.

I made the chat window smaller and resized the word document window to match it so they were side by side. I'd missed some of our conversation during the two orgasms (and who could blame me), but I wasn't going to miss anymore of what this guy was giving. Two orgasms and a potential book weren't bad for a morning's work. *"So what exactly do you dream about?"*

"You."

The guy was a better writer than me. One word, so much reaction. It had me squirming in my seat and my clit throbbing again.

Was I about to have Orgasm Number Three?

Bring it on, baby. If it worked for me, it'd work for my readers. *"You just met me. You haven't had a chance to dream about me."*

"Actually, I saw your profile a few days ago. Didn't you see that I'd checked you out?"

"I don't look at those stats."

"Why?"

"I figure if a guy's interested, he'll actually make contact. I'm not into the passive-aggressive check-out or the obnoxious 'flirts.' If you want to flirt, then flirt. Saying you want to do it isn't actually doing it."

"So I'm getting bonus points for IM'ing you."

"You're getting something."

"I want something."

"I gathered that."

"I want you."

And we were right back to making me wet and throbbing again. *"Right now, you have me."*

"Do you know what I want to do to you right now?"

Given my profession, I had a pretty good idea. Maybe even a few better ideas than he had, but this was his babysitter fantasy, so I'd let him run with it.

"Why don't you tell me?"

The IM window went down again, so I could only

assume that he was either typing out his fantasy on a document to cut and paste in a new window or jacking off.

Either one worked for me.

The window popped up full of words.

"I dream of having you in my bed, your long brown hair all over my pillow, your gorgeous green eyes half closed as the orgasm I just gave you shudders through you. Your nipples are hard, pointed from me sucking you into coming. I'll do that you, know. Play with them and only them until you're begging me to make you come. And then I'll tongue them so fast and so hard you're going to grab the sheets and hang on, gasping my name, begging me to touch you.

"But I won't. Not your clit. I don't care how swollen and wet you are, the first time is all about your tits. I want to hold them and taste them, and run my palms around and around your nipples until you're writhing on my bed, tangling the sheets around your legs."

"Mom, what's for breakfast?"

I jumped. *What's for breakfast*? One mom, fried and over easy.

Jesus. I was wrung out and hadn't even moved out of my chair.

"I have to go." God, I hated typing those words.

"Wait."

This guy's one word sentences were a powerful force.

"When can we chat again?"

Again? He wanted to do this again? Any more orgasms and I'd have a heart attack.

For a second I wondered if my ex had hired him to kill me, but then I realized my ex didn't have a clue that I could actually orgasm to death. Poor schlub. He'd missed out. And so, obviously, had I.

I didn't want to miss out on anymore of this.

Right now, in the confines of my own home, where no one but Scott Masters and I had to know, I could do this.

"Tonight? I have a full day with the kids and work." And showering and changing out my panties…

"Time?"

Oh geez, he was really pinning me down.

I wasn't so sure about that. I didn't want to be held to a time. Part of the fun of this was the spontaneity. If I had to show up at a certain point, it would seem scripted.

"How about you check back and see when I'm online. If I'm online." I didn't have to make it too easy for this guy. *"Kids. Don't know from one minute to the next when I'm available."*

That was a lie. Teenagers, especially those approaching twenty, didn't want to have anything to do with their parents, even if getting away from them meant walking to a friend's house. At some age it wasn't cool to have your mom drive you.

For the first time since the ex left, I was actually looking forward to an empty house. *Not* that I'd ever missed the ex. He wanted out? Good riddance. I had better things to do with my time.

Like "chat" with Scott.

CHAPTER THREE

I couldn't stop thinking about that chat all day.

Dropping one kid off at the pool for lifeguard duty, another at the fast food job, then getting myself to the nail studio, then to the grocery store so take-out wasn't our main staple… I just couldn't get Scott out of my head.

My body wouldn't let me forget either. He'd awakened parts that had been in hibernation for way too long.

Was it wrong that I was thinking about meeting him?

Of course it was. He was probably some psycho. A stalker. A sixty-three-year-old guy who sat home watching porn on his laptop before deciding to act on what he saw.

It was completely irresponsible—even irrational— to want to meet this guy.

He probably wouldn't even chat with me again.

***

I was more than a bit wrong about that.

I picked up my iPad off the dining room table, the catch-all place in our house for things we wanted to drop somewhere without the dogs being able to get to. Though, I'd begun to suspect as of late that the cats were bribing the dogs with treats from this table in exchange for opening the food bin in the pantry.

Too bad they didn't know what treat was awaiting me when I opened my email.

"It's been an hour and I can't get you out of my head." The email had come just as I'd left the house so I hadn't seen it before I headed out.

"Four hours since you rocked my world. I want to rock yours."

"Hey, gorgeous. I've been thinking about you all day and hope like hell you're online tonight."

Three emails by four thirty. I stared at my in-bin. Thankfully, the dating site forwarded them to my normal email program so I didn't have to go online to read them and risk another chat window showing up. One I might be tempted to open.

A new message popped into my inbox.

"You're reading my emails. Come online so we can chat."

Oh hell. I'd forgotten that a Read notice registered on the site when I opened the email.

So not only did Scott know I'd seen his emails, but so did the other dozen or so guys who'd reached out, guys I hadn't responded to. Guys with screen names like LetsMixItUp, YouFoundMe, PorscheGuy, Hotlipps1244, OneNightOfFun, HarleyBikerDude, Comeonurface—

Really? Did these guys *really* think those screen names would lure women?

I had to laugh. I'd been doing that a lot since I'd joined the site. I read their profiles—and not just the ones with the questionable taste in screen names—and I had to wonder who, exactly, they were looking for.

I mean, sure, I liked a guy who was into sports, and had outside interests, but did they really think that all women were into motocross, exercising six days a week, going to sporting events, playing pool and poker, hanging with buddies, and grilling five nights a week, while managing to do other things to do like, oh I don't know, take care of the kids, manage a home single-handedly, sleep...

But then, most of these guys were every-other-weekend

dads. No disrespect; it was what it was. But was there a constant need for them, once they came home from work, to clean up after four the-world-ends-at-the-end-of-my-nose teenagers who didn't know the meaning of the words "help out"? Or to get the kids to their jobs/games/practices/recitals on time, or run out (at ten o'clock at night) for last-minute poster board for a project due the next day, take them to doctors' appointments, and handle the everyday minutiae that didn't *quite* leave time for motor cross and playing poker...

Then there were the poets, the men who spouted lovely sonnet-like descriptions of how they were gentlemen and raised with old-fashioned values. I'd like that, I really would. But if the guy was so romantic and big-gesture-oriented, why was he divorced? Now, I knew from my own experience that sometimes the other partner just lost his mind and walked out, shattering dreams and the family. It was always possible. And it was possible for women to do it, too; mid-life crises were not gender-specific. But I was always a little leery of a guy who seemed too perfect on the page. Made me wonder what he was hiding.

Like the guy I went to dinner with who told me, as we were leaving the restaurant once we'd established we'd be having dinner again (no, we wouldn't; I'd only said we would as a polite end to the date), that he'd learned a lot about himself going through his breakup. He'd learned he'd been mean and he was working on correcting that.

Um, yeah... You might not want to bring that up on your next first date, dude, 'cause the woman will believe you've changed, why?

I was so not into this dating thing.

"Mystery Lady... Come play."

Damn Scott and his compelling invitations.

I went to my office door and stuck my head out. The two kids at home were in their rooms with the doors closed. Typical teenager behavior. I'd seen them more when they were toddlers who took two long naps a day and went to bed at seven p.m.

I sighed, both sad that they didn't want to hang with me and a little glad. Because now I could have some *me* time.

I opened the dating site.

And waited.

Scott's instant message didn't show like I'd thought it would.

I hovered the mouse over his image in my sidebar, debating whether I'd click on it or not.

Whoa. Hold on.

I released the mouse, shoving it away as if it were electrified. This was a game. Scott was a fantasy, not real. I meant, yes, he was a real guy (at least I hoped he was a guy; you never knew who was on the other end of that line), but if I initiated contact, that was putting the ball in my court.

I wasn't about to do that. That would give him the power. He'd know I was thinking about him. That his teasing this morning had gotten to me. I wasn't going to let that happen. This, while fun, wasn't real, and I had to get myself under control and remember that. I wasn't into dating. I wasn't going to meet him. This was not going to blossom into something because, even if he was on the up-and-up, he was sixteen years younger than me.

I'd heard some of my oldest son's friends calling me a MILF, and while that was flattering—and inappropriate—I didn't want to be a cougar. That moniker had connotations of predatory and dominant, neither of which I could ascribe to myself.

So I had to back off. If he initiated contact, well, I could justify that to myself. But I wasn't coming on to him. I'd feel… I don't know… desperate.

"Miss me?"

Damn him. The worst possible question for me to answer. It was a trap. Say *yes* and he'd have that upper hand, *no* and he could get annoyed. Not to mention, I'd be lying, and I did pride myself on not being a liar. Or a cheater. But that harkened back to my baggage with the ex.

"If I'd had time to breathe, I might have had the chance to." There. That gave a little, but not all. And it'd leave him wondering. I was, after all, the Lady of Mystery.

"Ah, I stole your breath. Good. I plan on doing that a lot—and leaving you gasping."

I clenched my thighs beneath my desk. I probably should've used my vibrator when I got home just so I wouldn't jump into this response right away.

Or… I could use my vibrator now. After all, he'd gotten himself off while we'd chatted this morning. I could have enjoy myself too.

"Hang on." I quickly shut down the screen in case one of the hermits upstairs took an atypical walk into my office and saw this. In the years since they'd become card-carrying members of the teenage race, they'd only ever been in my office to steal my printer ink. It'd be my luck that today would be the momentous day one of them sought me out for companionship.

I poked my head out, saw that all the cave—er, bedroom—doors were closed, and ran upstairs to my room. Then into my closet. In the back corner. Beneath the jumble of clothes destined for the local thrift shop. That's where I kept the vibrator so those hermits who had little to do with me wouldn't stumble upon it and embarrass all of us.

I tucked it in my bra. Yes, if they looked closely enough at my chest they'd see it, but that would mean they'd A) have to open their doors, B) actually look at me, and C) put their eyes in that vicinity, and if there's one place teenage sons weren't going to look it was at their mother's chest, so I was fairly safe until I got back to my office and reopened the screen.

"I'm hanging, baby. Low. But I'm hoping you're about to change that."

Good lord. Was everything sexual to this guy?

Then again, would we be having this conversation if it wasn't? I should be thankful.

And I was.

I think.

I locked my office door and pulled the blinds. Then I turned on the rotating floor fan that kept my southern-exposure office from becoming a sweatbox in the summer afternoons.

Though I had a feeling that the fan wasn't going to be very effective in the next few minutes. But the noise would at least, mask my vibrator's.

"I'm back."

"Glad to hear that. How was your day?"

I was waiting for the *honey* at the end of that because it sounded like such a normal conversation. But I hadn't had any so-called normal conversations with a vibrator in my hand that I could recall.

"The day was long. And hard." There. His volley.

"Funny about that… So was mine."

"Did you get any work done between your long and hard day and emailing me three times?"

"I actually did. Amazing what I can do when motivated."

Which allowed all sorts of possibilities to roll through my brain.

I unbuttoned my shorts.

Damn. I should have changed while I was upstairs. Put on that long T-shirt dress for easy access.

Then again, I was in my office with the blinds closed and my door locked. Who said I needed to even be *wearing* clothes?

My pussy got wet at the thought of sitting in my "professional" space naked.

Which made it a very good idea.

"And what exactly motivated you?" I typed right before I shimmied out of my shorts and (non-satin-tied) undies. The T-shirt and bra came flying off just as his IM appeared.

"Spending time with you this evening."

"How did you know I'd be online? I didn't know."

"I was hoping. I've been hoping all day that you'd come back."

Awww…

"So I could make you come again."

Ooooh…

I flicked on the vibrator.

Oh, crud. How was I supposed to type and use this thing?

I turned it off and dropped it into my lap, then typed, *"Awfully sure of yourself."*

"Hey, when I can get a girl off with just my words, I kinda think I've got something here. Can't blame me for that, Ms. Orgasmic."

"Not blaming. Smiling."

And getting wet as hell.

I had to do something with this vibrator. If only I had some way to hold it—

Well, duh.

"And what are you smiling about?"

I opened the two side drawers on my desk, propped my feet on them, leaned back in the chair, turned on my little pink friend Dickie, and inserted him just where I needed him to be. Well, where I needed some*one* to be.

Oh. My. God.

Sitting there, in my office, naked and spread, with Scott's words on the computer and Dickie in my pussy, channeling sensations through me—

I came.

Just like a rocket, I shot off, toes curling around the hanging file tabs.

Thank God the chair was leather and not fabric because I came all over it.

"Are you doing what I think you're doing?"

"what"

"do u"

"think im doing" I couldn't even type a full sentence.

"That."

"then whyd u ask"

Sanity was seeping back in slowly. And not nearly as fast as my juices were seeping out of me.

"Because I wanted to know. Since I'm sitting here stroking myself, I was hoping you were doing the same."

God damn it, couldn't the guy let me finish one orgasm before he started on round two?

"how r u"... *"typing"*

"One handed, baby. Guys are used to that."

He was the fastest one-handed typist I'd ever seen. Made me wonder how fast he was with that other hand.

Oh, Jesus, my pussy was clenching again.

"Tell me what you're doing. Where are you?"

"at my desk" I couldn't be bothered with punctuation and capitalization. My editor would have a fit—

Or not, actually. This was pretty hot stuff and if I could just remember it long enough to put it in a book, she'd love me.

Not that I was telling her any of this was real. I'd written plenty of paranormal erotic novels; my imagination was no surprise to anyone. They could all put this story down to that imagination. Only I—and the mysterious Scott Masters, if he ever stumbled across the book—would know it actually happened.

"I thought you were home? You're getting off at work?"

"work from home" Damn. First bit of personal information that I didn't normally give out.

"That's convenient. We should schedule nooners."

I'd never had a nooner in my life. Sex with the ex had been good (until it hadn't) and had left me wiped out and needing a nap, so midday hadn't been optimal.

But with Scott—

Hang on. I wasn't *with* Scott. My little pink friend could get me off all by himself. It didn't need Scott and his sexy words, and neither of them wiped me out so much that I couldn't function.

And I'd lost the thread of my argument. Maybe because I had a vibrating joy stick in my pussy and everything was throbbing.

"its not noon"

I retyped it. *"it's not noon"*

"Your orgasm must be subsiding if you're correcting punctuation."

What could I say? That lack of an apostrophe bugged me. *"Smarty."*

" ☺ "

Emoticons? Really? I had to laugh. This guy was full of surprises. *" :P "* I cyberly stuck my tongue out at him.

"Don't do that unless you plan to use it."

I just might want to— *"Kind of hard through a computer."*

"Actually, it's very hard beneath *the computer. And if you really want to use your tongue, we're going to have to meet. Which I'm up for. In every sense. What are you wearing?"*

No, I was not going to tell him. The guy had enough chutzpah on his own; he didn't need any help from me. *"Guess."*

There. That'd keep him, well, guessing.

"I'm picturing you naked."

I looked at the camera lens on my laptop. Please don't tell me it was on.

No. *Phew.*

But just to be safe, I covered it with a couple pieces of tape.

"Are you a mind reader?"

"Sweetheart, I wish I was because I'd jump inside your mind and figure out why the hell you won't meet me. If we're this good apart, imagine what we'd be like together."

I was. In vivid color. *"I'm not ready for that."*

"I get that. But you're obviously ready for something and if that's all I can get, I'm more than willing to continue.

So was I. *"Thanks."*

"My pleasure. And yours."

It certainly was.

I leaned back in the chair now that the threat of voyeurism was off the table.

Though… that was actually kind of hot.

Oh my God, who *was* I? I was turning into a heroine from one of my books.

But those were fantasies. In real life, a forty-nine-year-old did not engage a younger guy in cybersex to then have it work out happily ever after. That's why my genre was such a hot ticket. People thought about doing what I wrote about, but no one actually went out and did it with the expectation that it'd work out like it did between the pages of a book.

"Babe? You there? Or are you enjoying yourself without me?"

No. I was having cyber-second-thoughts.

"minute" What he didn't know wouldn't ruin the moment.

"Holy fuck, woman. I have got to meet you. You've had, what? five orgasms in the past six hours? How the hell are you still standing?"

It was four, but, again, what he didn't know wouldn't ruin the moment. *"not standing"*

"Oh? Are you lying down? On your back or your side? On your stomach? Doggy style?"

Yes, yes, and yes. Whatever way he wanted.

"sitting at my desk, legs braced on drawers on either side"

"Naked," was his response.

Did like a guy who got right to the point. *"No question mark?"*

"You already answered that and, baby, my mind is going places the rest of me wants to go. Desperately."

"Oh?" Hey, if I was supposed to have had five orgasms, I was down one. Maybe we could go for a two-fer this time.

I slid the vibrator back in.

"Yeah, I want to kneel in front of you and put your feet on my shoulders. I'll push that chair back against the wall so you can't go anywhere and then I'm going to lick my way from your neck, down to your breasts and suck on your nipples so hard you'll be begging me to touch you."

I was already there…

"But I won't."

"why" Had to ask that because I sure as hell was touching myself. I ran my thumb over my clit as I pumped Dickie inside me.

"Because you want it too bad," said Mr. Frustrating. *"I can't wear you out before I get to enjoy myself."*

"u aren't enjoying this"

"Oh hell yeah, baby. My cock is hard and throbbing. I'm running my fingers up the shaft and it's jerking to get more contact. But I'm imagining your soft lips around it as I stand in front of you in that chair, your head bent enough to lick the head, teasing me, but you won't take me in your mouth."

"yet" Jesus, the image he was creating…

"Yeah. Yet."

I wondered what he'd taste like. I'd only ever tasted one man. Only had had one man's dick in my mouth; what would it be like to have another's?

God help me, I wanted to find out. And I wanted that dick to be Scott's.

I almost said it then; almost typed that I'd meet him, but thankfully, sanity prevailed. I still didn't know this guy.

"And then I'm going to suck your tits one at a time, running my tongue around the tip until you're weeping."

"I don't cry when I'm aroused."

"I wasn't talking about tears."

Well shit. I'd missed that line. What kind of erotic writer was I?

A very very horny one whose brain was short-circuiting at the moment.

"And then I'll tongue-fuck your belly button, giving you a preview of what's to come."

I already knew what was coming: me. With the intensity of the ones I'd been having for the past several hours, an honest skin-to-skin orgasm might just kill me.

"You with me, babe?

"yes" I was working the vibrator inside me, fighting off the urge to just put it on my clit and send myself over the edge. Dickie inside me worked for me, but, dammit, it'd been so long since a man had been there that I almost didn't want the vibrator. It wasn't a substitute for hard, hot flesh.

I was getting dangerously close to telling him I wanted to meet.

"Not very talkative, are you?"

"no" I could imagine him laughing in his… office? Living room? Bedroom? I had no idea where he was or what he was or wasn't wearing yet the guy had gotten all of that and a position from me.

"what r u wearing" I needed the visual so I quickly brought up his profile.

He'd added more photos.

Shirtless ones.

Oh my God, the guy was a god. He couldn't be real. That couldn't be him with the six-pack and broad shoulders and just enough hair on his chest to give my nipples a joy ride every time I brushed up against him.

"You might want to check out my profile.

"am"

"Smart girl."

I wasn't a girl. I was all woman and in about thirty seconds I was going to roar. *"Nice"*

"I figured it was the closest I was going to get to getting naked around you for a while. Besides, I want you to see me. I work hard for that body.

I'd work hard for that body, too…

"shows"

"You like?

"id have to be dead not to"

"And you're definitely not that. Come yet?"

"no"

"Well, damn. I'm not doing my job."

"no you're sexting a 49 yr old"

"Who I'm imaging as my babysitter."

"that's just wrong"

"That's why it's fun. And it's only wrong if we don't do it right. Are you doing it right?

Oh yes I was. The one good thing about a vibrator, well, other than the no-towels-on-the-floor thing, was that it'd do just *what* I wanted just *where* I wanted, just *when* I wanted. I'd found my G-spot long ago.

"give me" ... "minute"

"Babe, take all the time you need. I just wish I was there to watch.

So did I.

That mental picture of him getting off watching me was enough to send me over the edge.

I had to fight to keep my legs from closing, but with them open, it was so much hotter. So much more intense.

My pussy clenched around Dickie, but I kept pumping him in and out, swirling him to catch my clit on a pass, and that only ratcheted up the intensity.

"Come for me, baby."

I was and if I could get close enough to the keyboard, I'd tell him, but my knees were locked as the waves rolled through me.

"I'm going to come too."

My eyes shot to that picture of him, bare-chested with a bottle of wine in one hand and a blanket in another. He took that picture this afternoon. I knew he had. Just for me.

I lifted my feet from the file drawers and felt the indentations from the metal tabs on the hanging files. Next time I was keeping my shoes on.

Next time.

I'd never look at my office the same way again.

I tugged the chair closer to the desk *"come for me Scott,"* I typed. I liked writing his name.

"am"

"long and hard?" I had to ask, still imagining sucking him to the back of my throat.

"thick... hot... gush"

My pussy throbbed at his words. *"I want to taste you."*

Holy shit. I yanked my fingers from the keyboard and fell back in my chair. I hadn't even been aware I was typing until those words showed up on the IM window under my screen name.

"mmmmmmmmmmmmmmmmmmm"

I could actually hear him coming from that line of non-specific mmmm's.

I glanced at his picture again, the one with the blanket. He was looking up into the camera, not head on, as if he had a secret to share.

The man was tempting me.

I was very tempted.

"God, baby, that was amazing."

"I know."

"Still shying away from meeting me?"

No. Yes. Hell. *"Scott, this is just a fantasy."*

"It doesn't have to be."

"It does."

"I'm going to try to change your mind, Mystery Lady."

And I was going to let him.

"Mom! What's for dinner?"

Shit. Fantasy over. *"I have to go. Kids."* Not to mention a little thing like putting my clothes back on. And taking care of Dickie since he'd taken such good care of me.

"Mom?"

"Be right there." Good God, teenagers were better birth control than the pill. Not that I needed to worry about that ever again, having had a nice little operation to take care of that problem—which meant one less worry should I ever decide to lose my mind and meet Scott.

"I have to get to my game. What's for dinner?"

I glanced at the clock on my desk as I yanked on my underwear and shorts. Shit, I had no time to be sexting with a guy young enough to be my, er, younger brother when I had kids to feed and a game I'd totally spaced on to get to. "We'll grab something on the way. Do you have your cleats?"

"And my shin guards and a jug of water. What are you doing in there? Come on!"

Thankfully, my daughter Katy's question was a rhetorical one; she didn't really want to know what I was doing anymore than I wanted to tell her.

I glanced at the screen as I pulled my T-shirt back on—shit. Forgot to do up my bra.

"I'll miss you."

Scott knew just what to say. And that was kind of freaking me out. Well, on top of the fact that I'd just had a sexcapade with a guy I didn't even know.

I shut down the computer without replying. When the fantasy got in the way of my real life, it was a problem. The kids came first and my feminine needs could just suck it up and deal with Dickie.

Dickie. Shit. I looked around for some place to stash him. because, with my luck, the kids would suddenly decide to come in and hang out.

The painted vase on top of my credenza. I wrapped him in tissues and dropped him inside. It'd have to do.

Chapter Four

I couldn't get Scott out of my head.

I sat on the bleachers, chatting with the other parents, laughing and smiling as if I weren't reliving the past twenty-four hours in my head, but I was and my body was on fire. Every time I'd forget for a few moments, I'd shift on the bleachers and the smallest movement would remind me that I'd had some of the best orgasms of my life today and certain body parts were still awash with the afterglow.

"Hey, Dana, did you ever think about online dating?" Chelsea, Katy's best friend Molly's mom, asked me.

"Online… dating?" I gulped around the word.

"Yeah, Kevi Marlings met her latest on one of these dating sites. I know a few other couples who hooked up that way."

"Um, no. Haven't tried that." I leaned down to tie my sneaker.

The one that didn't need tying.

"I wouldn't go near one of those with a ten foot schlong." Cathy Templeton had no filter. Never had, and during the neighborhood Friday night happy hours, her vocabulary could get really raunchy.

I loved her for it, though. More than one of my characters had been inspired by something Cathy had said.

However, Cathy would change her mind if she'd ever met Scott.

The thought was unsettling. Obviously Scott was no

novice when it came to sexting. No one just chatted up an older woman like he did and was able to go down this path on the first try. He'd honed his skill.

And I was the lucky beneficiary so what was I complaining about?

"You never know who's on the other end of that connection," continued Cathy, voicing my own concerns. "Sure, the photo might be good, but there's no guarantee it's really that guy. Much better to meet him in person."

"You mean at a bar?" scoffed my next-door-neighbor, Kim. "Yeah, that's so much better. You don't even know if the guy's giving you his right name."

"Gee, everyone." I patted the sneaker and sat up. "You all make it sound like so much fun. Which is why I'm still single." And it was. I wasn't into the bar scene. Especially the pick-up part. The thought of getting naked around someone new… This body wasn't the same as it'd been twenty years ago.

No, much better to pull out my vibrator and masturbate to a computer screen than actually let someone see the stretch marks and muffin top.

Yet another reason to remind myself that, no matter how tempted I was, meeting Scott was definitely out of the picture.

"At the very least, you could use the experience for book fodder." Cathy snuck a sip of the beer she'd packed in her youngest's insulated lunch box.

I rolled my eyes. Inappropriate partying was expected of Cathy; no one would think twice. Now if I were to guzzle booze at a kid's game, it'd be the scandal of the century.

Imagine what everyone would say if they knew what I'd been doing all day.

"How's the newest book coming, Dana?" Cathy asked.

Snickers accompanied that question.

I was used to it. There were always those sorts of comments, but I didn't mind. Every one of the women on these bleachers—and a lot of the men—read my books. They could snicker all they wanted.

"It's almost finished."

"When's it come out?"

"Not for another three months. Has to go through editorial and then copy edits. A few more steps."

"I think you should write faster. Get more books out."

Yeah, because I could just whip the word count out like that. I mentally snapped my fingers. I was a fast writer, but still, sometimes I needed inspiration.

Scott was turning out to be very good inspiration.

I already had the gist of the new story running through my head, and I hadn't forgotten one second of the love scenes I wasn't going to have to make up. I just had to put this stuff to paper the minute I got home before I forgot it.

Or had it overshadowed by whatever he came up with next.

Yes, I was going to continue this online thing. No meeting, but I wasn't going to stop chatting. Only the two of us knew about it and he didn't know who I was. I could come all I wanted in the privacy of my own home, helped along by one very sexy younger man.

Damn if my panties didn't get wet. These were polyester, not cotton. A little closer to satin, but without the price tag.

My phone vibrated.

One new message.

It was from the website. I'd forgotten I'd signed up for automatic email alerts when I'd set up my account.

Oh the things wine could make us do…

I opened the messages.

"Thinking of you."

Hmmm… A picture of him shirtless, a box of Chinese food balanced on his six-pack.

He was in a bed. His, I was sure.

"Talk to me. I know you're looking."

Damn. Forgot about those Read notifications. And there wasn't a way to turn them off.

I shut down the phone. Already that image of him was

turning me on and I didn't need to be squirming around on the bleachers with half my neighbors hanging around.

The phone vibrated again.

"Two new messages."

Oh God. I didn't even have to read them and I got wet.

But of course I was going to read them anyway.

"I want you, Mystery Lady. Come play with me."

Dear God in heaven, I was tempted. That six-pack—he'd removed the Chinese food and was staring at the camera with a smokin' hot gaze—was tempting me beyond belief. My ex had looked like that once. Many many years ago. He'd let himself go and since I wasn't exactly Miss Let's-Get-Physical anymore, I hadn't been able to complain.

But I liked what I was seeing.

"Boy, that must be some email," Cathy said. "What? Someone send you a cock shot?"

I was not one to be easily embarrassed but her almost dead-on comment had my face flaming.

I shook my head and closed the screen. "My ex." I got red when I got angry. It was close enough to pink to explain the flush I was sure was on my cheeks. And that was all I had to explain because the neighbors all got it. There was no love lost for the guy who'd abandoned his kids.

I never thought I'd be happy to have *that* as an explanation for my actions, but diverting the focus from the *real* email was worth using him.

The phone buzzed again.

"Geez, what's his problem? Did the bimbo wise up and dump his fat ass?" Kim had heard every last sordid detail when I found out about my ex's affair. We'd been conversing over the driveways for fifteen years, more so once I'd confided to her about the state of my non-marriage. She'd waved goodbye to him the day he'd loaded his shit into the car he should have left me, and drove away—with her middle finger raised the entire time. You had to love friends like that.

But I didn't have to tell them about r sexting a young hottie.

"He's contesting child support. Again." A long-running issue that I, for one, couldn't wait to be done with. Though I had to say, I thoroughly enjoyed making him pay. Even if it'd only been a nickel, the fact that he had to write out a check to me for the next two and a half years put a smile on my face like nothing else.

Well, that'd been true before this morning. Now? Those orgasms were the thing I was smiling the most about.

"I want you to come all over my face."

The screen lit up with Scott's latest message.

"Must be some email. I'm not sure whether you're ready to laugh or cry."

Come, actually, but even Cathy wouldn't be so blunt.

I was feeling blunt. I was also feeling horny as hell. "Just give me a sec to respond."

I slid to my right, away from the group, and typed back, *"That'd be kind of tough to do since I'm sitting on a row of metal bleachers next to half my neighborhood."*

"Just think of the show we'd give them."

OMG. Seriously? This guy was beyond any character I could write. I couldn't come up with half the ideas he did and I'd won a lot of awards for my books. This one might finally get me on the *New York Times* bestseller list.

If I told people it was the truth, it *definitely* would—though on the front page instead of the review section.

"You're bad," I typed with a smirk on my face.

"So bad I'm good."

"And modest."

"Got me there."

No, he had me. Enthralled, enraptured, ensnared. This guy was my dirty little secret that I was going to enjoy every minute of. But not now. I didn't exactly relish having an orgasm in front of my neighbors and their kids. That would get me banned from the PTA for sure.

Not that that was a bad thing, but while my role in life, according to my teenagers, was to embarrass them, coming in public might just be a little too much. *"I gotta go."*

"No, you gotta come. Come for me, Mystery Lady. Later. When you're home, in your bed alone. Open the app and talk to me."

"Do you do anything but sit on your computer, emailing strange women on a dating site?"

"You're not strange, you're sexy as hell. And I'm not on my computer. I'm on the app on my phone."

"I thought you were in a bed with Chinese food."

"That was earlier. Right now, I'm actually at a park, watching my niece play soccer."

I was actually at a park, watching my daughter play soccer. Wouldn't it be funny if he was at the same game…

Hell no, that would not be funny. That would be too real. Too weird. Too freak-me-out.

I was almost afraid to type my next sentence, but I had to know. *"What park?"*

"I'm not stalking you. Unless you're at a park in my hometown, you're safe."

"I didn't think you were stalking me."

"Yes you did. And I get why. All this sexting could get your guard up, but I really am a normal guy. I just saw you and my imagination went wild. What can I say? You haven't exactly been fending me off… No, scratch that. You have, but you've kept coming back for more. Kept coming, period."

He had a point and I couldn't exactly cry double standard. *"When you're forty-nine and some hot young-'un emails you, let's see how 'fending off' you'll be."*

"I don't plan to be on this site when I'm forty-nine. I plan to be firmly ensconced in my lover's bed, making her scream with pleasure."

The floodgates opened between my thighs. I wanted to be that screaming woman. Granted, we'd still have the age difference, but if we'd been together all those years, I wouldn't give it a second thought.

So why was I thinking that now? I was never going to meet this guy.

"Yo, Dana!" Marybeth, another neighbor, yoo-hoo'ed me. "I think that's the longest you've spoken to the dick in the last three years."

It was the longest I'd *thought* about a dick in the last three years. *"Gotta go. The natives are getting curious."*

"I still say we ought to put on a show."

I was *this close* to swiping the phone closed, but I wasn't going to let him have the last word. *"So why don't we? But just for each other."*

Now where in the *hell* did *that* come from? Just because one of my characters would say something like that didn't mean *I* had to.

I shut down the phone and if it wouldn't have raised too many eyebrows, I would've thrown the thing into the trees. Scott Masters, LAX7615, had short-circuited my brain along when he'd rewired my body.

And I was enjoying every second of it.

Chapter Five

Tonight of all nights, the kids wanted to chat.

Seriously, they might have had a collective fifty-eight-minute conversation with me over the past month, and now all of them wanted to hang out in the family room and interact with me.

And I was such a bad parent for wishing that they'd wanted to do this *last* night when I'd been sitting in front of my favorite train-wreck of a TV show, watching women behaving badly.

If those women were real, then what the hell was I?

Right now I was the Bad Mom, wishing her kids would remember they were teenagers who knew everything and hated me so I could go off and have my cyber fling where everyone got off and no one got hurt.

Then again, I'd kill for time like this with all four of them tomorrow because this was an aberration. So I told Horny Mystery Lady to put her hormones on ice, then sat back and enjoyed my kids.

"What took you so long?" was Scott's first email when I got into bed and opened the site later on.

"Kids wanted to hang with me."

"Lucky kids."

"You're sweet."

"No, I'm not. Because what I'd do to you if I were hanging with you is anything but sweet. It's raunchy and dirty and a hell of a lot of fun."

And here I went getting wet again. At least this time I wasn't wearing any panties.

I wasn't wearing anything. I was in the mood to *par-tay,* and he'd just given me the perfect opening. *"Oh, really? And what, pray tell, would that be?"*

"Jesus, Mystery Lady. Every time I think you're going to back down, you don't. Do you know what that does to me—what you *do to me?"*

"I have a fair idea, but why don't you tell me?"

I'd propped the iPad on a pile of pillows beside me in my big, empty king bed, the Bluetooth keyboard on a standing picture frame holder in front of it so it'd be easily accessible for one-handed typing. I'd propped myself up on another pile of pillows and now slid my hand down my naked body to rest just above the landing strip I'd recently gone to a spa for.

I had no idea why I'd suddenly subscribed to that new social custom two years after the dick had left (and three years after the drought of sex had commenced), but it made me feel sexy.

"I start by putting your right foot on my shoulder."

He didn't beat around the bush—

I giggled. Yeah, I guess he kinda did.

"And for your left... I'll suck on each toe, tugging so the sensation shoots up your leg right to your pussy."

As it was doing right now.

"Then I'll put that one on my other shoulder and skim my fingers up your calf to your thigh, circling my way slowly down to your pussy, where I'll slick your juices over your engorged lips. Lips that are just begging for my tongue."

How the hell was he typing all of this one-handedly?

He had to have typed it beforehand. That's the only way he could get the words up so fast even with two hands.

He'd been thinking about this for a while. Planning his every move. Writing it down and probably fine-tuning it for maximum effect.

I was so ready for this ride.

"I'll slide my drenched finger slowly over your clit, stroking it until it's pulsing for more attention, and then I'll slip it inside you. One finger at first, then two. Three if you're a good girl..."

The cursor pulsed on the screen in time with the pulsing of my clit.

"Four if you're bad."

I'd never in all my life wanted to be so bad.

"And then, when you're writhing on the bed, your hair spread out on my pillow, tangling around your shoulders, your back arched in supplication, I'll flick your clit with my thumb, scraping it gently with my nail, drawing gasps from you as you try to come. But I won't let you. Not yet."

Yet, please. Dear God, let it be *yet*…

"I'll lean in close, my hot breath fluttering over your swollen clit, and I'll kiss your thigh. Drag my tongue along it. Take a little nip with my teeth.

"You'll grab my head, trying to get me to lick you, but I won't. Not yet, Mystery Lady. You're not going to get off that easily."

Oh yes I was if he kept this up. My own hand had no such reservations in not touching my clit and I was stroking away. A couple more sexy promises and I'd be seeing stars.

"I'll pull out my fingers. You'll whimper. Maybe even beg me to fuck you with them again, but I won't."

Why? Why wouldn't he?

"I'll use my tongue instead."

I was so close I could taste this orgasm.

I wanted to tell him, but I had a death grip on my mattress and there was no way in hell I was prying my fingers off my clit. I stroked harder, flicked it with my nail—made my toes curl right into the sheets.

So I did it again.

Dear God, I could feel an orgasm start to spiral in my belly. Scott better wrap this up or I'd be coming without him.

"You taste amazing, Mystery Lady. The scent of you is

driving me wild. I want to tongue-fuck you, so I shove your legs up and wide, baring you to my eyes. You're so pretty and pink and plump, slick and wet, just waiting for me to eat you out."

Yes, dear God, yes…

"I plunge my tongue inside you, hard and fast, and you try to close your thighs around me, but I won't let you. You have to take this. Take every sensation, every thrilling pulse of blood through your veins, want and need and down-and-dirty lust streaking along your nerve endings, never letting up, pushing us on, over and over, as I lick your pussy lips, until you beg me to suck you in, my tongue fluttering against you until you can't breathe. Until the sensations roar over you, hot, wet, electric, like a rogue wave tumbling you to the shore."

My toes were still curled, my pelvis tilted, my backside clenching as if I could feel him inside me and didn't want to let go

Damn, I should have pulled Dickie from his hiding spot, but I'd been too horny to think straight when I'd arrived home earlier.

And with good reason.

"Then I'd slide my fingers back in. Just two this time, so the others can spread your lips wide for me.

"You'll pull your knees to your chest—a chest I'm going to get to, Mystery Lady, I promise. You have gorgeous tits and I intend to enjoy them for hours.

He might kill me if this went on for hours.

I should have reminded him that I was older than him, but I had both hands in on the action between my legs and didn't want to stop to find the keyboard. My knees were pulled back and I was pulsing toward the ceiling, whimpering that I wanted a man where my fingers were.

I wanted Scott.

"And while I finger-fuck you, I'll crawl on top of you, keeping your legs wide so I have clear passage to plunge deep inside you.

"And then, I do.

"Over and over, your pussy clenching my dick tightly. I rim you with my head, flicking it along the underside of your clit, my pre-cum coating us both. You hook your arms beneath your knees, offering yourself to me."

Oh hell yeah.

"And I take you."

He took me all right. The image of him from today, the one with the blanket, filled my iPad screen, that sexy smile speaking to me alone, and I imagined him above me, that chest brushing against mine every time he fucked me.

My nipples were hard, begging for attention, and it was my biggest regret that Scott wasn't here right this minute to suck on them. It'd been so long since a man had sucked my tits. That wasn't something Dickie could do for me. I needed the real thing—a hot mouth on me, licking and sucking and biting.

I dragged one hand up my body, my juices leaving a trail that I wanted Scott to follow. I circled one nipple, slicking the wetness over it, and moaned. God, to have a tongue here…

I pinched the tip, the sensation shooting straight to my pussy, and I could feel the orgasm coming on.

I palmed my nipple, circling, the bud getting tighter.

I could feel that same tightness in my clit.

Jesus, I wanted him here with me.

And then he was.

"ur awfully quiet mystry lady."

He was typing live now.

"cum 4 me"

One more stroke over both my clit and my nipple and I did. The sensation rocketed through me until I couldn't stroke myself, I couldn't move. My fingers were clamped around my nipple, my other hand was buried between my legs, every pulse of my clit right against the pad of my thumb, my legs rigid as my orgasm overtook me.

The IM window winked out.

I wanted to reach over and ask Scott if he was coming, if he'd been stroking himself to completion, but I couldn't move.

The tension finally released my locked muscles and I sank into my mattress, sweat trickling down my temples and under my breasts. It might have been between my thighs as well, but I was so wet that I couldn't tell.

God, I missed sex. I missed the intimacy of having someone play my body like a finely-tuned instrument, bringing me to a crashing crescendo.

I took a shuddering breath. I had to get a grip or I'd be spouting off something stupid on my next IM. Something like I wanted to meet him.

The screen winked on.

"finished?"

I chuckled and shifted closer to the keyboard, my arm lethargic as I raised it to type. *"I've only just begun."*

"aw, baby, you know just the thing to say."

The thing was, if he'd read my books, he'd see that I *did* know the thing to say. As long as I kept this fictional, I could do this. So, yeah, meeting him was out.

Or so I was desperately trying to convince myself.

"I want to send you a picture but not on this site."

Alarm bells went ringing through my head. I was not about to give him my personal email address. Hell, it was through my website, so he'd know immediately who I was—

Wait. There was the address I'd set up for all those websites who want you to join before you can buy something. It was a generic name that no one would ever connect to me.

I considered the ramifications… There weren't any.

I typed the address in.

"ok give me two minutes."

I'd just given him twenty; what was another two?

I stretched my hands above my head, arching my back. My body felt alive, almost as if Scott had been the one stroking it.

Almost.

"ok go look"

I wiggled back into my pillows, propping myself up a bit

more, and pulled the iPad onto my stomach, navigating to the inbox where Scott's personal email address blinked at me.

I opened the message—

Oh. Dear. Lord.

He was naked. Not that I hadn't expected it, but still, to see him there, so beautifully naked… His body literally took my breath away.

It was a selfie, taken with the camera above his head as he lay on his bed, a full body shot over sculpted abs, lean hips with that line by his obliques that did amazing things to my insides, and a cock jutting toward me as if begging me to lick it.

Scott was a very big boy and my mouth watered at the thought of taking him inside.

I'd never particularly enjoyed oral with my ex—too many times he'd grab my head and I'd feel as if I was merely an extension of his hands, not someone giving to her lover.

But Scott… one hand was thrown over his head, the other taking the picture and I knew he'd let me do what I wanted to do without taking matters into his own hands.

"like?"

"hell yes" I wasn't about to censor my reaction since he hadn't censored his camera.

"lol"

"nothing funny about that picture. ur hot.

"sweating actually. and sticky from my cum. wanna lick it off?"

"yes"

I stared at the IM window and waited for his reply.

And waited.

Another picture popped into my email inbox.

Scott with a hand around his cock and the caption, *"Waiting for you, Mystery Lady."*

I was never one for dick shots with my ex; seemed pathetic when it was trying to jut beyond the beer belly, but this… Hell yeah, now I got the appeal.

I was mighty glad Mr. LAX7615 had chosen me to run with the babysitter fantasy.

"like?"

"I'd have to be dead not to."

"don't die on me; we have too much left to do."

"I think that might kill me."

"nah, you can take it."

I wanted to take him.

The thought slammed into my brain and there was no denying I was tempted to meet Scott. Someplace no one would know me, where I could be this mystery lady and saunter up a flight of stairs to his bedroom and pull him in after me, taking off his clothes with each step toward the bed. Tugging him down on top of me as I lay back, all turned on and wet, ready for him to fuck 'til I couldn't see straight.

Hell, I was halfway there already.

"babe?"

"here"

"are you coming again?"

"I don't think I can."

"we're going to have to test that theory."

"lol"

"I'm not kidding. Turn on your webcam."

"I'm on my iPad."

"Even better. Let's Facetime."

I dropped the iPad flat on my stomach. If we were Facetiming right now, Scott would be staring at my bedroom ceiling.

I wanted to do this. Wanted to bring up the visual and get each other off that way.

I propped myself up on my elbows and looked around my bed. A couple of books on my nightstand—none of them mine. My phone charger, a box of tissues (they'd come in handy), a lamp, and a picture of the kids—um… that would have to go.

I reached over and turned it face down.

And then I realized… I'd made my decision.

I picked up the iPad.

"babe?" was typed three times in the IM screen.

"here"

"Sorry. pushed for too much, I guess. I don't want to scare you off."

"You didn't scare me."

He didn't answer for a few seconds.

"Oh?"

"Yeah, oh."

"I don't know what that means. Kinda hard to figure out without inflection."

"It means okay."

"okay?????"

I smiled at the question marks; I could hear the tentative hope in his question.

I took a deep breath. Did I really want to do this? Did I really want to go from this arm's-length fantasy to arm's-length video?

Naked arms-length video?

With a guy sixteen years younger than me?

Who was, essentially, a stranger I'd met online?

Who can get you off with words alone. Imagine what he'll be able to do with his voice when you're not worried about having to type.

I was imagining it. A lot.

My finger hovered over the onscreen keypad.

And then I typed the first letter.

And the next.

And the next.

Until my whole answer was there.

"Okay, Scott. Let's Facetime."

Chapter Six

"Okay, Scott. Let's Facetime."

I pushed the Send button for the instant message.

Almost immediately my breath caught in my throat. What was I doing? What had I done? I'd committed to FaceTiming with a guy I'd just met this morning through an online dating site—a guy who'd made me come at least half a dozen times just with instant messaging.

I was out of my mind.

Actually, no. I was firmly in my mind—one that was awash with sensual pleasure and the image he'd just sent me of his naked self in his bed, his dick hard and calling to me.

"I need your number."

Yeah, he did. And that was a problem. I didn't want to give him my personal information. It was one thing to meet him online where I could be anonymous, but another to give him real contact information.

Hang on. I had an Internet number; I didn't have to give him the real one. I'd set that up for fans who invited me to cyber book club meetings or signings or when I gave remote workshops for writers' groups in other states.

And I, semi-savvy Internet user that I was, had linked it to my iPad.

My identity was safe.

My nudity, however, was an open book when my screen lit up with his call.

I should have put make-up on. I shouldn't have eaten the last of the kids' fries when we'd done the drive-thru. And I definitely shouldn't have been laying there with my nipples as hard as pebbles.

Yet none of that made me flip up the sheet as I hit Accept.

A very good call on my part because there was Scott, in all his naked glory.

"My God, you're gorgeous." His words, not mine, though I could certainly say them back to him. The man was even better in motion.

"It's the lighting." And thank God for it. Just from my iPad, low enough to hide wrinkles and stretch marks. Hopefully.

"You should light a candle. Ambience, you know."

Sit up and walk around naked in front of him? Not happening. "Why not a glass of wine and a bunch of grapes while I'm at it?"

Pictures didn't do his smile justice. "I'm all for that."

He was all for something all right. The guy might as well run the Stars and Stripes up that flagpole.

"Didn't you just get off?" I slapped a hand over my mouth. It was one thing to type my every thought, but typically I didn't voice them.

Scott's smile got wider. "I did, baby. See what you do to me?" He palmed that thing between his legs.

Holy hell. I didn't think I actually *could* put all of him in my mouth. He wouldn't fit. "Then I guess it was a good thing I *wasn't* your babysitter. You never would have come out of your room."

Scott shifted and, man, what that movement did to that six-pack. *Sexy* just rippled all over it. "Well, I did do a lot of coming *in* my room, but if you'd been around, I would've been on the sofa next to you, watching whatever soap opera you wanted."

"I didn't watch soap operas. I was always outside playing basketball or taking a walk."

"Ah, I wouldn't mind a little one-on-one action."

"I bet you wouldn't."

He encircled the flagpole just to make a point—that the old wives' tale about big hands/big dick had been told by *happy* old wives for a reason.

"And I'll put nature walks on our list. I already have the blanket, as you saw in the picture."

"Our list?" I was having a little trouble concentrating on the conversation. Sue me.

"Of all the places we're going to make love."

If I'd been sipping that wine, I would've choked on it. "Um, exactly how long is this list?"

He ran his hand up his cock. "This long."

That was a long list. "You're presuming an awful lot."

He stroked his thumb across the head. "I'm hoping an awful lot."

"Why?"

"Seriously? You have to ask that? Look at you."

Oh hell, I'd forgotten we were having this conversation naked.

I did look at myself. Prone, I didn't look half bad. Tits weren't as perky as I'd like. Then again, no woman's *natural* breasts were perky when she was on her back.

"Yeah. You get it." His voice was husky.

I looked at the screen. If it was possible, his dick had gotten harder. And now his palm was rolling over the head. "Feel good?"

If he said "duh" I was hanging up my erotic writer pen.

"God, baby. So good. But I wish you were doing this."

So did I.

Well, hell, I was the writer here. I knew how to put actions into words. "Slide your hand down your shaft to the base." It was what I would do.

He did.

"Now pump."

He did, arching slightly, his eyes closing on a long, "mmmmmm."

Mmmmm was right. I could feel my creative juices flowing. Along with a few others. But I was warming up to this, and not just with a fire in my veins. My imagination was running full tilt; it was time to put out or shut up. "Use your other hand too. Circle the head."

Good boy that he was, he propped the iPad against some pillows and listened to me.

And I got to listen to him enjoying himself.

His breathing kicked up and he licked his lips. Made me remember him wanting to lick *my* lips and darn if I didn't get wetter just imagining his tongue on me. If he and I ever *did* get together, there'd be no friction whatsoever between us because I was wetter than I'd ever been.

And so, quite suddenly, was he.

"Jesus." He panted through the orgasm, thick cum coating that six-pack. "God damn, woman. I can't believe how quickly you can get me off."

"Technically, you did that."

He peeled open his gorgeous blue eyes and stared into mine. "Make no mistake, Mystery Lady, that was all you. Now that I can see your lips moving, I can really imagine them sucking me off. Do you swallow?"

He said it as if he were asking me the time of day, but for him, hell yeah, I'd swallow. Well, in this cyber world. In real life? We weren't getting together in real life so I could live in this fantasy one. "Sure."

He groaned again. "*Sure*, she says as if it's no big deal. Do you know how many women won't do that?"

Yup, because I was one of them. Swallowing was actually a topic of conversation among the neighborhood crowd and either no one was owning it, or none of the guys were enjoying it. I voted for the latter because I'd never seen the appeal.

Well, not before today. Now, however, looking at Scott still pumping his shaft... I actually did wonder what he'd taste like. Just one more sure sign of our smoking hot affair—

Affair. I'd never been a fan of that word, and since my ex had had one, I *really* didn't like it.

"You are single, aren't you, Scott?"

He rolled onto his stomach and tugged his iPad close to his face. Gave me a great view over his shoulder of the nice set of glues curving behind him. "What do you take me for?"

Was he just a little *too* angry? Maybe protesting too much? I didn't know, and call me jaded, but fantasy or not, this was something I needed clarity on. "I don't take you for anything. I don't know you. You're just some guy who picked me up online."

"Some guy?" His eyebrows veed. "You do this with other guys?"

"Um, Scott? If you remember, we just 'met'"—I one-handedly air-quoted the word—"this morning. Not that it's any of your business, but I don't have cybersex with every guy who IMs me. If I did, I'd never get any work done."

"Yeah, I can see how you'd be popular. You're gorgeous. Every guy's dream."

Not one guy's, apparently. But that was my ex's loss. Because right now, I was a thirty-three-year-old hottie's online fantasy.

So what the fuck was I doing trying to destroy the interlude with reality?

Good thing I wasn't writing this, or my editor and her red pen would be having a field day. It was time to head back to the fantasy realm. "So… *every* guy's dream?"

Grinning, Scott waggled his eyebrows. "Most definitely mine. Right now, I'm dreaming about kissing those freckles on your chest."

Oh shit. I'd forgotten exactly what he was seeing. My flaws in all their naked—literally—glory.

My hand flew to those "freckles": four birthmarks that ran together into a blob. My ex had suggested—a few months before I found out about his affair—that I get a tattoo to hide them. I'd actually considered it. I'd always wanted a tattoo, but he'd been adamantly opposed for years.

Turned out, his change of heart was because the bimbo had one. Should have been my first clue.

So the tat was off the table. Well, a tat on my chest. I was still considering getting one someplace else. Just because I could.

"Don't hide them, baby. They look like a shamrock. One I want to trace with my tongue."

Okay, definitely *not* getting a tat there. From now on, whenever I looked in the mirror, I'd think of Scott doing exactly what he wanted with them.

And then with me.

"Slide your fingers down, baby," he said, his voice going low and husky.

My nipples were already begging for attention, so I gave them some.

"Oh, yeah, that's it." He sounded as if his breath was caught in his throat.

I knew the feeling.

"So fucking hot." He stroked himself.

"*That's* hot, Scott."

"Tell me your name."

I shook my head. "That would make this real."

"Baby, in case you haven't realized"—he arched an eyebrow—"this *is* *r*eal. I've got my cock in my hand, and I'm watching you play with your tits. The only way it could be more real was if I was there."

I imagined him beside me. What would it be like?

Well, hot, obviously. It couldn't not be hot.

And it'd be real. Skin-on-skin contact that I hadn't had in way too long.

Jesus, I missed that.

It was on the tip of my tongue to tell him who I was. Where I lived. Exactly what I wanted him to do.

"And I'd lick every inch of you."

Saved by cybersex before I did something I'd regret.

Oh I don't know… After that comment, you might regret not *telling him where and who you are.*

That was not my conscience talking. My conscience was the one throwing Caution and Hazard signs all over the place. My libido on the other hand, was the one flinging rose petals and welcoming Scott with open arms.

And legs.

My legs slid apart, and if I hadn't had the damn iPad in my hand, I could touch myself.

What the hell was I doing with an iPad in my hand anyway?

I exhaled and set the thing on a pillow so I could fully attend to the matter at, well, hand.

"I want to see you. Can you change the angle, baby?"

I hesitated, but only for a second. A little late to get stage fright now.

"God, you are one beautiful woman. I'm glad you *weren't* my babysitter… I wouldn't have been able to handle you back then."

"*Handle* me? I'll have you know, young Mr. Scott Masters, that I am not a woman to be handled. I'll do my own handling, thank you very much."

His grin was sexy as hell as he leaned closer to his iPad and whispered, "Then get working on it, babe. I want to watch you come."

Damn it, I blushed. How could I still blush? I should be beyond blushing by now with what we'd done together.

"Are you blushing?"

"No." Of course he'd ask that, just to pile on the embarrassment.

Funny how I could be so into the moment that I'd get myself off in front of a complete stranger, but the minute he said something about it, I turned pink. If I hadn't had my operation, I'd swear my hormones were going wild.

"Prove it, babe. Slide a hand to your pussy."

"And that's going to prove what?"

"That you are the woman of my dreams."

Okay, I could be that. If only for tonight.

"Great minds." I smiled and did what I'd been planning to do anyway.

"And great bodies. You are one sexy lady."

"I feel sexy." Boy, did I. I arched as my fingers slid between my folds, my skin slick and hot, and I couldn't keep a moan from escaping.

"Ah, yes, baby, that's it. Tell me what you feel."

"Wet. So wet."

"Lick your fingers."

Say what? That wasn't something I did.

But this whole scenario wasn't something I normally did and I was thoroughly enjoying myself, so why not?

I did lick my fingers, and it was incredible how sexy that made me feel. Especially when I watched his reaction. His eyes widened and his breathing actually stopped.

Then he drew in a shuddering breath. "Oh fuck yeah." He jerked his cock, the tempo increasing with each pump. "I want to taste you, baby. Want to feel your legs tighten around me. Feel your feet flex and your toes curl. I want to bury my face between your legs and not come up for air until you come."

My fingers went back between my legs.

"Fuck yourself, Mystery Lady."

"Yes." I couldn't keep the gasp in as I pulled my knees back and plunged two fingers inside, still working my clit with my thumb.

It wasn't enough.

I spread my pussy lips with my other hand, giving myself total access, fingers stroking and fucking as sweat trickled across my stomach, my tits smashed together, nipples tightening in the breeze from the fan. "Oh, God, Scott."

"Yeah, baby. That's it."

I found my G-spot, working it fast, curling my fingers to just the right spot, and stars erupted behind my eyes. I called out—I think it was Scott's name but couldn't be sure because the rush of pleasure between my legs was so intense I couldn't breathe. I couldn't think. My muscles clenched my fingers as I came. Dear lord, I wanted a cock in me.

"I'm coming too, baby."

I managed to pry my eyes open despite the stars and saw Scott staring at me, his eyes intense, not blinking as he pumped that thick cock, aiming it right at me.

"I want to suck you."

"I'm imagining it." He reached out to stroke the screen, and if I'd been able to tear my hands from my body, I would've moved the iPad to my lips.

Jesus Christ, maybe I *should* meet him because this attraction hadn't faded. If anything, the it had grown.

I wanted Scott Masters inside me now.

***

"I think that deserves at least a first initial."

His voice hummed along my spine as I stretched, post-orgasm lethargy seeping through my veins. "D," I said before I thought about it.

"Ah, D. As in delicious."

I giggled and rolled my eyes. Then I rolled over and grabbed the iPad, bringing it close. Now that the afterglow was fading, I wasn't exactly feeling my ultra-sexy best to lie there naked in front of him. Which probably made no sense given what we'd just done, but this was totally new for me, so I was allowed to vacillate.

"Seriously?" I asked.

"Seriously." His grin was wolfish, that was the only word to describe it. "You are one delicious lady."

"I wasn't very ladylike just now."

"Are you kidding me? You were all woman just then, Ms. Delicious. Or would you prefer Ms. Divine? Dazzling? Decadent? Definitely desirable."

"I guess demure is off the table." Because I'd been almost off the bed in my excitement.

"Baby, there is nothing demure about you."

Not this cybersex me. The real me? Like I said, this

wasn't me so I could be whoever I wanted. I was enjoying this whole Ms. D thing, but I wasn't sure I could keep up with her on a daily basis.

"What are you thinking? You're looking too serious for a night with me."

He'd caught me. "Sorry. Reality intruded."

"Don't let it. Let's enjoy the fantasy. Unless you want to make it a reality?"

I propped myself up on an elbow. "That's just it, this isn't me. This *can't* be me."

"Sure it is. Otherwise who was with me just now? People have different sides. This is just one you haven't explored before."

Was he right? *Could* this sexy, out-there woman be me? Was being with a stranger a byproduct of the divorce or had the fantasy been latent inside me all along, just needing the right man to bring the sexpot out to play?

I mean, my ability to write brazen sex had to come from somewhere. It wasn't as if every writer could just decide to write an erotic story and there it was, good enough to garner a publisher and an audience. I had to have tapped into something inside me, right?

It was a thought worth considering.

"I can hear you thinking. I hope you're not trying to talk yourself out of this."

I smiled at him. I was actually trying to talk myself *into* it. But that was a conversation for me, myself, and I. If I let Scott have a say, we know which way he'd go.

I yawned, then glanced at the time. Crap. I had to get up in four hours and not in the way I'd just been *up* for the last forty-five minutes. "I have to go, Scott. Tomorrow comes too early."

He ran his fingers over the screen and I could almost feel the heat on my skin.

"I hear you, Mystery Lady." He kissed his fingers and put them back on the screen. "Sweet dreams."

"You, too." I closed out of Facetime, my body still trembling from the orgasms, my mind still trembling from what I'd been doing. I was an almost fifty-year-old suburban housewife who, up until a few years ago, had had a normal life. Kids, husband, dogs, mortgage, happy hours on Fridays with the neighbors. Nowhere in that list was cybersex with a stranger. Of course, dating wasn't in that list either. Nor was single-parenting. So I guess when my reality shifted, cybersex entered the mix.

My phone dinged. I had an email.

I knew before I opened it that it was Scott.

"I'll be thinking of you."

He'd just guaranteed that I'd be doing the same about him. Not that that was in question. One did not have multiple orgasms with a guy and *not* think about him.

"Back at ya." I closed my email, then pulled the sheet over me. The kids hadn't gotten up in the middle of the night for over a decade, but if tonight was that night, there was no reason to scandalize them. Mom never slept naked.

Mom might not, but Ms. D sure did.

And she liked it.

CHAPTER SEVEN

"Good morning, Delicious Lady."

It was silly that his greeting made me smile. Then again, I was sure I'd worn a smile the entire night while I slept. And I was sure I'd be keeping it on all day, but we couldn't have a repeat of yesterday. One day out of time was excusable, but I'd promised my readers a release date and if I didn't finish the book, I couldn't get it to my editor on time and that would delay publication.

"You too. Have a nice day. I'm going to be busy."

"So no nooner?"

Dammit all, he made me wet *again*! *"You are bad for my productivity."*

"You are very good for all of me."

And I was supposed to argue with that how?

"So you have a nice day, Mystery Lady. I'll be thinking of you."

"Me too." That was all I was giving for today. The last twenty-four hours had been nice—well beyond nice—but it was time to get back to my real world.

Which just so happened to be one of fantasy, but what could I say? I loved my job.

***

I loved it even more when I got to the love scene and could borrow Scott's moves. With last night's Facetime session firmly embedded in my brain, the scene just flowed.

So did the wetness between my thighs and damn if I didn't have *another* orgasm.

Jesus, how was that even possible? I'd never had them before when I was writing. Sure, I got aroused—I'd better or my readers wouldn't—but to come? Never.

Which I could no longer say.

And, actually, that might be a good thing. If I got off while writing it, maybe my readers would while reading it and then there'd be some buzz. I had yet to hit the NYT—maybe Scott was my ticket. I was glad I'd answered his IM for more reasons than one.

I finished the scene, my pussy sensitive as I sat back in my chair. I didn't know if I'd ever written a scene so quickly. I glanced at the clock and checked my word count for the morning. Yup, that was one for the record books.

I needed a break. Writing at breakneck speed wass great for productivity, but it could wear me out. Having an orgasm on top of it only added to the drain on my system.

I opened my email. Of course there were messages from the dating site. Five of them. Three from Scott.

I didn't open those. I'd never get anything accomplished if I did.

My editor had also sent me an email. Carrie was a dream to work with and we'd put out a lot of good books together. She knew my style, knew how I worked, and I didn't have to fight her over every comma or em dash because she got my voice. Editors like her were as important to a writer's career as a story line

"Hey, Dana. Any chance you can speed up the delivery on Call of the Wild? *A slot opened up at the end of the month because someone had to pull out"*.

So much for getting ahead of the game with my writing, but I wasn't one to turn down an earlier publication date. Quicker publication meant more books for my readers and maybe, finally, a vacation for me after three years of working more than anyone should have to to put food on the table.

"You know me, deliver or die. You'll have it." I added a smiley face. It was a joke between us; we said the smile was so big because that the *smiler* was grinding her teeth.

I did get out of my chair for a quick walk, even though my deadline had just been pushed up. Sitting so long made my thigh muscles ache—though they'd gotten quite the workout last night and weren't as sore as they normally were by this time of the morning. Still, walking helped both my mind and my body.

Six more emails showed up when I got back. None, however, from Scott.

I had to admit to a certain disappointment. Which was ridiculous. It'd be one thing if he and I had a relationship, but cybersex was not a relationship. And I didn't really want one. Not with a thirty-three-year-old. I'd be the laughing stock of my neighborhood if I actually started something with a guy his age. "Cougar" would be flying around faster than I could type the word and I was a fast typist.

I hovered the cursor over his first email, but didn't open it. There were those darn Read notifications and I'd told him I had to work.

But it could be fodder for the story.

Nice argument, but I had enough fodder for *three* stories. And all in twenty-four hours. If I kept this up, Scott could keep me in stories for the next ten years.

Of course, he'd probably kill me with orgasms in half that time.

I shook my head and closed down the email program. I was a professional. I had to work. My readers depended on me. My kids depended on me. My mortgage company depended on me. I had a lot of things depending on me, which was why it'd been a relief to just let it all go with Scott, both literally and figuratively.

My responsibility-overload was almost a reason to take those nature walks he'd mentioned.

Almost.

***

The chapters flew from of my fingers the rest of the afternoon. I'd known these characters for a while and had the basic framework of the story. Filling in the scenes was what took up the most time, and since the book was heavy on sex, I had to be in the mood to writer those scenes. Not a sexy mood, though that certainly helped—as I now knew from first-hand (hands?) experience.

But people always asked me how I got inspired to write those scenes and if they were from personal experience. My standard answer was that I had a good imagination, leaving it to theirs to take it further.

And even though after this book I could say, "Why, yes, this is personal knowledge," there was no way in hell I was going to cop to the truth. I *did* have a good imagination—which Scott and I had used to our advantage these past twenty-four hours.

"Hey, Mom. What's for dinner?"

And just like that, the flow of creativity shut down. Hard to think about multiple partners and multiple orgasms when teenagers were asking to be fed.

"Give me a sec," I hollered back, winding down the ménage scene I'd been working on. One that hadn't been inspired by Scott, because if I had more than one of him in my life, I'd never get anything done.

I finished the scene with a lot of "FINISH THIS" notations in the margins and went to enjoy my kids and our dinner.

"You wouldn't believe what happened at school today," said my youngest as she plopped her backpack on the kitchen table. Katy was a junior and the Perez Hilton of her school. More than once I'd been called in to discuss her cell phone usage. I swore the kid was going to be an entertainment news reporter when she grew up, if I could just get her to pass her classes. She was more interested in gossip than in history, not that I could blame her. But still, I had to be the responsible parent (given that I was the only one) and keep her focused on school work.

However, now that I *got* the lure of being online, I was going to have to put on my Hypocrite hat just to get her to graduate.

"What happened?"

"Lisa Leno got caught sexting an older guy."

I dropped the spoonful of mashed potatoes I'd been scooping into a bowl and had to wipe the look of horror off my face before I turned around. "What? How?"

"She was showing people! She'd say all these wild things and then he'd post back and when he sent her a, um, picture, well… the principal heard about it and she got called down and then her parents had to show up and we're going to have to talk to the administration tomorrow and maybe even the police."

Oh God, my daughter had seen some guy's dick online? *So had her mother.*

Yes, but that was different. I'd wanted to see Scott's. I'd made the conscious decision to. I knew what I'd be getting into and God knew, I'd seen enough dicks in my time. But my seventeen-year-old daughter?

"Yeah and now we're going to have this whole big thing on Internet safety and sexting and all this other stuff. It's so bogus." She flopped into a kitchen chair as only a teenager could. "She's an idiot."

She or me?

"I dunno," said Rick, my twenty-one-year-old. "Sexting's pretty hot."

I dropped the bowl of mashed potatoes in front of him. "Richard Thomas Jenkins, please tell me you do not sext."

Pot, meet kettle.

"'Course not, Mom. I just said it's hot. Doesn't mean I do it."

No, but his mother did.

I was feeling worse about this by the minute. I should

never have sexted with a stranger. Just because I was thirty years older than these kids didn't make it right. Or smart. Jesus, what if Scott had had a webcam set up and recorded what we'd done? Thank God I hadn't given him my name, but those damn freckles on my chest were a dead giveaway. They were perfectly visible above the necklines of my t-shirts.

That was it; I was getting a tattoo there tomorrow. Hide the evidence before it became evidence.

"It's not hot, it's disgusting. Who wants to see a guy's junk in math class?"

I set the meatloaf I'd made earlier and a bowl of green beans on the table. *Yeah, Katy, you go with that thought.*

I, on the other hand, was having vivid flashbacks to Scott's thick cock. I wouldn't have minded seeing *that* in math class. Maybe then I would've enjoyed calculus.

I shook my head. Completely inappropriate thoughts.

"So, did she get suspended?"

Katy picked up a green bean. "Dunno. It just happened and since Mom won't let us use our phones at the table—"

That'd been one of my rules since their dad had left because it'd been too easy to lose ourselves in electronics when we needed to stick together. It sucked having to be mom, dad, breadwinner, trash taker-outer, bill payer, and every other "er" that came with home ownership and parenthood, but if I didn't step up to the plate, the plate would remain empty. I was keeping it together for my kids, which was why there'd been no dates and no sex. Scott had come along at just the right time.

Or so I'd thought.

"The guy's an idiot, though," said Matt, son number two. "He should've picked someone his own age."

I swear, if I didn't know any better, I'd think the kids knew.

"Nah, he should've picked an older woman," said Luke, my recent high school graduate. "I hear cougars are all about sexting."

Seriously, had someone been spying? I wanted to shrivel

up in mortification. Instead, I shoveled in some mashed potatoes in an effort to look like I didn't have a clue what they were talking about.

"Ew, that's just gross," Katy said. "That'd be like Mom sexting someone."

The mashed potatoes just would *not* stay in my mouth. "Uh, can we please change this subject? It's not dinner-table appropriate."

"Yeah, you're creeping Mom out, Katy." Luke helped himself to a big mound of mashed potatoes. Better in him than all over my plate. "Mom wouldn't do something like that."

"Hello?" I waved my fork around. "I'm right here. And I just said I wanted to change the subject."

Rick wasn't saying anything. Not that the kid was a chatterbox, but he was a lot like his father. Sat back and contemplated things. I hoped to God he wasn't contemplating my reaction.

Shit, I had to stop this. No more Scott. I needed no further proof than the four kids at this table that I needed to stay firmly grounded in reality. I'd forgotten who I was. What my responsibilities were. There wasn't any time in my life for a Scott, and if my pushed-up deadline didn't prove that, the kids put everything in perspective.

Rick helped me clean up.

That should've been my first clue.

Actually, it was and I dreaded what he was going to say.

"You know, Mom, if you want to date, I can watch Katy."

I had my back to him while I was at the sink and I kept it that way. Talk about awkward. This must be what "The Talk" had been like for him. "Thanks, Rick, but that's not happening."

"I know. You've been so busy with us since the jerk left that you haven't had time. But if you haven't noticed, we're all grown now. You can leave us alone to go on a date."

I pasted the brightest, happiest Mom smile on my face and turned around. "Thank you, honey. I appreciate that. But to date, you have to meet someone, and I don't have the time."

"You could always try an online dating site."

What did he know?

"Those cost money. And who do you really meet on them?"

"Maybe other people like you who are just getting back into the dating thing and don't remember how to do it?"

Oh I remembered. It was just that hanging in a bar at twenty-two was way different from doing it at forty-nine.

"It might be good for you to get out. It'd be fun to have someone treat you well occasionally."

I kept that big ol' happy smile on my face and walked toward my eldest. When had he grown up?

I cupped his cheek and stood on my toes to kiss his other one. "Thank you, honey. I'll keep your offer in mind."

"'Kay, Mom. I love you."

"I love you too." I walked past him. "I have to get back to work. My editor pushed up my deadline. I'll be in my office if you need me."

With the door wide open so I wouldn't be tempted to go online.

And maybe to prove to the kids that Mom wasn't sexting.

Chapter Eight

Mom was, however, horny as hell when she shut down her computer for the evening and called it a night. I might be finished with Scott, but the images of last night wouldn't go away and they'd turned my normally steamy novel into an inferno. *Call of the Wild* was definitely my hottest book to date. Too bad I couldn't thank the guy responsible.

Or meet him.

No. Bad idea. That whole dinner conversation... What was I, a fifteen-year-old boy thinking with my sexy parts and not a responsible almost middle-aged mom? Jesus...

I kissed the kids, then went upstairs and got ready for bed. I looked in the mirror. For an almost middle-aged woman, I wasn't doing so bad. The skin was still wrinkle free. Oh, there was a frown line or two on the forehead and smile lines by my mouth, but no crows' feet yet and the neck hadn't started to go. Tits weren't bad—they'd never been that big, so there wasn't enough to droop—and the muffin top was more like a pooch that I knew other women wouldn't mind, but since I'd always been concave in that area, it bugged the crap out of me. I should start doing sit-ups.

Ass was still tight—the walking helped. Thighs had never been a problem and I'd luckily escaped the cankles that some of my first cousins had. All in all, not a bad picture. I could at least hold my head up high because my much-younger sexting partner hadn't had a troll to look at.

But that was all finished now. He could go find a twenty-something with firmer parts and a concave belly and sext her 'til she couldn't walk. I was done.

Ding.

My cellphone screen lit up with the email's arrival.

I crawled into bed and pulled the covers over me, making sure to leave my bedroom door wide open. That way I wouldn't be tempted.

Because I was.

Ding. My cell always reminded me a second time when I had an incoming message.

I opened it. I mean, it *was* only right that I let Scott know that this was over. I mean, we *had* gotten pretty personal. I didn't have to leave him hanging—especially since he hadn't left me hanging.

Excuses, excuses…

I chose to ignore that annoying voice in my head and clicked on his earliest email.

"I can't get you out of my head. You are so gorgeous. And sexy. And fun. I seriously had a lot of fun last night."

Was that what they were calling it these days?

"I hope you have a great day and I'd love to just chat if you can take a few minutes from your schedule. But if not, I understand. Not everyone has the same freedom I do with their day."

That sounded interesting. Why did he have so much freedom? What did the guy do for a living? He still hadn't answered me.

"Ciao for now, Delicious Lady."

I had to smile. I mean, who wouldn't?

I opened the next email.

"Just saw the news that the walking path overhaul down at RiverWalk is done. They're opening them this weekend. I'd really love to take you there."

He wanted to go out? To meet? No. Absolutely not. This was crazy. And at a park? Serial killers did all their best work at parks. Jogging paths, secluded bushes…

Except RiverWalk was a day-trip shopping mecca and the walking trails ran along the river, out in the open.

I probably had a better imagination than I needed right now. Aside from the fact that Scott had jumped in with guns blazing (no, that was not a euphemism, but I might turn it into one for the book) with a woman he didn't know, and we'd done things that weren't exactly first-date material, I didn't get the sense that he was serial killer material. Not that my gut was necessarily reliable. I was sure Ted Bundy's dates didn't sit there wondering when he was going to off them.

God, I was getting psycho—and starting to creep myself out.

I opened another window on my iPad and brought up his Facebook page. Again, not a sure-fire indicator of non-criminal activity, but there were pictures of his friends and family and—

Holy hell. How'd I miss that? We had a friend in common.

Granted, I had thousands of Facebook "friends" given that my page was my author page and I pretty much accepted everyone—never knew where my next reader was coming from—so the chances were statistically good that we'd have someone in common, especially living only twenty miles apart, but still…

I clicked on his friends list. It was a guy I used to work with at a past day job. Kevin Patterson.

I scrolled through Kevin's pictures. There was Scott and him at a baseball game. Scott at Kevin's backyard barbecue. I'd been invited to that but hadn't gone since it'd been right after the dick had left and parties hadn't been high on my list of priorities.

There was a picture of Scott with Kevin's sisters, and one of Scott and Kevin's dad.

He was a family friend. Maybe had even dated one of the sisters?

Okay, so he was looking a little less psycho-ish now.

But how did I call Kevin and ask? And then ask him *not*

to tell Scott that he knew me? And how would *that* story come out?

Yeah, that wasn't happening. I was not going to ask Kevin about Scott.

But at least I felt better knowing that someone knew him and well enough to have him at family gatherings. And that picture with Kevin's father… Who took pictures of random friends with their parents unless that random friend wasn't so random?

Okay, so I was feeling much better about Scott. But still, why had he IM'd a forty-nine-year-old?

It had to have been for kicks and giggles—and a couple of orgasms, because, yeah, he'd gotten those. Had that been what his IM'ing had been all about? A fantasy of his to put a cougar notch in his belt? I certainly couldn't take issue with that because I'd enjoyed our little tête-à-tête (ahem) just as much as he had and I wasn't about to claim double-standards violation.

I opened the next email.

"I know you said this isn't real for you, but it is for me, Mystery Lady. I want to get to know you in ways other than the biblical sense, though, make no mistake, that's still definitely on the table—and maybe we could even find a table. LOL. I think you're hot, I think you're adorable, I love your profile, and I'd really like the chance to get to know you. Please say yes."

I was tempted. So tempted.

I opened the email that'd come through just a few minutes ago.

"I've scared you off, haven't I? I don't want to. If it's too fast, okay, I'll slow it down. But I've been thinking about you all day and I want to talk to you. Talk. It doesn't have to be about sex. Not tonight anyway. ☐ Please can we Facetime? I promise to keep my clothes on."

Now that was a damn shame.

But I had to appreciate the effort, mainly because he was saying things I wanted to hear.

My earlier argument went out the proverbial window as I emailed him back. *"Okay."*

My iPad screen lit up in two seconds. Damn. I should have better positioned myself in bed. Fluffed my hair. Put some makeup on.

Except he'd already seen me at my sweatiest and he was coming back for more. Well, not more since he'd said sex was off the table. But then what the hell did we have to chat about?

The screen kept "ringing."

I ran over to shut my bedroom door—locked it—then hit Accept once I climbed back into my bed.

Scott's face filled the screen. "Hey, beautiful."

"That doesn't begin with a D."

"I thought Dollface might be too irreverent."

"Boy, you're quick with the one-liners. Are you a stand-up comic in your other life?"

"I'm definitely standing up, but there's nothing funny about it."

I could see only his face and his shoulders—shoulders covered in a blue T-shirt—and the pillows behind him so while I knew he was reclining in bed, I had no idea if he was "standing" at the moment. Or if he even had pants on. I know he said he'd keep his clothes on, but they could be unbuttoned. He could be touching himself…

Jesus. Why'd I have to go there? Sure, I was sex-starved after three years of drought, but could I at least have one decent conversation with the guy before I wanted to get down and sweaty with him again?

"I've been thinking about you all day."

Apparently I couldn't because the minute he said that, I flashed back to last night, to me writhing on the bed, coming as he talked me through it.

My fingers wanted to steal down to my pussy, but I clenched them so they couldn't. "I've been thinking about you too."

"And what were you thinking?"

It'd be so easy to slip into the dirty talk. To go back to what we did so well. But, come on, I had to have some self-respect. The fact that we actually had a friend in common took this to another level.

But was it one I wanted to go to?

Kind of late now, unless you'll never go to one of Kevin's parties again.

Oh great. I needed an exit strategy from a relationship I wasn't even having. Not that I went to a lot of Kevin's parties, but if I wanted to, I wanted to be able to. What if I did go to Kevin's in the future and Scott was there? Better to end this go-round on a good note and not have the awkwardness then.

"Babe, I don't know what's going through your head right now, but don't over-think this, okay? Let's just take it one day at a time and see where it goes."

"That's just it, Scott, where do you want it to go? You're thirty-three. I'm not. I can't have kids and you're in prime family-building mode."

"I thought you had kids."

"I do. But I no longer can. And I don't want more."

"Um, Mystery Lady? I didn't come on the site to find a baby mama."

"I get that. I'm just saying that starting a family is a normal part of being in your thirties. You won't get that with me, so it's pointless for you to be spending time with me."

"I don't think it's pointless, and you already have a family. If this goes anywhere, I'd have them as my family too."

"But don't you want your own kids?"

Wait. How the *hell* had we started talking about kids? This had gotten personal way too fast. More personal than putting my naked body out there for him to see.

"I think we're getting ahead of ourselves." Amazing that a guy so much younger than me showed more maturity than I did. "Let's just talk about our days and not worry about what the future holds. I want to enjoy the beautiful woman I met yesterday and see what makes her tick."

He did. Big time. Especially with the level of maturity he was showing while I was freaking out.

I pulled myself together. I was not responsible for Scott's happiness or his future, and if he wanted to waste prime baby-mama-hunting time on me, then I was going to enjoy it because this really was the perfect relationship at this point in my life. Some cybersex, some flirtation, no strings. It worked for the heroine in my story and it ought to work for me.

"You're right. Too far ahead of ourselves." I shifted to a more comfortable position. "So how was your day? It's kind of hard to know what to ask you since I don't know what you do other than play video games and flirt with women old enough to be your babysitter."

That was what'd started this whole encounter and I wanted to get back to that. Keep it light between us.

"You're the only one I'm flirting with." He exhaled. "Sorry. Had to swallow what I was going to say since I promised to keep this sex-free tonight."

Swallow was not a good word in this context. Or rather, it was, it just wasn't one I wanted to be considering right now. But I worked past it. "So what do you do? Do you work from home all the time?"

"I work with the markets, some investing, financial stuff. That sort of thing."

"Oh. That sounds… interesting." No, it didn't. To the creative side of my brain, it sounded like gobbledy-gook with a few *blechs* and *icks* thrown in. I couldn't imagine a more boring job than staring at financial statements all day. But, hey, if it made him happy and he could make a living at it, she couldn't fault the guy.

"How about you? What do you do?"

Crud. Here was where I either had to get creative or come clean. But the minute I did, he'd want to know my pen name and if he could buy my books in his local bookstore and all the rest of what came with the job. It never failed; at parties my books always became a topic of conversation when a new person joined the group. I couldn't count how many times one of my neighbors would open one of my books on their smart phone and start reading the steamier scenes aloud. Not that I had a problem with people reading what I wrote for everyone to hear, but invariably the inappropriate comments would start, and with the amount of alcohol that had to be flowing for someone to muster the courage to read those scenes aloud in the first place, not much was beyond limit.

"Wow. I didn't realize that was such a heavy question. If you tell me, are you going to have to kill me?"

I smiled. Scott was right; I was making way too much of this. "I'm an author."

"Oh wow, really? As in, I could go to my local bookstore and pick one up one of your books?"

He might get some funny looks, but yes, he could. "Yes."

"That's cool. I have a friend who knows an author. He used to work with her near where you live. Maybe you know her? He said she writes the really steamy stuff. Says she makes a good living at it and that—"

He was a smart man. Too smart.

I hadn't realized Kevin would talk me up with his friends. Not that that was a bad thing since word of mouth was always good advertising. But in this case, it was too good.

"It's you, isn't it? You're Kevin's writer friend."

I could deny it, but what would be the point? He wasn't stupid and all it'd take would be a quick glimpse at Kevin's Facebook friends and he would know exactly who I was.

I should've stopped while I was ahead. I should never have started this Facetime session.

Unless you wanted to get found out. Now you have no excuse not to meet him since he knows who you are.

"Guilty as charged."

He wasn't smiling.

That wasn't good. "Scott?"

He shook his head. "Sorry, just trying to wrap my brain around it. I hadn't expected to be research."

"Research? Are you kidding me? You're the one who started with the sexy come-ons." Seriously? He was going to throw double standards in my face? "I was trying to dissuade you from that conversation if you recall. If I'd wanted you for research"—I spat the word out—"then I sure as hell wouldn't have been trying to talk you out of this." I was highly insulted that he'd even think that.

Of course, the fact that I'd ended up actually using him as research was completely irrelevant. I hadn't started this conversation with that in mind and if he'd kept it out of the sexy realm, I wouldn't have.

"Sorry. You're right. I was out of line saying that."

"Yes, you were." Now I had to tell him what I was doing, though. He came clean; now I had to.

"But if you want to use it, I wouldn't mind."

Or maybe just come period. "Want to say that again?" I needed to make sure I heard him correctly over the blood roaring through my ears as it all headed south.

"It'd be sexy as hell to see what we've done written in a book. Can you use it? Was it steamy enough? I've never read one of your books."

Was it steamy enough? Was the guy for real? "Um, yeah, it'd work in my books."

"So are you going to use it?"

"I try to keep my personal life separate from my professional one."

"Yeah, but you have to get your ideas from somewhere. I wouldn't mind being that somewhere."

"Really? You want me to put what we've done out there for the masses to read? You don't have a problem with that?"

"Hell no. Why would I? It's not like you're going to publish it as non-fiction and name names. I think it'd be really hot for you to write what we did and let everyone read it. Only you and I would know it was real. Kind of like exhibitionism without people seeing us."

"Oh great. Now you're an exhibitionist."

"You're complaining? We were both putting on quite the show last night if you recall, Mystery Lady."

"It's… Dana." My pen name was Mallory, but that didn't begin with a D and all he'd have to do was ask Kevin.

"Dana." He said my name on a groan.

And even that got me wet. I was having an uncomfortable discussion/revelation and yet him saying my name got me wet.

This guy was one talented individual. But then, I'd already discovered that.

"Your secret is safe with me, Dana." He smiled. "Even if you decide to share it with your readers."

"You really want me to, don't you?"

"Yeah. I do. To know women are fantasizing over something we did together… I'm going to have to read your books."

I felt a blush flame over my face. Which was weird. I had no trouble with my friends and neighbors knowing what I wrote—people I attended soccer games and PTA meetings and church with—but Scott, the guy I did kinky things with, *him,* I had a problem with. I shook my head. I was alive and well and living in Double Standards Land.

"You might want to wait until my next one comes out. I think you'll like it."

"Oh?" He arched an eyebrow. I'd always thought that was a sexy move on a guy and I was proven right when he did it. "Does that mean some of this might make its way into the story?"

"Possibly." Yeah, like *all* of this.

"I'll have to keep an eye out for it. But in the interim, I'm going to be doing a lot of reading. It seems I have some catching up to do. Don't want to disappoint you."

"Not happening."

"Oh, I don't know. Remember what I said about the babysitter leading the younger guy to sexual fulfillment? I wasn't too far off, was I? I mean, after all, this is what you do for a living. You probably know lots of things you could teach me."

I should be uncomfortable with this line of reasoning, but it was just turning me on. Here he was, accepting what I did. My ex had had a problem with it. Then again, the argument could be made that *he'd* had reason to have a problem with me writing about wild sex since I wrote fantasy and he hadn't been that fantasy.

Scott, however…

He was definitely fantasy material.

"Or maybe I'll just stimulate your creative juices."

Not touching that with a ten foot poke, er, pole. "You're really okay with this? With me writing about us?"

"Babe, I'd be a moron *not* to be okay with it. Why, was your ex not okay with it?"

"Let's just call him a moron, shall we?"

"I'd rather not call him anything. Guy's an ass if he left you. A dumb ass. Not only do you look like every guy's dream *and* give good cybersex, but you write about it. If you need research material, I'm your man."

Um, yeah, I could definitely work with that. "Okay, so now that you know what I do for a living and you know who I am, I guess this *is* real."

"Yeah, it is. But I don't know who you are. Not really. I don't even know your last name."

Kevin knew my real name, but it wasn't my Facebook name. Dammit. See? This was what happened when I did something outside my comfort zone. I ended up with sex, er, *six,* degrees of Kevin Patterson.

Good God, I couldn't have planned this any worse.

"Don't over-think this," said Degree Number One.

"Kind of hard not to."

I was waiting for him to make reference to something else that was hard, but he surprised me.

"Dana, come on. It's not a bad thing. I wanted to know who you were even before I found out what you do. Before I found out you know Kev. If it helps, he's said really nice things about you."

"You were *talking* about me? You didn't even know me."

"Hey, when a guy tells you he knows a woman who writes erotica, you pay attention. I mean, I'm a guy. You can't fault me for that."

"I guess."

No, I definitely couldn't fault him for being a guy. I could fault him for not knowing the difference between erotica and erotic romance either, but that knowledge would come in time if we continued this.

If.

"Hey, come on. It's not the end of the world. I mean, you write the stuff for a living. You have to know people are reading it."

"Well, yeah, it's just… this. How we met. What we're doing. I hadn't planned for this to get real."

"And I've been trying to change your mind, remember? I've thought you were one hot lady and I was the luckiest guy in the world to find you."

"I'm noticing some past tense going on."

"You're over-thinking it again."

"Look, Scott, you're—"I wasn't going to say *young*—"not as bogged down with responsibilities as I am. You don't have kids, but I do. That's why this can't be real." I should have just shut down the conversation before it'd gone this far. Hell, before it'd gotten to the whole "did you take them off with your teeth" thing. It was my own damn fault.

"Your kids don't know what you write? I thought they were older. They *have* to know. Even if you didn't tell them, they have to know."

"They know." They weren't overjoyed with it, but since it kept us in this house, they didn't complain. Not much.

"Then what's the problem?"

"What I write is fantasy. You're real."

"Ah, and here I thought I *was* your fantasy."

Okay, that got me to smile. "Fishing, are we?"

He shrugged, and that sexy dimple winked into his cheek,

giving him an innocent look that I knew was far from the truth. But on him, I didn't care.

"Hey, I'm human. And contrary to what you seem to think, I don't do this all the time. Matter of fact, you're the first woman I've done this with."

Now it was my turn to raise an eyebrow. "I find that hard to believe."

"Why?"

"Because you're too good at it."

If I thought the dimple-wink was cute, his smile was downright deadly.

"Now *that's* a compliment," he said.

"Oh brother. Here you go getting a big head."

I knew the minute the words left my mouth that they were the wrong thing to say. Or maybe the right one.

"Do you want to say it or shall I?" Scott waggled his eyebrows.

I sighed. "Don't. No need."

"Come on, Dana. You're a beautiful woman and shouldn't be hiding behind your computer screen. Live a little."

That was what my friends had been saying for the past year—but I bet not one of them had foreseen this scenario.

"Besides," Scott said, "now that I know who you are, that you're real and not a psycho, it just makes you hotter."

"Not a psycho?"

"You think women are the only ones who think about that? I purposely don't own a bunny for just that reason."

I had to laugh. The age gap wasn't so big after all if he'd seen *Fatal Attraction*. Probably on Netflix, but at least he could come up with the reference.

"Good, I made you laugh. I'll just add that to the list of things I can make you do."

"How do you do that? Take everything back to sex?"

"It's you, Dana, it's easy. You bring out that side of me. I'm telling you, I don't do this on a daily basis. But when you mentioned the babysitter thing… It struck a chord with me. I'd never had a babysitter who looked like you and what if I'd had? I'd either never have come out of my room, or I'd be following you around like a lovesick puppy. So I went for it."

His words were a twist on my motto: You can always ask; the worst someone can do is say no. In Scott's case, I'd said yes. Bingo Yahtzee for him.

And, yeah, for me.

"Okay, so let's say we decide to go somewhere with this," I said, not even choking over those words. "Where do you see it going? I told you, I'm not having any more kids. That phase of my life is over."

"You let me worry about my biological clock, okay? I hear you loud and clear. But you need to hear me: I'm not looking for a baby mama, so let's get that off the table right now. I'm interested in *you*, not your reproductive parts."

We looked at each other for a silent beat.

He smiled. "Okay, not the internal ones. Better?"

Definitely better since I'd done away with those internal parts. But as I'd said to my niece when she first saw me after the operation and asked me if I was still a girl, the fun parts were still there.

And they'd quite enjoyed themselves with Scott.

I curved a smile onto my lips. Those "fun parts" were getting interested in this conversation, and Scott certainly was into it. I was the only one with any hang-ups and I shouldn't have any left since we'd pretty much annihilated the hang-up thing last night.

"You have a great smile," he said.

I'd been hearing about my smile ever since my parents had spent two-K on it back when I was in junior high. I'd hated the braces back then, but was glad for them now. "Thank you."

"No, thank you for sharing it."

"Thank you for putting it there to begin with."

"I did that?"

"Yup."

"Why? Because I'm not interested in your internal reproductive parts?"

"Nope."

"Because I'm interested in the external ones?"

"Among other reasons."

He raked a hand through his hair. "Jesus, Dana. I said I'd keep sex out of the conversation, but you're making it hard to keep my word."

"Am I making something else hard?" Okay, call me a hypocrite, I didn't care. All I knew was Scott was saying the right things and sometimes I just had to say fuck it and enjoy myself. All work and no play made me a very lonely, cranky, frustrated woman.

He arched an eyebrow at me. "Are you giving me permission to break my promise?"

"Just this one."

"Oh, man, baby. Yeah, you've definitely made something else hard. I was lying here, wondering how I was supposed to *not* touch myself. Right now I think I'm fucking a hole in the mattress."

"Lucky mattress."

He dropped his iPad.

I giggled.

I *giggled*? I hadn't giggled since I was twelve yet with Scott I was giggling.

"Whoa whoa whoa. No fair." Scott flopped over onto his back and held the iPad above him, giving me a great shot of a tight-fitting T-shirt stretched across a muscled chest.

His biceps flexed. "Jesus, woman. When you change your mind, you really change your mind."

"I'm not changing it so much as deciding to not hold back. I was definitely thinking about it. You're right, we've already gone places that we might not normally have, but that doesn't make them bad or wrong. I think you're sexy and I like watching you. I certainly like the orgasms I get from watching you, and we're both consenting adults, so why the hell not?"

"You really are a woman after my own heart."

It wasn't his heart I was after.

Seriously. I wasn't looking to fall in love. I'd only joined the dating site because I was lonely and feeling sorry for myself. Didn't mean I wanted to take on someone else's bad habits and mood swings. But some sexy? I wasn't stupid.

"And maybe after a few other things." I gave him my sexiest smile as I kicked off the sheet.

He groaned and closed his eyes, one arm dropping from the iPad, to fall onto his stomach.

And then moving lower.

"You're touching yourself, aren't you?"

He groaned a long "mmmmmmmmmhmmm."

"Show me."

Yup, pretty much tossing my embarrassment card out the window. And that was how it should be in my fantasy world.

He set the iPad on the pillow, wiggled around some—he *had* been wearing shorts—then tilted the iPad so I had a full-on shot. And I did mean *full-on*. They say the camera added ten pounds; if it did, it was being added all in one place. Scott had nothing to be embarrassed about in that area.

"Like what you see?"

"Yeah. Very impressive."

He chuckled. "I'll show you impressive." He squeezed his hand around the shaft and pumped.

He got bigger. The head got thicker.

And my mouth got dryer.

I licked my lips.

"Damn, Dana, I want to do that."

I wanted him to.

"Is that cum on the tip?" I was practically panting the question, my no-longer-dry mouth now salivating at the thought of licking him.

"Yeah, baby. Want a taste?"

He slicked his thumb over his slit, then brought it closer to the iPad… only to slip it into his own mouth.

"I want your mouth on me, Dana. I want to feel you slick your tongue all over my head. God, it's so sensitive. My fingers aren't anywhere near as good as your mouth." He was back to pumping himself, his thumb rubbing his head, coating it with pre-cum.

His hips flexed, keeping time with his thrusts. "I want to fuck your mouth. Feel you take me to the back of your throat. I want to come in you, have you swallow me as I pump into you. Can you see it, Dana? Can you imagine it? Your gorgeous hair covering my cock, caressing my balls…"

He was doing some pretty impressive one-handed motions on himself that I couldn't peel my eyes from.

"Rake your teeth along my cock, swirl the head with your tongue." He was doing it to himself, his nails playing the part of my teeth, ever so gently sliding up his length.

I wanted to reach through the screen and do it for him.

"Ah, yeah, Dana. That's it. Take me in your mouth." His hand closed over the tip, his fingers milking his shaft, his palm rubbing the head…

My pussy pulsed in anticipation. I wanted that head pounding inside of me. I wanted to wrap my legs around that tight ass and feel our sweat-slicked bodies slide against each other, each pounding thrust taking me higher.

My hand stole down to my pussy. I had to touch myself. Had to make myself come along with him.

"That's it, Scott. Pump yourself, baby."

He opened his eyes, staring right into mine. "I want you, Dana. I want to touch you. Know what you smell like. What you feel like." His back arched, and he gasped. "What you taste like."

He pumped faster and my breathing picked up along with his, my gaze darting between the smoking hot image of him getting himself off and the ecstasy on his face.

"Yeah, Scott, that's it. Come for me, baby."

"I want to come on you. In you." He arched some more and I wanted to slither through the screen and straddle him, taking that big thick cock inside me, riding him until we both screamed.

I worked my fingers faster against my clit.

"God, Dana…" The iPad shook with his rhythm.

I slid my fingers into my pussy. I wish I had Dickie with me, but I wasn't *that* adventurous to bring toys into our cyber session.

Maybe someday…

And the fact that I was considering a *someday* with this guy was a little startling. But it couldn't be any more startling than us doing what we were doing, so I'd worry about *someday* later.

"Talk to me, Dana."

"I'm so wet. I think about you pushing inside me, filling me. I haven't had a man in me in so long."

Oh shit. I hadn't meant to go there.

"How long, baby?"

"Too long." I wanted to leave it at that and get back to my fantasy.

"Does that mean you're nice and tight?"

With the way my muscles clenched around my fingers, I was going to go with a yes on that. "Yeah."

"Oh God, Dana. The image…" He slammed his hand up and down his dick, the swollen head popping out of his fist, the sound of skin hitting skin reminding me all too well of what that felt like.

My orgasm started, not as a wham-bam-thank-you-Sam sort, but one that rolled through me like waves on the shore. Gentle at first, but picking up speed as we neared the shoreline, then crashing over me with a roar, knocking the breath right out of me.

"Christ, woman, you do know how to do an orgasm."

I bit my lip, the tremors shaking me. I didn't want to talk. I just wanted to stay inside my head feeling this, seeing the image of him jerking himself, cum glistening on his head—

He hadn't come yet.

My eyes flew open.

He was watching me. His breathing was shallow.

"Scott?"

"Yeah, Dana?"

"You didn't come yet?"

A quick shake of the head with a bit of a grimace was my answer.

"Are you planning to?"

"Yeah. But I wanted you here with me."

"I'm right here."

"Not for a few moments you weren't."

True. "But I'm back. So let's take care of you."

"It's not going to take much."

"Well that's no fun."

"Trust me, I'm having a ball." He palmed himself. "Two actually."

I rolled my eyes. Had to love a guy who could make you laugh while making you come.

"Nothing to say to that, Dana?"

I chuckled. "Nope. Don't think I can top that. I just want to watch."

He groaned. "You like to watch?"

"Well I like to participate, too, but since watching is the closest I'm going to get right now, yes, I'll take what I can get."

"Take this, baby. Take me." His breathing ratcheted up and he pumped himself faster, his hips rising to meet his fist, thrusting as I imagined him thrusting inside of me, his backside clenching, a perfect set of glutes and hamstrings… Scott was one long line of muscle. With one very long and firm muscle in particular that I was dying to feel.

He worked himself, quick. Slow. A long stroke, a flutter over the top. I couldn't take my eyes from him. He planted his feet on the mattress and lifted himself, fucking the air with each thrust.

I imagined myself on top of him, bearing down, taking that long dick inside me, my hands planted on his abs, his hands gripping my hips, dragging me onto him, only to lift me off before I ground myself onto him again.

God, I ached. Again. How was it possible for this man to make me so incredibly horny? What would happen when he finally touched me?

If *he touches you. If, remember?*

I remembered. But I didn't want to remember the *if*. Scott was so fucking hot, I just wanted to jump through that screen and be with him so all those sexy things he was doing to himself, he could do to me.

"Oh… God… Dana…" My name was a long moan as he came, cum spurting onto his abs, every muscle taut and stretched as his orgasm surged through him.

I wanted him surging in me.

He inhaled and relaxed back onto the mattress. The iPad slipped so I could only see his side, with a glimpse of that God-given sexy line by his hip. The human body truly was beautiful, especially when it was made like Scott's.

I stretched, arms over my head, tiredness seeping through me. Between the two of us, we'd had more orgasms in the past twenty-four hours than I'd had in the past two months, and that was including the ones I'd had with Dickie. I was worn out.

"Hey, pretty lady." Scott's voice was that after-sex growl, low and intimate enough to get my nerve endings paying attention again.

"Hey, yourself." I smiled softly and brought the iPad up to my face.

"That's better. Now I can see you."

"You could see me before. A lot more."

"I know, and while I like your body and you're sexy as hell, this is better. More intimate. Perfect for post-coitus cyber cuddling."

"You know, five years ago those words wouldn't have made sense."

"Gotta love technology."

We were babbling, saying nothing of substance. The kind of thing lovers said afterward as they snuggled into the covers, arms around each other, spooning.

I missed spooning.

He stroked the screen sleepily and I could *almost* feel him with me.

His eyes closed and his fingers drifted off the screen. I didn't want him to go to sleep. I didn't want this to end. If he were here, if we were together, he could fall asleep and I'd lie here, feeling him around me, enjoying the connection. But the only connection I had now was verbal and I wasn't ready to let it go.

"Hey, sleepyhead, what are you thinking about?"

His eyes still closed, his gorgeous smile crawled over his face. "You don't want to know."

Which ensured I did.

If I were with him, I'd nudge my backside into his groin. That'd get his attention.

I sighed. "Yes, I do."

One eye opened and that smile got bigger. "Sure?"

Even more so now. "Yup."

"Okay." He snuggled more into his pillow, the iPad shifting so I had that view over his shoulder again where I could see his perfect butt. "Ice cream."

Okay, that was one I couldn't have called. "Um… Any particular flavor?"

Both of his eyes were open now. "Seriously? *That's* your reaction?"

I shrugged. "Why? What was I supposed to say?"

He now propped himself up on his elbows. "Don't get me wrong, it's a good answer. I just wasn't expecting it."

Like I was expecting *ice cream*. "You've lost me."

"I gave the same answer to that question to a woman I was in a relationship with, and she went off on me."

I was fairly certain that even in cybersex relationships, mentioning another partner was frowned upon.

I shoved myself back so I was sitting up some more and pulled the sheet up. Being naked and sated wasn't a feeling worthy of covering myself, but being naked and angry was. "So why would you give *me* the same answer? Was this a test?"

"No test. I actually *was* thinking of ice cream. Cold, creamy ice cream—that I want to drizzle all over you and then lick off."

Okay, that answer worked, but still… "Was that what you were thinking with the other chick too?"

He grimaced. Good. It was what he deserved for bringing someone else into this.

"Guess I shouldn't admit that, huh?"

No he shouldn't.

No—wait. I was in no position to tell anyone what they should or shouldn't do because if any of my friends had told me she was contemplating doing something like this, jumping into cybersex with a stranger, I would have told her she was out of her flipping mind. But having experienced "this," I could honestly say that *not* doing it was more the reason for a mental evaluation. And, honestly, I had no claim to Scott, nor was I making one. I had no grounds for moral indignation. And definitely none for emotional indignation either. If I was a consenting adult, then I ought to act like one.

"You're not still seeing her are you?"

"Seeing—? Oh geez." He exhaled and flopped onto his back. "Look, Dana, I'm sorry. I shouldn't have mentioned it. She was a long time ago and I'm not a serial dater. I told you I wasn't doing this with anyone else. Damn it, I need to stay away from that particular fantasy. It gets me in trouble every time."

"Hold on. Ice cream is a valid fantasy. I guess it doesn't matter which body is beneath the ice cream if you're into licking it off someone. I'll have to remember that."

"Hey!" He sat up now and pulled the iPad to his face. "The body beneath *is* important. You did hear that I was in a relationship with her, right? She wasn't some random chick I—"

I wondered at what point he was going to see the hole he was digging.

"Dana, it's not like that—"

"Of course it is, Scott. I *am* some random chick you picked up online. Let's not gild the lily here. It is what it is, and I am what I am. And frankly, I wouldn't mind if you licked ice cream off of me. I wouldn't mind if you licked anything off me, as long as your tongue was on me. Anywhere. Everywhere." I moaned, imagining it. And I imagined real good. This entire whatever-you-wanted-to-call-it cyber thing was based on imagination. I had to remember that. That other chick wasn't important.

"Holy fuck." Scott sank back against his pillows. "I have to meet you, Dana. We have to get together. Please. You can't be this perfect fantasy on the other end of a tablet and nothing more. I have to feel you. Touch you."

"Yeah, I know, taste me." Boy, the butterflies in my stomach went wild at that. It was even hotter when *I* said it.

"And lick ice cream off of you."

He had a great smile. It did things to my insides… And I could only imagine what it'd do to my outsides.

That's right; I could *only* imagine it.

"I have to go, Scott. I have to get up early, and two nights of this on this old bod are doing me in."

"That *old bod* is hot and I think you could do a lot more. But I ruined it, didn't I, by mentioning her?"

"No, you didn't. It just got real, and the reality is, I have things to do tomorrow. I need my sleep."

He sighed, nodding. "I understand." He kissed his fingers, then put them against the screen. "Goodnight, Ms. D. I hope your dreams are of me." He ended the Facetime session before I could respond.

Which ensured that I'd be thinking of him.

As did his text. *"Vanilla or chocolate? Or both?"*

Both. Definitely both.

But I didn't answer him. Let him stew about it. Let him wonder.

Let him dream about me.

Now *that* I liked.

I shut down my iPad and plugged it back in. The battery was going quicker than usual these days—did cybersex use more power?

I knew that wasn't possible but it did make me smile and I snuggled down onto my pillow, my body still tingling.

Scott Masters left quite the lingering effect.

Chapter Nine

The effect was still in existence the next morning.

I woke up to the *ding* of a message.

"Thinking of you, Ms. D. Call me when you get up."

I waited. Sure enough the next message popped right up.

"Because I'm already up."

Of course he was.

I smiled and got out of bed. If I replied, I'd never get anything done. Multi-orgasms were addictive and I could easily turn into a junkie. Good thing he *wasn't* here; I'd be distracted all day and get no writing done whatsoever.

I showered and got dressed, took care of the pets, grabbed my hot chocolate that I ran through the cappuccino machine, and sat at my computer, ready to write for the day.

Ding.

Darn, I'd forgotten to turn off the phone. I typically kept it on mute while the kids were in bed so I could sink into the story and not get pulled out. Most of my friends and family knew not to bother me in the morning unless someone was injured, and even then, there'd better be blood.

Only one person wouldn't know not to contact me.

I, against my better judgment, looked at my phone.

"Have a great day. I'll be thinking about you."

No kidding.

I smiled. I liked him thinking about me and I liked thinking about him.

I was thinking about him a lot—and that made writing the next scene tough to do because the characters in the book were now at odds with each other. The big emotional moment where everything looked like it was going to hell and they'd never fix it. Putting characters I loved into painful scenarios and writing about them always zapped my energy and rubbed my emotions raw. It was much more fun writing them as they fell in love.

For a bunch of reasons.

Ding.

I smiled. Normally I'd be annoyed, but I couldn't be with him.

"Are you mad?"

Oh, geez. Hadn't thought he'd think that. *"No. Just getting into my writing cave. Once I go in, I don't come up for air for hours and I have a lot of writing to get through. I'll touch base with you later."*

"I'd rather you touch something else."

That line was going into the book because if it did for my readers what it did for me, I was going to sell more books than I ever had.

"Talk to you later."

I answered him with a smiley face emoticon. Didn't want to give him any more opportunity to play with my words and get me thinking of sex scenes instead of emotional, heartbreaking ones.

"Once last thought for the day..."

The guy seriously was going to be the death of me. Didn't he get that I needed to concentrate? I said I'd talk to him; he needed to back off—

A body shot.

He'd sent me a body shot.

Well, his face was in it, but that body...

The camera stopped short of a dick shot—thank God. I really wasn't into those. On video, aroused, me having an orgasm... sure. But a static, "Here's my dick!" just wasn't my cup of tea.

"Have a great day."

If I didn't have bed head, no makeup, and a threadbare T-shirt on, I'd probably return the favor. He did say he liked looking at me after all. But not like this. I was keeping the fantasy firmly in fantasy realm.

"I will now. Turning off my phone."

And I did. Well, after I sent that picture to my email account and then brought it up on my computer. Who knew? I might sail through this emotional scene and segue right on in to the make-up, mea culpa, let's-fix-this scene where hot body shots could provide the perfect inspiration for the end of the book.

His did.

I sat back six hours later, my arms aching, my fingers stiff, my ass numb, and my body emotionally and physically spent.

The book was finished. I wrote twelve thousand words and got to *The End*. That'd never happened before. The most I'd ever written in a day was ten thousand and it'd taken me over ten hours to do.

Scott Masters was good for my productivity.

Well, he was good for a lot of things, but definitely a plus for my writing career. Too bad I couldn't keep him.

Who says you can't?

I did. I wasn't sure what the protocol was for cyber sex romps—couldn't call this a relationship or a romance, so *romp* was the best word I could come up with—but they didn't lean toward happily-ever-afters. Especially when he was thirty-three and I… wasn't.

I drummed my fingers on the desk. This was getting out of control—and I wasn't fighting it.

No, I was liking it.

I opened my email program. I still had Kevin's email address. I could just shoot him an email, asking him about Scott—

Yeah. Right. What was I going to ask? *Do you recommend the guy for a fling?*

I closed the program. There was no logical way to get info out of Kevin on Scott without revealing my hand. And I didn't really want to do that. Not yet. Not unless it went somewhere.

Define somewhere.

That was the thing; I couldn't. Where did one take a cyber romp? To reality? A motel?

I shivered at that thought, a completely involuntary, unplanned shiver—that was as delicious as the idea of seeing Scott in the nude on the bed beside me.

Kevin was friends with the guy. I'd known Kevin for more than five years; he was a nice guy. A friend who was close enough to be in family pictures would at least be as nice as Kevin, right?

Scott's better than nice, woman.

Yeah, he was. And the fantasies he inspired were *way* beyond nice.

I leaned back in my chair, stretching my arms over my head, enjoying the shivers still running through me as I looked at that last scene on the computer screen.

Ice cream. That was one I hadn't used before. But it played well. Hot and cold, the sugary sweetness, having it melt into the heroine's navel so the hero could lap it up... Then it tracking down her abdomen and between her thighs...

I looked at my office door. I'd locked it. I didn't even remember doing it—I never locked it when the kids were awake—but I had.

I'd been planning ahead obviously.

I spread my legs and slipped my fingers between them.

I also hadn't put on panties today.

Smart girl.

I re-read the scene as I touched myself, imagining I was the heroine and Scott was doing all those delicious tongue-twirling things to me. He was spooning the ice cream onto my breasts, the cold shocking to my aroused nipples.

I let go of the computer mouse and stroked my nipples through my t-shirt.

His warm mouth closed over one nipple, the ice cream melting against my skin…

I had ice cream in the freezer.

I opened my eyes. No. I wasn't going to get it.

It would be messy.

Sticky.

Sticky and messy would be fun *with* someone, but not by myself. In my office chair.

An ice cube on the other hand…

I looked at the clock. The kids were all out at their jobs or with friends, enjoying the last days of summer vacation, and wouldn't be home any time soon.

I wanted to enjoy *my* day.

I stood up, tugged my T-shirt dress down over my thighs, and scooted over the dogs who were camped out by my door. Normally I let them in with me, but since Scott had come along, I wanted my privacy. Even from the dogs.

Oh, wow. I hadn't realized I was neglecting the animals because of my newfound fantasy life. It was getting out of control.

But I couldn't complain.

I shrugged. The dogs were going to sleep anyway and they were content outside my door. I was going to enjoy this ride for as long as I could.

I ran into the kitchen—literally ran. I shook my head and laughed at the way I was acting. As if I was a teenager again.

And that, my friend, is a good thing.

There. Absolved by my conscience.

I grabbed a glass and dropped some ice cubes into it. No, I wasn't going to use all of them, but I wanted to make sure I'd have enough to last me.

My pussy clenched, and I felt the slide of wetness between my thighs. Probably wasn't going to take me all that long anyway.

One of the dogs raised her head, a lazy grunt accompanying the motion when I headed back to my office.

"Go back to sleep, Bandit."

I shut the door and locked it—no need to tempt fate. Then I made certain my office blinds were closed and peeled off my dress.

There was just something so deliciously forbidden about being naked in any room other than my bedroom or the bathroom. That alone turned me on.

I walked to my office chair and set the glass on the desk. I scrolled back to the beginning of the ice cream scene.

The cold tightened her nipples and made her gasp.

"Hey, pretty lady. I want to make you make that noise."

Jenna nodded at the spoon in his hand. "You did, babe. Now what are you going to do about it?"

I swirled an ice cube around my nipple. Yikes. Cold.

But very very hot.

"This."

Bradley knelt over her and licked the first droplet of the ice cream from beneath her breast. Then he dragged his tongue up, flicking her nipple and, God, the sensations of hot and cold were incredible. She trembled with pleasure.

I didn't get that hot part after the cold. And I wanted it, damn it.

I put the cube right on my nipple—it was so cold it did burn, but in a delicious tingling sort of way.

I squirmed in my chair. I didn't need to re-read the scene; I'd just written it. I could work from memory.

I closed my eyes, imagining Scott here, running the ice cube over my nipples, first one then the other. Water dripped between my breasts and down my stomach, another sensation I hadn't counted on. The feel of it pooling in my navel… I was suddenly full of erogenous zones that hadn't gotten a workout since the last time I'd had sex with my ex.

And even then, he hadn't paid this kind of attention to those zones.

I grabbed another ice cube, one for each hand.

One for each nipple.

Around and around I swirled. I arched my back, needing someone to suck on my tits. No matter how I tried, I couldn't manage it.

I groaned Where the hell was Scott when I needed him?

Put on cyberhold for some stupid reason.

I thought about calling him, but that would set a precedent I didn't want. If I let him in during the day, my productivity would be shot to hell and as much as this could be called research, I didn't think my mortgage company would grant me an extension because of it.

Instead, I slid the ice cubes together, gasping as the melting water trickled down my skin.

Some seeped down along the crease to my thigh.

But by then it had warmed up.

What would that cold ice fell like in my pussy?

Oh, wow. I'd never thought of ice cubes before. Like Ben Wa balls only dissolvable.

I spread my legs and slicked one ice cube over my pussy lips. I shivered, but not from the cold. Rather, the contrast of my heated skin and the cold ice made me shiver with want.

I slid it inside me.

Holy hell. The sensation was… incredible. Indescribable. Unbelievable.

I clenched my muscles, holding it in as the wetness trickled out—wetness I didn't think was entirely from the ice.

I took the other ice cube and slicked it over my clit.

Ah… So painful it felt good.

I did it again.

God, yes…

I stroked myself with ice, spreading my labia with one hand and working the entire area. Jesus, the sensations had my toes curling and my muscles clenching so much it was as if… as if…

Holy hell, an orgasm ripped through me.

I twisted in my chair as if some guy were holding my knees in place and eating me out unmercifully.

I shuddered and cried out—something I never did while masturbating, even with Dickie. I'd trained myself to be quiet, but this… I couldn't control my reaction. The fact that I still held the ice cube on my clit was amazing because I wanted to grab the arm rests of the chair and hang on.

Pulse after pulse slammed through me, the surge of my orgasm lifting my ass off the chair. My juices poured from me—this wasn't the ice cube. I'd had a few squirting orgasms before, though they'd been more like a long flow of fluid, and this was definitely that.

But I'd never had one by myself before.

I felt the ice cube slide out of me and that signaled the beginning of the end. My muscles contracted and relaxed so I could lower myself back onto my chair. Right onto the ice cube.

No, I was not going to try ice *there*.

I chuckled and wiggled 'til I felt what was left of the cube slip off the chair.

Jesus. That'd been intense. Amazing, but intense. I didn't know if I'd do it again, but for a one-off, it was definitely something to try.

But, God, it'd worn me out.

I dropped the ice cube that I'd used on my clit into the glass with the others and threw my hands over my head, trying to catch my breath. My heart was pounding in my chest. Definitely not one to try with a weak heart.

But maybe one to try with a younger one…

I wanted to be with Scott. The idea was no longer growing on me; it was a full-blown desire. I didn't care some would call me a cougar—that'd only be if anyone found out. No one had to. God knew, no one had known about my ex's affair for months; surely I could pull off a one night stand with Scott?

Maybe two?

Ding.

It was him. Of course it was.

I reached a shaky hand for my phone. If I could've mustered enough energy to pull myself up to the computer I would have since I typed faster on it, but right now I was just chilling. Enjoying the tremors.

I opened Scott's message.

"I hope you're having a productive day. Enough so that you can meet me online tonight."

Well duh. That'd been the point of shutting him down during the day; I wanted no distraction other than the one he was providing when we got together tonight.

"But I'd rather meet you in person. Will you? Can I take you to dinner?"

Dinner? The offer was tempting. Really tempting. Really *really* tempting.

But that couldn't happen. Restaurants were public places and we already knew one person in common. What if we knew more? What if one of those people saw us together? What if one of my *neighbors* saw us together?

I didn't want to be the cougar of the neighborhood. It was bad enough my ex had left me for a blue-eyed blonde in her early thirties; I was already a cliché, but one of his making. Getting caught dating Scott, I'd be one of my own making.

So much for my full-blown desire.

"I'm pushing too hard, aren't I?"

Not in the way I wanted him to.

"I'm not going to apologize for it. I want to meet you, Dana. I want to see where this goes. Being online is hot and fun, but I want more."

If the guy were even ten years older, all of this—the attention, the sex, the fun—would be amazing. I'd jump on it—him—in a heartbeat.

You're letting a number *dictate your actions? Everything else is perfect and you're letting a number put the brakes on? Really?*

Well, when I put it like that…

Why *couldn't* I go out with him? Because society would call me a name? Was I that shallow? That insecure? I'd always prided myself on being my own woman. I'd owned that in my career choice; why couldn't I own it in my life?

"I know you're reading these."

The damn Read notifications.

"And since you didn't jump on and tell me I'm out of my mind, I have to hope you're at least considering my suggestion. Are you? Can we do dinner?"

I wanted to do dinner. And breakfast. And every minute in between.

So why the hell didn't I?

"No, Scott. We can't."

I sat back and waited for the reaction I knew was coming.

"NO????? Jesus, woman, what do I have to do to get you to go out with me?"

My fingers hovered over the keyboard, and I took a breath. *Here goes.* I was about to make Scott Masters one very happy guy.

CHAPTER TEN

"Plan a weekend instead."

Scott stared at his phone, almost unable to believe what Dana had typed.

A weekend. The hottest woman he'd met in a long time—maybe ever—wanted to spend the weekend with him.

Hell, he'd been hoping for a dinner; a weekend was… unimaginable.

He couldn't get his fingers onto the keypad fast enough.

"Does this weekend work for you?" Probably not since she'd have to make arrangements for her kids with only a day's notice, but it couldn't hurt to ask.

"Actually, it does."

The hell with the killing he'd made on the stock market today; he'd just won the lottery with her answer. The financial district would drop their collective jaws if they heard him say that; Scott was very aware of his reputation as a financial whiz kid and while he liked that professionally, this was all personal.

"Any place in particular?" His mind was racing through the possibilities. There was the one with the champagne glass bathtub—cheesy but somehow still sexy—and the one with the theme rooms. Also cheesy, but man, the fantasies they could inspire. Then there was the swanky place that would cost him a day's worth of trading, but he wouldn't mind a dime of it if he got to see Dana writhing amid eight-thousand count sheets.

He got hard just thinking about it.

"Surprise me."

Oh he'd surprise her all right. The woman didn't have a clue what she was in for. She thought their cyber sexcapades were something? Scott was thoroughly going to enjoy showing her what sexy really was.

"How early can you be ready?" God knew he was ready now. He had to admit he was surprised that he was. He wasn't twenty anymore and with Ellen, his last girlfriend, sex had gotten rote. Then again, it'd never been as hot as it was with Dana, even when he and Ellen had begun seeing each other. They'd grown comfortable, then complacent, and, well, he hadn't been too upset when she'd said she'd wanted more excitement in her life. The thing was, Scott wanted that too; they just hadn't had it together. So the breakup hadn't been bad, it just hadn't been... anything. He still saw her occasionally, and when he did, it didn't feel as if they'd once been together for three years.

But with Dana... He'd taken one look at her picture on the dating site and had to make contact. Even her age hadn't dissuaded him. He wasn't big on numbers anyway unless they pertained to a stock he was trying to buy or sell. Age was a state of mind, and after watching his father die so young, he counted the years he had left, not the ones that'd already passed.

"Have to drop the kids places. Earliest I could leave would be 6:30."

"6:30 it is." Earlier if she could make it, but he respected her obligations.

He actually liked her obligations. He liked that she was a mom. No pressure for him. He wasn't sure he wanted kids; being the oldest of a family of nine, he'd pulled enough diaper duty to last him a lifetime, especially after Dad had died. He'd put all his work in early; now was the time to enjoy life, and with Dana, he planned to.

"I'll text you directions... unless you want me to pick you up?" He added a smiley face emoticon to let her think he was joking because he understood her trepidation. Couldn't be too

careful these days and, even though it was *him* she was cautious about, he liked that she was. Thank God she knew Kev, who would vouch for him, otherwise this weekend wouldn't be happening. Scott knew that as surely as he knew he was going to go out of his skull waiting for tomorrow night.

"You can pick me up. You know Kevin and what I do for a living. Not much is a secret about me now."

"Oh you have some secrets left. Like how you taste. How you feel. How you smell… And I plan to learn everything I can about you."

He couldn't wait to hold her. Just hold her. Feel her body against his. He wanted to bury his face in her hair and inhale the scent of her. Wanted to run his hands over her curves, feel the weight of her breasts in his palms.

To start with.

"Can we Facetime?" He wanted to see her again. He'd stared at her profile pictures for so long he'd memorized them. But there was nothing like seeing Dana in motion. The way she smiled, the way her eyes crinkled, the sound of her moans vibrating at the back of her throat—

Damn, he could come right now if he wanted to.

He didn't. It was lonely coming by himself. Even what they'd done online, while great, wasn't what he wanted. And it wasn't just getting off; he wanted Dana with him. Masturbation was biology; he wanted that connection with someone that took jacking off from physical to something more. A bond. He was tired of being single. Tired of coming home to an empty house.

"Can't. Love to, but I now have a ton of stuff to do before tomorrow night if we're going to do this."

"Oh we're going to do this, Mystery Lady. I'm not letting you back out now."

They said their goodbyes and for a moment Scott just stood there, the phone resting in his palm, his other resting on top of it, almost as if he could feel her essence.

He looked around his place, as if someone were watching

him. It was ridiculous because no one was peering in his windows, but he just felt so… exposed.

He laughed and tucked the phone into his back pocket. Exposed? Standing in his living room fully dressed? He'd been exposed last night on the internet with Dana yet he hadn't felt one whit of self-consciousness.

He should've. He hadn't been playing her; he'd never done that with anyone before, not even Ellen. But with Dana, the words had just come out of his fingertips of their own volition, as if it'd been the most natural thing in the world.

He looked at the phone. He wanted to call Kev. Find out more about her. But then Kev would start asking questions and he had a feeling Dana wouldn't want anyone to know. She was hung up on their ages; he was going to have to show her that the numbers didn't matter.

He was going to start with their mode of transportation tonight. His Audi was hot, but Dana was hotter, and once he was with her, he didn't want to have to worry about mundane things like driving.

Limo was the first order of business. Then the champagne, and the flowers, and the ritzy hotel. He'd save the champagne glass and theme rooms for when they knew each other better and she wouldn't be so self-conscious. He remembered Kevin's comments about her when they'd worked together.

"Dude, you totally wouldn't expect the stuff that comes out of her pen to come from her. Sure, she's a hot older woman and obviously has had sex, but she's so normal, you know? Nice, a good mom, does the whole PTA thing. Calls out when her kids are sick, goes to family resorts on vacation. Just by looking at her, you wouldn't expect her to even know about half that stuff, let alone write about it."

He was going to get her books. But not until after he met the real Dana. He didn't want anyone confusing anything. She wrote fiction; he got that. Writers had good imaginations. Just because she wrote that stuff, didn't mean she did it.

But could she? And would she write about them?

He got hard*er* thinking about that. About seeing on paper what they'd done on screen. And what they were going to do this weekend.

He had visions of making love to her in front of a fireplace—had to make sure the suite he reserved had one. And on the bar. Another must-have. And one of those padded benches at the bottom of the bed; he'd bend her over it and take her from behind, holding those gorgeous tits of hers as he drove into her—

Jesus. He couldn't even fantasize about her in the middle of his living room without wanting to finish himself off.

He looked around the room again. He had a fireplace. And an ottoman that was bigger than a bench. He had the bar. And a sectional sofa with recliners built in.

He wanted to bring her here. He hadn't shared this house with anyone; it'd be all his and Dana's. He could make love to her all over this place and embed her scent in every corner.

He imagined her sitting naked on his kitchen countertops. He'd come out of his office, raking a hand through his hair, numbers running through his brain, and then he'd look up and see her sitting there. Naked. Open. Waiting just for him.

He'd forget the pressures of the market, the incessant number-crunching that went on in his head, the constant barrage for interviews and tips. He'd drop his pants right there, stride over to her. Ditch the briefs. Peel off his shirt. By the time he made it to the kitchen, he'd be as hard as the granite she was sitting on. He'd walk up to her, tug her forward, and plant a kiss on that sexy mouth of hers while he thrust inside her.

She'd wrap her legs around his waist, her heels digging into his ass, and she'd moan into his mouth, her pelvis rocking against him, her pussy clenching him.

It wouldn't take long. Not the first time. Maybe not subsequent times. Hell, right now he *was* as hard as the granite, and no relief in sight.

Fuck it.

He strode over to the sofa, dropped trou along the way,

released the lever on the recliner as he dropped into it, took his dick in his hand, and imagined Dana as she'd been last night.

Her mouth was the first thing he remembered. Her lips, pouty and full from when she'd bitten them after she'd gasped. She's slicked her tongue over them and he wanted her to do that right before she took him in her mouth, sliding down him slowly, taking every inch of him.

He ran his palm over the head of his dick. His hand was nowhere near as smooth as her slick lips and tongue would be, but it was all he had at the moment.

He cupped himself with his other hand, stroking gently as he imagined Dana would do. He scraped his nails along his sac, shivering at the sensation, imagining it was Dana doing that to him.

He spread his legs wider, stroking behind his balls—where he wanted her tongue to be.

His balls tightened at the image, and damn if he didn't feel his orgasm starting. If Dana could do this to him in his imagination; he could only imagine what she'd be like in person.

He was imagining now. Seeing her long brown hair flowing over his thighs as she ran her tongue along that sensitive flesh, then taking each ball into her mouth, tonguing them, sucking them, licking them.

He squeezed the base of his dick as his balls tightened and got heavy. He didn't want to come just yet. He wanted to see this scenario through to the end because, God willing, it'd be the last time he'd have to imagine Dana sucking him off—he wanted to *remember* it.

She'd lick her way up his dick, along the pulsing vein, her tongue fluttering enough to tease but not finish him off. He liked the teasing, liked the anticipation of her sucking him in, but Dana would take her time. She'd drive him nuts and he was completely down with that.

She'd run just the tip of her tongue around the rim, flicking, fluttering, sending his nerves crazy.

Like now. He was using just his fingertips to pull gently

at the head, catching the underside, sending jolts of electricity streaking down to his toes.

Then she'd lick the head, her tongue fucking his slit—Shit. Pre-cum.

Scott swirled it over his head, the slickness making the image of Dana's tongue more defined.

He wanted her on him.

Her teeth would scrape the head, not enough to be painful, but enough for him to want it to be.

Then she'd close her lips over him, taking him in slowly, the suction pulling every thought in his head to that one spot.

He slid his hand up his shaft. No way it could compare to a woman's mouth, but it'd have to do.

Until tomorrow night.

Shit again. The image of tomorrow night, of Dana in the back of the limo and what he was going to do to her until they got to the hotel… He was going to go down on her and taste every part of her sweet, sweet pussy. He was going to make her come so good, she wouldn't be able to walk when they finally got to the hotel. Hell, he had to remember to pay the driver to get lost for a good half hour.

He worked his dick faster, squeezing as he pumped. He closed his eyes, seeing himself between Dana's thighs, tasting her, watching her back arch and her nipples tighten as she tried to catch her breath. He loved how a woman's stomach fluttered when she was about to come.

He'd spread her wider and take her clit between his lips, sucking until she couldn't manage to get out his name. Then he'd tongue her so fast, she'd scream it as she came, pulsing against his mouth, her juices coating the fingers he'd slide inside her at the last minute, curving them to give her another orgasm just as the first one was ebbing.

It was a special talent he had, and Dana was going to benefit from the hours he'd spent perfecting it.

He pumped himself faster, imagining Dana convulsing around him, her slickness coating him.

Ah, fuck… His orgasm built low in his sac. Scott jerked himself faster, harder, wanting it to be Dana working him. *One more day.*

Hell, one more night.

Scott dug his heels into the foot rest and focused on what he was doing, imagining he was holding Dana's head as she slid her mouth over him, the warmth of her breath on his cock… He palmed the head, needing the pressure, pretending it was the back of her throat and—

Holy fuck, he came. Thick, hot streaming lines of cum surged out of him, coating his palm, and trailing down his shaft, giving him some much-appreciated lube.

He pumped faster, squeezing again, working the sensation through himself. God, he was shuddering. He hadn't given himself an orgasm like that in a long fucking time.

It was all Dana's fault.

He shoved back with his calves, bringing the chair upright. Yes, it'd been Dana's fault… And she was going to have to pay the price for making him want her so badly.

Chapter Eleven

Scott sat on the edge of his seat as the limo pulled up to Dana's house. God, he might think this was his first date, first prom, and first time all in one, he was that… Nervous? Anticipatory?

Horny…

Yeah, that, too.

But this wasn't just about sex. He wanted to get to know her. Yes, on a physical level, but also an intellectual one. He wanted to hear what made her tick, how she thought, about her kids, her life, her job. What she wanted for her future and where he could factor in.

Because if she was everything he thought she was, he *was* going to factor in.

He hoped to hell she'd let go of her worry about their age difference. It was a non-issue. And he planned for her to believe it after this weekend.

The limo pulled to a stop at the curb in front of her house. A nice, normal-looking house. Just as Kevin had described Dana. It had a wooden swing on the front porch, pots of flowers on the steps, big old oak trees shading the yard… Pure suburban normalcy.

If her neighbors only knew what they'd been doing. What they were *about* to do.

Nah. If her neighbors knew, Dana wouldn't do it. For all that she hadn't been shy with him online, he'd bet no one else knew the side of Dana he'd come to know.

He was very glad about that.

He cleared his throat as he got out of the car and straightened his collar. He'd dressed up somewhat—a button-down, but he drew the line at ties. He had a jacket in the car solely for dinner at the restaurant.

He lifted the bouquet off the seat. He didn't know her favorite flowers, but roses were too cliché for tonight. He'd gone with an assortment of lilies, some tiger, some golden, some calla, with irises thrown in—an array of wild abandon, exactly what she reminded him of.

Hell, he was half hard as he walked up the path to her front door. Dammit, he didn't want to be. Not yet. He wanted to be able to talk to her without thinking about ripping her clothes off.

Then she opened the door.

Yeah, that wasn't happening.

"Hi," she said, swishing her hair forward over her shoulder. Not in any affectation, but to hide… her blush.

She was blushing. He smiled at that. Imagine, his Dana blushing after all they'd seen and done and said together.

His Dana.

He liked the ring of that.

He also liked the dress she had on. No little black number for her. No. She was in vibrant green. The color of a golf course that hugged those curves he couldn't wait to get his hands and mouth on, the perfect backdrop for her gorgeous dark hair and green eyes.

Eyes that were even prettier in person.

"You look… breathtaking."

Her blush deepened. "Thank you."

He stared a few more seconds—she honestly was stunning. The camera didn't do her justice, and he'd be dammed if he could tell she was forty-nine.

Dana had just shocked the hell out of him. And after what they'd already done together, Scott hadn't thought that was possible.

"Those are for me, I'm presuming?"

"Uh. Yeah. Yes. Sorry." Jesus. He was stammering. He hadn't stammered around girls since… well, *ever*. He held out the bouquet. "I wasn't sure what flowers you liked, so…"

"These are perfect, thank you. Do you want to come in while I put them in water?"

"Okay. Great."

This was *not* how he thought their first in-person meeting would go. She was blushing and he was stammering despite having seen each other at their most vulnerable.

Maybe that was why they were nervous.

He followed her back to the kitchen. The woman had a walk like the most graceful ballerina with just enough *oomph* in her backside to keep him following after her. And it was all natural. There was nothing fake about Dana.

"Sorry about the mess. Kids."

"It's fine. Lived in." Reminded of his house growing up, though actually much neater than he was used to.

She opened the top kitchen cabinet for a vase, but the heels—Jesus, those heels!—she had on didn't help much.

"Here. Let me." He reached above her head to grab it.

God, she smelled good. If it was perfume, it didn't have that sting of alcohol after it, and if it wasn't… He was going to buy stock in that soap or lotion company.

He pulled the vase off the shelf and she took a step away—

No way in hell.

Scott took a step toward her and held the vase between them. "Here you go."

He almost smiled at the way her eyes darted at him then away, the little nibbles on her bottom lip making him stare until he realized he was making her nervous.

He didn't want to make her nervous; he wanted to make her comfortable.

"Dana."

She looked up at him. God, she had gorgeous eyes. He could lose himself in them.

"It's okay. I don't bite." He let his smile come out to play just a little. "Unless you want me to."

She blushed again, but not before he saw the flare of desire in her eyes.

Good.

She tucked some of her hair behind her ear. "Let me put these in that vase and then we can get out of here."

So she wasn't shying away. Good for her.

And good for him.

Scott stepped back, gave her some breathing space. She'd better take advantage of it because this might be the last time for the next forty-eight hours.

"Where's your bag? I'll take it out to the car."

She turned on the faucet. "On the sofa in the family room. There are two."

"Of course there are." He smiled at her as he headed out. He'd never known a woman who could make it with one bag.

"Scott?"

He turned around.

"Don't judge a book by its cover."

He cocked his head, not sure what she was getting at. "I never do."

"Good." She nodded and turned back to the flowers, kicking her hip to one side, not so shy anymore. "Because I'm not like any of the women you've met before."

That, he knew.

It was all Scott could do not to put a bounce in his step. That spicy woman he'd been talking to was in there somewhere; he just had to coerce her to come out and play.

Chapter Twelve

He had his hand on the limo's trunk, about to close the lid, when she walked out of her house, her dress swishing around one of the nicest set of legs he'd seen in a long time.

"You rented a limo?"

"Got it in one, Mystery Lady." He slammed the lid and rounded the car. "Ready?"

One word, so many implications.

"As I'll ever be." She practically skipped down the path—well as much as a woman could skip in those hot-as-shit fuck-me pumps that had him imagining doing just that.

She'd be keeping those on later.

He reached for her hand as she made it to the sidewalk. "Here, let me help you over the grass. We don't want you to ruin those shoes."

"*We* don't?" She gave him a sexy, come-hither look that he really didn't need to get turned on.

He spanned her waist and lifted her over the grass, setting her down in the few inches between the curb, the car, and him.

He didn't let go. "Right. *We* don't. I have a vested interest in those shoes."

She rested her hands on his biceps and heat seared through his sleeve. He was surprised the fabric didn't catch fire. Because he sure as hell was hot enough to spark one.

She flicked her tongue over her bottom lip. "And what would that *vested interest* be?"

She was daring him—but she didn't know him as well as he wanted her to if she thought he wouldn't take her up on it. He hadn't gotten to where he was professionally by playing it safe, and winning Dana was going to be the personal equivalent.

"I don't want to get grass stains on the sheets."

He smiled when she gripped his arm a little tighter, his comment taking her out at the knees. Go him. If a few of her neighbors weren't staring out their windows, he might just sweep her up in his arms. But she'd have to face enough questions because of the limo; no need to add fuel to the gossip fire.

He took pity on her. "Was that too much?"

"After what we've done? Hardly."

He leaned in a little closer. "Something's hard all right."

She tilted her pelvis toward him. "I can see that."

"You're even sexier in person, Dana."

"I'm glad you feel that way."

He ground himself against her. So much for the neighbors. "You can feel what I feel like."

She gripped his arms a little tighter. "You need to stop that, Scott, or there's no way I'm going to wait for the hotel."

"What makes you think we're going to?" He opened the door behind her. "Get in."

That came out a little harsher than he'd intended—he certainly hadn't planned to order her around—but she just smiled that sexy smile and climbed right in.

Then she tugged on the front of his shirt when he got in.

Almost made him wish he'd worn a tie.

"I'm assuming the driver can't hear anything?" she asked, sliding her fingers between his buttons as he tugged the door closed behind him.

He palmed her cheek, brushing her hair off her face, and tilted her head back. "I hope so because I plan to make you scream," he whispered just as he went in for the kiss.

Her lips were as luscious as they looked, and the taste of

her—holy fuck, the woman was all his favorite flavors wrapped up in one curvy, sexy, package.

He ran his tongue around her lips, stroking that full bottom one until he had to suck on it. Her tits tightened against his chest, nipples hard. He wanted to rub them against his naked flesh.

Everywhere.

He speared his hands through her hair, threading his fingers through it, grabbing hold. He threw one leg over hers and cradled her head as he laid her back across the seat.

She moaned when his dick surged against her, and she spread her legs—but not as far as he'd like because of the seat back blocking the way.

He wanted her on a bed, spread wide with no impediment whatsoever. Well, maybe some silk ties for her wrists if she'd let him.

Jesus, he almost got off on that thought alone.

Not a good way to make a good first impression.

He dragged his lips from hers, stroking his tongue along her jaw, down her throat—she smelled *so* damn good—to that hollow where her neck curved into her shoulder. He loved that part of a woman.

But then her dress got in the way.

He pushed himself up on his hands. "Let's get you out of this dress."

"Don't you think you should tell the driver to get started?" The smile she gave him was part imp and part temptress.

The driver. The limo. The hotel. He wanted to smack his forehead, but then he'd have to sit up and he was fine right where he was.

Oh hell, he had to sit up anyway to push the call button.

Exhaling, he climbed off her. Normally, he'd hate the fact that the button was by the seat facing them, but he didn't want to accidentally hit the thing while he and Dana were otherwise involved. He wouldn't necessarily care if the guy got an earful, but Dana would, and he didn't want to give her any reason to be uncomfortable.

Although… yes he *did* want to make her uncomfortable—he wanted her writhing beneath him, trying to come.

"Quick question."

She arched an eyebrow at him. "I didn't think you were the quick sort of guy, Scott."

A smile crawled across his face as her sexy voice crawled across his nerve endings. "When it counts, I'm not. But… How do you feel about seafood?"

She shrugged. "I see food, I eat it."

Now he chuckled. He liked her for many reasons and her humor was just one of them. "I mean, is there anything you won't eat? Can't? Any allergies to anything? Any special requests? That sort of thing."

"I take it we're having seafood for dinner."

"Unless you're allergic. Can't have you getting sick this weekend."

"Then you'll be happy to know that seafood is just fine, and I don't have any other allergies. I'm not picky when it comes to food." She tapped the seat with the toe of her fuck-me shoe, almost making him forget what he had to do.

He pulled out his cell and texted the manager at the restaurant to set their dinner in motion, then he hit the call button for the driver. "We're ready to leave."

"Very good, sir," said the disembodied voice from the front.

Scott had arranged for the guy to stay in the front seat for this trip, telling him he'd handle their luggage.

The driver had been more than happy to take the tip for less wor, and Scott had been happy to alleviate something that might cause Dana embarrassment.

Which he did now, making sure the call button was off before facing her.

She hadn't moved. Well, that wasn't quite true. Her hand was in her hair, that jumbled mess of silky brown waves that was spilling over the edge of the seat, and her right leg was propped up, her dress doing a slow slide toward the crease of her thigh, but other than that, she hadn't moved.

He liked the few changes.

"Now where were we?" he uttered, shocked at how low his voice was. He knew he wanted her, but hadn't realized he'd barely be able to speak with the wanting.

She crooked her finger at him. "Right here."

He was across the open space in no time, and back in position just as quickly.

"God, you feel amazing beneath me."

"Yes, I do." She smiled and he had to chuckle.

"It's just like the other night online, only better."

"Definitely better." She nibbled her bottom lip again. "Kiss me again, Scott."

"My pleasure, sweetheart."

She said something, but it got muffled as his lips covered hers. God, he didn't think he'd ever get tired of kissing her.

Her tongue danced with his, then took over for a bit as she grabbed the back of his neck and pulled him closer.

He wanted to get closer. Hell, he wanted to get inside her so badly he couldn't think straight.

Thinking was overrated at times.

He skimmed the hem of her dress up her leg—holy fuck, she was wearing thigh-highs.

He pushed himself up then knelt between her legs.

"Scott—?"

"Shhh. I have to see." He brushed the flowing hem of her dress up and—

She was wearing red satin panties. That tied on the sides.

"You didn't." He looked at her.

Her smile was pure come-on. "I did."

"I like."

"I know."

"I'm taking them off with my teeth."

"I certainly hope so."

"That's why you wore them."

"Hey, I might be older than you, but I'm not senile."

And there it was. Dana's issue. Well, he was going to nip that in the bud—before he nipped *her* bud.

He ran a finger along the top of her panties. "Do you like this?"

Her stomach fluttered. Of course she did.

"Yes."

Her breathing got shallow.

He fiddled with the satin ties. Not enough to undo them, but enough to make it easier when he did eventually get down to business. "How about this?" He spread his hand over her hip.

Her skin was sinfully smooth and silky.

He wanted to nibble on her hip, too.

And he would. But first, he had to address this age issue. "That's good."

"Just good? I'm wounded." He put his other hand over his heart because there was no way in hell he was moving this one. Heat rolled off her in waves and the scent of her arousal perfumed the air. A few inches down and he'd feel her wetness.

"Better than good, and you know it."

"Yeah, but you're the writer. You're supposed to be good with words."

"On paper I am. In the heat of the moment? This moment? Words aren't exactly what I'm focused on."

"What are you focused on, Dana?" He slid his fingers toward her clit. "This?"

"Yeah." Her breathing picked up, upping the tempo her breasts were moving.

"You should have worn a button-down dress."

"This one zips down the back."

"Good. I like zippers. I'm even better at undoing those with my teeth than I am with satin ties." She shuddered—and he smiled. "Like that, do you?"

"Scott, I have a feeling there's not going to be anything you do that I *don't* like."

"How about this?" He slid his finger beneath the edge of her panties. "Do you like that?"

She licked her lips—not provocatively this time because he could tell that they were dry, but it still turned him on some more.

"Yeah. I do."

"Want me to go farther?"

"Yes."

"I like a woman who knows what she wants."

"Then you're going to love me because I want you, Scott."

Every muscle in his body froze at her flippant comment. Love her?

"Oh, shit. I'm sorry. That didn't come out right." She struggled to sit up, but he pressed down on her hip.

"Don't move." His voice came from somewhere deep inside him—he hadn't realized he was capable of that low of a baritone, but—Jesus.

Love her?

He wasn't in love with her. Love didn't happen at first sight like it did in chick flicks. He'd seen a hot woman and had had to get to know her. There wasn't enough to know about her yet for him to love.

But he sure as hell was willing to find out. And *that* was what shocked him.

"Scott?"

He ran his gaze up from the sexy panties and thigh-highs, to the flatness of her stomach, to the not-so-flatness of her tits, up the curve of her neck to that face… "You're gorgeous, Dana. The most beautiful woman I've ever met."

"Uh… oh." She sank back on her elbows.

"And it's not just the outside, though, don't get me wrong, you are incredibly hot and sexy and can turn me inside out when I just think about you moaning my name. But your ability to be so open and honest and genuine… And then there's the courage and strength it took for you to agree to come away with me. I know the kind of woman you are. Even if Kevin hadn't told me how normal you are, how nice you are, I can see that from talking to you. The courage it took to not only admit you wanted me, but to actually do it… It's incredibly sexy. You are one amazing lady. From the moment I saw your picture, I imagined being with you. But you know what?" He tightened his fingers on her hip, wanting to sink down into the cradle of her thighs and pound into her, showing her what she did to him. "I'd never imagined it being like this. You being like this."

"Like what?"

He slid his palm around to her ass—he just had to. "This. Sexy as hell. A total turn-on. When I look at you, I don't see an older woman; I see a woman. All woman. Who can turn me on with her laugh, and make me ache with a look. As far as I'm concerned, your age is a non-issue. I've dated woman who weren't your age and they can't even compete. So let's drop the number, shall we? We're here; you and me, and that's all I care about. Deal?"

"Deal." She held out her hand as if to shake his.

He looked at it. He would've preferred a kiss, but they'd get back to that. He put his hand in hers.

She yanked him back down on top of her.

"Hey!"

She nibbled his earlobe. "You complaining?"

"Hell no." But he did adjust the way he'd fallen over her. Her hip was fine for his fingers to grip, but his dick didn't want to be there. Not when where it wanted to be was so close.

She swirled her tongue along the shell of his ear and damn if it didn't send his nerve endings into overdrive.

He shifted, taking his weight on his right elbow, leaving his left hand free to skim up her side, and find her breast.

She gasped into his ear, her breath sending shivers through him.

"Like that?"

She growled her answer when he rubbed her nipple. It hardened instantly. God, he wanted to get his lips around it.

She sucked on his neck, and Scott was hoping she'd leave

a mark. He wanted her so crazy with wanting him that she lost control. Nail marks, bite marks, hickies… he'd take it all. He wanted Dana with a passion he didn't know he had in him. No wonder things hadn't worked with any of the other women he'd been with. If anyone had made him feel even a tenth of what he was feeling now, he wouldn't be here.

Thank God no one had.

Her hands gripped his ass and he felt that touch straight through his balls. His dick got so hard it was painful, throbbing like he was going to come, but it was too fast.

He backed himself onto his knees, enjoying the way the skin on his neck stretched when Dana wouldn't let go.

She even got onto her elbows to follow him over—until he pinched her nipple.

She gasped and let go, her eyes wide and aroused as she stared at him.

"You like that." It wasn't a question, but she nodded anyway.

"Take off the dress, Dana. I want to see your tits. Play with them. Suck them."

She couldn't scramble around fast enough, but scramble she did.

And, hey, if her dress just happened to get caught around her waist so her gorgeous ass flashed him, all the better.

He wanted to undo those little bows on her hips.

"Unzip me." Her voice was husky.

Scott stared at the back of her dress, enjoying how it curved in by her waist, then out over the flare of her hips.

He brushed her hair to the side and breathed a soft kiss across the nape of her neck.

She turned to look at him over her shoulder. "Scott."

He nuzzled her ear. "Yeah, babe?"

"Are you ever going to undo the zipper?"

He pressed a soft kiss against her cheek, just by the corner of her mouth. She jerked her head back to get closer, but he pulled away. He liked teasing her.

"Of course I will." And he slowly, deliberately, held her gaze while he lowered his mouth to the zipper.

He took the piece between his teeth, bringing both hands up to the neckline on either side of the zipper, and tugged.

Dana's breathing was almost louder than the rasp of the zipper.

He tugged again, revealing a few more inches of skin.

She dropped her head back, her hair falling in his way, but Scott didn't care. Dana's breathing had gotten even more shallow and faster.

He dragged the zipper down some more, then released it to run his tongue along the skin he'd just exposed.

Her head fell forward and she moaned.

"You taste so good… Here." He licked her again, then nudged the zipper down more with his chin, pressing kisses as he went.

"I thought you were going to use your teeth," she whispered.

"Oh, I will. Don't worry." To prove it, he nipped her skin. "See? Teeth."

Her chuckle reverberated against his lips as he pushed the dress down to the middle of her back. She wasn't wearing a bra.

"You're a funny guy, Scott Masters."

"I'm a horny guy and you are just the woman to help me with that problem." He nipped his way down some more.

"I don't see that as a problem."

"See? Just the woman." He nudged the dress to the side to find the dimples in the small of her back, another part of a woman he found sexy. He swirled his tongue against one, smiling when she shivered, then he kissed his way across to the other one.

Then he grabbed the zipper tab and tugged it the rest of the way down, ending right above her sweet, delectable, perfectly shaped ass.

He had to restrain himself from licking his way down that

as well. First things first, and the first order of business was to get her naked.

He knelt and slid his hands up her sides, his fingers curving around to the front so that he brushed the undersides of her breasts, then up over them, pausing to take her nipples between his fingers and squeeze just a little.

She moaned again, arching her back, thrusting those tits into his hands.

He palmed them, then cupped them, his thumbs stroking her nipples until Dana surrendered and leaned back against him.

"Look at me, Dana," he said hoarsely. For all the play he'd started this with, he wasn't playing anymore. He wanted this woman with an intensity that was almost shocking, and it was only because he wanted to make her come first that he was able to stop himself from flipping her onto her back and thrusting inside of her.

But he'd get to that.

She opened her eyes, passion clouding the beautiful green.

"Jesus, woman, do you know what you're doing to me?'

She smiled quickly, then moaned when he flicked her nipple. "I know what you're doing to *me*; why don't you tell me what you're feeling?"

"You, woman. I'm feeling you and you're the most amazing thing I've ever felt." He kneaded her tits, imagining his face between them, inhaling her scent, taking each nipple into his mouth and sucking hard—

Fuck it. What was he waiting for?

He kissed her lips and slid the dress off her arms, his hands feeling every part of her skin on the way down, beneath the top of her panties to her… landing strip.

Jesus, the woman had a landing strip. She wasn't feeling forty-nine if she was doing that.

Good. Just how he wanted her to keep thinking.

"Touch me, Scott," she begged when they came up for air.

"Trust me, sweetheart, I'll touch you. I'll touch you so much, you're going to scream."

A sexy smile curved across her face. "I'm counting on it."

He kissed her again, quickly this time. "Hey, let's get you out of this dress." He wrapped an arm around her waist and lifted, tugging the dress out from under her, then he turned her to face him.

She reached for him, trying to put her arms around his neck, but he grabbed them, and held them out to the side. He rocked back onto his heels and just stared at the most beautiful thing he'd ever seen.

"My God." The breath left his body. Her tits were gorgeous. Sure, gravity was probably tugging on them in a way she didn't like, but right now, they were tight and aroused and begging for attention. Her waist still curved in. She was a little poochier there than she probably liked—he had yet to meet a woman who was completely satisfied with that area of her body—but as far as he was concerned, Dana was curved in all the right places. Soft to his hard.

And her hips… Sweet God, her hips. They were just the right proportion, curved just the right way, and made him want to bury his face between them.

Which was where he planned to start.

He tugged her forward so she was on her knees.

"Scott—"

"Shh." He kissed her. Hard and brief.

Then he bent down to her right hip… and took the edge of the satin tie between his teeth.

He tugged.

The breath whooshed out of his lungs when the fabric folded down over itself.

Dana gripped his shoulders. Her stomach fluttered as he nibbled his way across it.

He shifted on his knees so he could reach the other side.

He tugged again.

Her panties fell away with a whisper.

Scott stared at her.

The woman didn't have a thing to be embarrassed about. She was perfect. Like a woman should be.

Especially kneeling there in just her thigh-highs and those shoes.

"Sit back, Dana." His voice was hoarse.

At least it wasn't trembling. Not the like the rest of him. He wanted her so badly.

She slid onto the seat, and when he looked up, she was staring at him, her pupils dilated so that her eyes were almost black.

"I want to taste you, Dana."

"I want you to, Scott."

He didn't need any other words.

He turned his head to the side, never taking his eyes off her face, and kissed her leg, the silky stocking turning him on even more. He was tempted to remove it with his teeth, but he liked it on her too much.

He flicked his tongue against her skin where the thigh-high ended.

She exhaled on a moan.

"Like that?"

She took her bottom lip between her teeth and nodded.

"That's not good enough, sweetheart. Tell me you like it."

"Mmmm, Scott. I love your tongue on me."

Okay, he'd gotten a little more than he'd bargained for. His dick got even harder—if that kept happening, he wasn't going to be able to wait for the hotel either. And he didn't want that happening; the first time he was inside Dana wasn't going to be in the back of a limo with a time limit.

Time limit. Shit. He'd better get busy.

He kissed his way up her thigh. Next time he did this, he'd do the other leg, but he had a time limit and with how aroused she was, he had to make sure he got her off before they got to the hotel, or he might have a pack of guys panting after her through the lobby.

He smiled at the image as he reached her pussy lips. Those other guys could eat their hearts out; he was going to eat her out.

"Scott," she whispered harshly, when he breathed against her.

"Yeah, babe?" He made sure to breathe against her flesh. He could smell her arousal, see the way she swelled in anticipation.

"Please, lick me. Touch me. Do something."

He chuckled at the desperation in her voice. He knew the feeling.

He licked her clit.

Her legs jerked.

He licked her again.

Her knees fell together.

He couldn't have that.

Scott straightened his shoulders—she was going to stay open for him until he'd wrung the last response from her.

"Please, Scott. Again." She sounded desperate.

He took pity on the poor woman… and thrust his tongue between her pussy lips and licked his way upward.

"Oh, God, yes." Her head fell back and he felt her sink into the seat.

He did it again.

Dana spread her legs wider.

That's a girl. Just want he wanted.

He moved in closer, his tongue flicking the lower part of her clit—and it swelled to attention.

"Scott…" She threaded her fingers into his hair and pressed him against her.

He hadn't planned to go anywhere but he liked her desperation, so he left her hands where they were.

He slid *his* hands over her shoes and up her calves, then down her thighs, slipping them beneath her ass. Then he drew his thumbs down the slick folds of her pussy… to her two openings.

He licked her clit and slid his thumbs inside.

She released his head and her hands slammed to the seat, her body going rigid. "Oh. My. God."

He circled his thumbs and his tongue.

Her juices coated his tongue, slicking down to his hands. God, she was so wet. And she tasted so fucking good.

He licked her again, the entire length, swirling again over her clit as it quivered against his tongue.

"Scott… please…" she panted.

He liked her panting.

He pulled back to look up at her, his thumbs still moving inside her. "Play with your tits, Dana. "

She dropped her head and opened her eyes, her hair falling around her shoulders, damp strands clinging to her cheek. "Huh?"

He leveraged himself onto his elbows, never moving his hands from the sweet places they were, and licked her nipple. "Play with your tits for me. Pinch your nipples. Enjoy yourself."

"Oh. Okay." Her voice was husky. Slow. As if she couldn't comprehend his words.

Good. He wanted her out of her mind with desire.

She put her hands on her chest. The sight of her graceful fingers, circling, stroking, plucking at her own tits…

Shit. He was going to come in his pants if he wasn't careful.

He bent his head, focusing on her pussy. He buried his mouth between her folds, her juices coating his lips. She tasted fucking amazing.

He licked her clit, feeling it swell again. He sucked it between his lips, his tongue running along each side before finally stroking the top of it.

"Faster, Scott. I'm going to come."

Damn right she was—right against his mouth.

He licked her harder, faster. Sucked her clit while his fingers clenched her ass, his thumbs circling inside her. He pumped them, feeling her clench around them. Her legs shuddered against his shoulders, but Scott didn't stop. If anything, he picked up the pace, feeling her pussy start to contract around him.

She gripped his head with one hand and held him there, his tongue swirling over her clit, and she dropped her legs back, so utterly open and wanting—hell, practically begging—that he was so turned on he just wanted to get out of these damn clothes and plunge inside her.

He fucked her harder with his thumb, removing the one that'd been in her ass so he could spread her lips further, touching every nerve ending she had there.

She pulled her knees back then, those heels grazing his shoulders, opening herself to him even more.

He replaced his thumb with two fingers, fucking, pumping them in and out of her like his dick was begging to be able to do.

"God… Yes… That's it… Oh… Scott…" Her words came in gasps, each one punctuated by a shudder of her pussy, then a clenching, and Scott knew she was close.

Then the limo hit a pothole, slamming her down onto his fingers, and that was it. She erupted around him, her muscles clenching him, throbbing around him, her clit going rigid as her juices flowed as she came.

He didn't stop licking her and her orgasm didn't stop; he could feel the waves of it roll through her. Just when he thought she'd finished, she'd shudder and he'd feel her spasm around him again. He lost count at four and wondered how in the hell he'd managed to do this to her.

But he sure as hell wasn't about to complain.

Nor was she.

Finally, the last round subsided as the limo made a wide curving turn, and Scott slid his fingers out of her pussy slowly, enjoying the way the muscles reacted, still clenching as if they wanted him back inside. He could only imagine what it'd feel like around his dick, and he had a feeling he wouldn't be pulling out.

"I guess I better send a thank you to the department of transportation for their shitty road maintenance, huh?"

She opened her eyes slowly—as slowly as the smile spread across her face. "I would've come anyway."

"Oh I know. We weren't getting out of this car until you did."

The car stopped.

"And not a moment too soon." Scott rocked back onto his heels again. She looked so pretty sitting there like that. Open and wet and sexy. Her hair was a mess, her thighs brush-burned from his cheeks, one of her stockings rolled halfway down her thigh, and those heels…

God, she turned him on.

The limo's engine, however, turned off. They had arrived.

And she was still naked.

Chapter Thirteen

"Um, Dana?" Scott gripped her ankles, and as much as he hated to do it, he drew them together and put them onto the floor in front of him. "We need to get out of here."

It took her a couple of seconds, and if this weren't their first time together, he might laugh at the panicked look on her face.

"Oh shit." She scrambled off the seat, trying to grab her dress.

He really liked the way her tits swung in front of his face as she leaned past him.

"Scott! Help me into this thing!"

He couldn't help chuckling then. "Relax, babe. The driver knows better than to open the door."

"But the bellhops might not."

Good point.

He took the dress from her and held it open so she could step into it, bent over as she was, enjoying the look of her stocking-covered legs with those sexy-as-hell fuck-me pumps moving in front of him. It was a damn pity to have to zip the dress and hide all that gorgeousness. But he'd see it later.

He swiped her panties off the floor and shoved them into his pants pocket.

"Hey, give me those."

"Nah. You don't need them. Besides, they're wet."

"In case it's escaped your notice, so am I."

"Trust me, Dana, I'm very aware of how wet you are." He scraped a hand across his cheek. He'd already checked in before picking her up, so they could go to their room and straighten up a bit, but if they did, they'd never leave. And while that idea sounded great, he wanted to build the anticipation. Tonight was going to be a night Dana would never forget.

He adjusted himself, then smoothed his shirt into his waistband. "Ready?"

"Do I look ready?"

She looked ready for something, but it wasn't dinner.

Still, he wasn't about to tell her. He had a special meal planned, and he wanted to sit across from her looking like she did, her hair just a bit out of place, her nipples fully outlined against the fabric, knowing her juices still coated her thighs, with her panties in his pocket, and that he'd done it to her.

Hell, it'd be a dinner *he'd* never forget.

"You look beautiful."

She looked even more beautiful when she blushed.

"Come on, Dana. Let's get some sustenance. We're going to need it."

He opened the door and climbed out first, wincing against the sun. He should've made the date for later, but even six-thirty had been pushing it because he'd wanted to see her so badly.

He held out his hand.

One long, perfectly-shaped, sexy stocking-covered leg slid out of the limo.

Jesus Christ, his dick went full mast.

He couldn't believe it; he'd made sure to get himself off twice before he'd picked her up just so he *wouldn't* be as horny as a teenager, but apparently, around Dana, it didn't matter how many times he jerked off.

Her fingers gripped his and Scott gave up trying to get his dick to give up the fight. It was a losing battle.

She gave him her other hand and he tugged her up, her dress flowing around her thighs.

"Ready?"

She chuckled. "I'm not sure. My legs feel watery."

He slid a hand down one of them. "No, they don't."

She swiped at his hand with a smile on her face. "Don't. Someone will see."

"And that would be a bad thing?"

"Of course it would. I don't want to be on display."

"Sorry, sweetheart, but you're gorgeous. You're going to be turning heads the minute we walk through those doors."

"You're kind."

"No, I'm not. I'm honest. I don't think you know how utterly beautiful you are."

She blushed again and it was all he could do not to back her up against the limo and kiss her senseless. He didn't care who saw what.

But he respected her wishes, so he closed the limo door, then went around to the trunk and smacked it twice as he'd arranged with the driver.

The trunk opened and Scott removed her luggage just as a bell hop showed up with a wheeled cart.

"Room 2401," he said, handing the bellhop Dana's suitcases and a big enough tip to ensure the bags wouldn't get lost.

"Very good, sir." The guy touched the brim of his hat and took that detail off Scott's plate.

Scott held out his arm. "Shall we?"

Dana smiled and slid her hand into the crook of his arm. He liked that, in her heels, she was almost as tall as he was—he also liked how much shorter she'd be out of them. He wasn't exactly sure *when* she'd get out of them because those were staying on in bed later, but at some point she'd have to—probably too dangerous to shower in.

Son of a bitch, his dick liked that idea a little too much.

Thankfully, they arrived at the hotel door so he could open it for her, then walked in behind her, giving himself a chance to calm down. They couldn't get to their table fast enough. At least then he'd have the tablecloth to hide his raging hard-on.

Not that he thought anyone would notice because he'd been right; Dana was turning heads.

And he was proud to be the man with her.

He was going to have to thank her ex-husband some day. Guy was an idiot to let her go.

Ah well, the guy's loss was definitely Scott's gain.

He led her to the hotel's restaurant, Le Circlet, thankful he could afford to take her here. He wanted to treat her like a princess and give her everything she wanted.

Which was a first for him. He knew what he looked like, knew that his car got him attention, and that, thanks to the media coverage of his success at a young age, his wealth wasn't a secret. He always kept an eye out for opportunists.

Dana wasn't one of them. She might not earn what he did, then again, he had no idea what authors made. She could afford to have a nice home and take care of her kids, so she had to be doing well, but what he sensed about her was what Kevin had said: Dana was normal. She wasn't pretentious; she didn't have an overblown ego. She obviously wasn't the bon-bon-eating stereotype. She was a normal woman who worked to take care of her family and who'd decided to give herself the treat she deserved. It was all Scott's idea to go overboard with the limo and the swanky hotel and the restaurant without prices on the menu and the other surprises he had in store for her.

"Mr. Masters, so good to see you again," said Henry, the manager. "We have your table ready as requested. Madame, right this way, please."

Dana arched her eyebrows as she looked over her shoulder at Scott and mouthed, "*Your* table?"

Scott smiled. "Enjoy it, Dana."

She looked a little uncertain, but when he nudged her in the small of her back, she followed Henry to their table where the broccoli-mascarpone soup the chef had suggested was already waiting.

Henry held out Dana's chair, but Scott was quick to step in behind her and help her scoot closer to the table, then took his seat across from her. He'd debated sitting next to her, but they actually would need to *eat* the meal, and if he were within touching distance, he wouldn't be able to keep his hands on the utensils.

"Scott, this is incredible. You shouldn't have gone to all this trouble."

The tablecloth was gold—all of Le Circlet's were. Their theme was high opulence and Old-Hollywood glamour with an international flavor. Gilded chandeliers and candelabra, a shiny black Steinway on a raised LED-lit rotating platform, the incredible flower arrangements on the table, as well as throughout the rest of the restaurant… Scott hadn't had to go to any trouble other than making the money to pay for it, but that wasn't what she meant.

"It was no trouble. A few phone calls."

"And a lot of thought." She held her hands out for Henry to slip the napkin across her lap.

That's the last time another man is getting that close to her.

Scott cleared his throat. Jesus. Where had that caveman thought come from? He was a civilized guy. Completely confident in himself and his appeal to women. To Dana. She was going home with him tonight—well, upstairs. The penthouse suite. Only the best for the best.

Henry handed him his napkin, then disappeared without a word. Just like Scott had requested. The staff was to be as unobtrusive as possible tonight because this was all about him and Dana.

"Of course I gave it a lot of thought, Dana." He took a sip of his soup, hating to dilute the flavor of her on his tongue, but he'd get another chance to taste her later. "I haven't thought about much else since you answered my instant message."

The woman could still blush. After all they'd done, and after the hottest limo ride he'd ever taken, she could still blush.

He had to say, he liked the dichotomy of her sexiness and her shyness. It only made him want her more.

He toed off his shoe and ran his foot up her leg.

Her hands hit the table and those gorgeous eyes of hers opened wide.

"You okay, sweetheart?" he asked, oh-so-innocently.

With a devil's grin.

And then moved his foot up another couple of inches. A few more and he'd be at her knee.

He loved kissing a woman in the bend of her knee. He couldn't wait to do that to Dana. Preferably while she was on her stomach, her ass curving in front of him, as he licked his way down her leg. He'd kiss one, then the other, then nestle between her legs for the rest of the night.

Jesus Christ, he was fucking hard—and he wanted to *be* fucking hard. Pound inside of her.

"Scott, what are you doing?" she whispered hoarsely.

"You don't know?"

"Well, of course I *know*. Every nerve ending I have is on fire right now. But why? Anyone could see us."

"Would it matter?"

She took a shaky sip of her soup. Then she ran her tongue over her lips.

He couldn't wait to do that, too.

"Of course it'd matter. I'm not an exhibitionist."

He raised an eyebrow at her. "You sure about that? You put on quite a show for me."

"That was for you, not the entire town."

He looked around. "I think the town's much bigger than this."

"You know what I mean." Her color was bright, but it wasn't a blush.

He thought it might be anger. "Whoa, sorry. Didn't mean to cross the line."

"I… What?"

"That. Then. I stepped over a boundary and I apologize. I guess I have to learn those with you. Kind of backwards, though. Usually I find out the boundaries *before* I decide to get involved."

"Why didn't you wait with me?"

A waiter showed up from seemingly out of nowhere and poured the champagne. Scott didn't know her preference in wine—that'd be taken care of this weekend—but he figured he couldn't go wrong with champagne. Especially Cliquot.

The waiter poured without ceremony, so Scott didn't have to take his eyes off her for a second.

She didn't take her eyes off him.

He was going to have to tip the waiter more because the guy handled the situation perfectly.

"How do you do that?" she asked when it was just them.

"Do what?"

"Make everything perfect?"

Scott exhaled. He hadn't realized he'd been worried until just that moment. And now she thought things were perfect.

"It's how I want this weekend to be for you. For us." He saluted her with his champagne flute. "Perfect."

She stared at him a bit longer.

Don't go there, Dana. Get off the age thing.

He could see it simmering there, just below the surface, the insecurity or questions or doubt in her eyes.

"Because *you're* perfect, Dana. Perfect for me."

There. He'd said the worlds. She'd either believe him or she wouldn't. He just hoped she was curious enough to stay.

She hesitated, then sipped the champagne. Well, more than sipped it.

His lips twitched as he tried to hide a smile when he picked up his spoon. She'd finished more than half the glass. Granted, the flute didn't hold much, but she'd definitely had more than a polite share of the stuff.

Wait. Did she feel the need to get drunk to make it through the night?

It was a sobering thought. He set his spoon down. "Dana, if you want to leave—"

"Why? Do you want me to?"

"No, but—"

"Because if you're having second thoughts, Scott, that's okay. You can tell me. I'll understand."

"What, exactly, will you understand?" Damn it. She wasn't over the age thing.

"I'll understand if you're re-thinking this. Me. Us. I mean, I know the limo ride was amazing, but, well…"

"Well, what? *Well* that you're sixteen years older than me? *Well* that you're older than me by enough to have been my babysitter? Dana, if tonight, if this, hasn't shown you that I don't give a damn about your age, then I don't know what more I can do. I want you. *This* you. The *you* who was in that limo with me. The one who Facetimed me. The one who texted me. The one who was daring enough to return my IM and give as good as she got. Jesus, don't you get it, babe? You're real. Honest. Who you are. So many people online are fakes or jacking-up their profiles to be something they want to be but aren't. But you… You're exactly who you portrayed yourself as being. And so much more. There wasn't a hint of this sexy side to you in your profile. I just thought you were beautiful and liked what you had to say. That, alone, was enough to interest me. But you, Dana… You're more than enough to keep me interested. To make me hungry to know more. To make me hungry, period." He ran his foot the rest of the way up her leg, tucking his toe between her thigh and the chair, feeling the heat rolling off of her.

"I know you want me. And it's okay. Don't over-think this. Don't worry about things we can't control. I don't give a damn about your age; all I care about is who you are. The years between us made you who you are. If anything, I'm grateful to those years, that experience. Because if we were the same age, you'd still be married to your idiot of an ex and I wouldn't be here with the most beautiful woman I've ever met. And I don't just mean on the outside."

He took a deep breath. He hadn't meant to say all of that

to her. Not yet. Not now. Those were things he'd wanted to say to her in the privacy of their bed, when he could trace her face with his finger and punctuate his words with kisses. Where she could wrap her arms around him and roll into him and he could show her exactly what she did to him.

"Slide your foot up my leg."

"What?" Her eyes flared open.

"Do it. What I'm doing." He wiggled his toes, then picked up his spoon and ladled his soup. "Do it. You'll see just how much I want to know you."

"You want to play footsie in this restaurant?"

"Sure. Why not?" He slid is foot across her knee and nudged it between her legs, bringing his spoon to his lips as if they were just having a normal conversation. "Don't tell me you don't like this."

She hesitated, blinking at him. He could see the war going on in her head.

He wiggled his toes again. "Let me in, Dana."

She did. Her knees fell apart and a look crossed her face…

He'd won this round.

He just hoped there weren't many more to get through before he could convince her that age truly was just a number.

He angled his leg for better access, and slid his foot along the inside of her thigh. "Have some soup."

Her eyes widened, but she did what he said.

Then he touched her.

She wasn't wearing her panties.

She sucked in a breath instead of her soup.

Probably a good thing. "Like that?" he whispered.

She nodded, then managed to eat some of the soup.

"Your turn."

She licked her lips—he liked that—then he felt her thighs move.

They clenched around his leg as she used one foot to remove that sexy high heel.

Then he felt her stockinged foot slide up his leg under his pants leg.

Man, did he wish he'd worn shorts.

He was going to have to get her to do this when they were in their room. Naked.

He flexed his foot against her and smiled when she closed her eyes for a second. "Feel good?"

When her eyes opened, there was no more Shy-Dana. Sexy-Dana had come to play. "You know it does."

She slid her foot from his pants leg. It was all Scott could do not to shift in his seat because he knew what was coming next.

She helped herself to some more soup while her toes slid up the outside of his pants, then along the inside of his leg, taking her torturously sweet time while he tried to eat some of whatever he'd ordered for this first course.

He gave up when her toes hit his knee, setting his spoon across the rim of the bowl and shoving the bowl to the edge of the table.

Dana followed suit. But she didn't remove her foot.

Thank God.

"Are you ready for the next course?" the waiter asked.

"Yes." Scott was ready for dessert actually, but he'd set this up; he had to finish it. Even if it killed him.

Their *coquilles Saint-Jacques* appeared as if by magic. Thirty seconds later, they were alone again. Management had trained the staff well.

He'd apparently trained Dana *too* well because her foot hadn't moved.

Scott set out to rectify that situation because if there was one thing he wanted—and, sadly, it wasn't the scallops which could be cardboard for all he cared—it was that he wanted Dana moving against him.

"A few more inches," he said, nodding at her.

Dana licked her bottom lip from the sip of champagne she'd just taken, and set her flute down as a sly smile curved at the corners of her mouth. "That's what she said."

He laughed, loving that it didn't kill the moment. "God, woman, you drive me nuts."

Then she touched his nuts. His hard, aching nuts.

"Yeah, I can tell."

He shifted then, putting her foot *exactly* where he wanted. His nuts weren't the only aching part of him. "What can you tell now?"

"That we're going to have one hell of a weekend." She tapped her toes against him, then ran them up the length of his dick.

He almost came from that alone.

She picked one of the scallops, and ran it across her bottom lip. Slowly. "Undo your zipper."

Hell. He felt some pre-cum leak out and he had to suck in a breath to keep from blowing his wad.

"Scott? Do it."

He couldn't open his mouth. But he sure as hell could open his zipper.

Without taking his gaze from hers, he reached beneath the table, ran a hand along the top of her foot, all the way up her toes to where they rested against him. He worked his zipper down beneath her foot.

He was commando. On purpose. And thank God for it.

He pressed her toes against him.

They both sucked in a breath.

"Feel good?" *He* was asking *her*.

She swallowed, nodded, then set her fork down. "Yeah. It does."

He allowed himself a momentary indulgence and closed his eyes, focusing on her heat against him. That silk stocking felt unbelievable against his skin.

She slid her foot up.

Scott couldn't stop the groan and his eyes shot open.

There was a smile on her face he would've paid to see. Actually, given this dinner, and the hotel room, he *was* paying to see it, but he didn't care. He was getting a bargain.

She nibbled her bottom lip. "Did I actually make you moan?"

He chuckled. "I'd say it was more of a groan."

"I'll have to work on that." She pointed her toes and ran her nails across his head.

More pre-cum came out.

Her toe caught it and she smiled that sexy-ass grin that made him harder.

She noticed. "Hmm… Someone's ready for dessert."

"Sweetheart, I have such a sweet tooth, you wouldn't believe. And I intend to indulge it all night."

"Hope you're *up*—"she stroked him again—"for that."

"Trust me. We will have no issues in that department." Coming before he wanted to, however… Whole other story.

She stroked him again and his cock jerked. Jesus H. Christ, the silk was incredible.

"This is fun." Her eyes twinkled when she smiled as she picked up her champagne for another sip.

"Glad you're enjoying yourself. Because I sure as hell am."

She stroked him again. "I wonder…" She licked her lips. "How far can I go with this?"

"Sweetheart, any other time, I'd tell you to take it all the way, but the first time I come with you, I want to be inside you. I want your legs wrapped around my waist and you moaning my name. I want to feel your orgasm take you and know that I did that to you." He picked up his fork, trying like hell to get his body to slow the fuck down. "Then you can get me off anywhere you want."

Her foot dropped to the floor, her champagne flute hit the table harder than was probably prudent, and her mouth fell open.

Scott smiled and picked up his champagne again. Then he saluted her and took a sip.

And pressed his toes against her pussy.

Dana's breath shot out, and her legs clenched around him as she—holy fuck!—came against his foot.

She gripped the edges of the table, clamped her mouth shut, her eyes never leaving his until her orgasm trailed off and her thighs relaxed.

She grabbed the Cliquot from the ice bucket in the stand beside their table, picked up her champagne flute yet again, poured herself some more, then saluted *him*. "Well-played."

He nodded. "My pleasure."

She arched an eyebrow at him. "Actually, mine."

He shifted again, well aware that his dick was still hard as a rock and naked for all intents and purposes—and it had some very well-thought-out intents and purposes.

Which he wanted to get to.

Maybe this five-course meal wasn't such a good idea.

He picked up his fork and waved it in a circle over the whatever-the-hell-he-was-supposed-to-be-eating. "I think I'd better get some sustenance in me. I plan to work off every calorie."

"So the more we eat, the more we can…"

He paused in raising the scallop to his mouth. "The more we can, what?"

She took a sip of her champagne. No, not a sip. A long, lingering taste. That didn't lower the contents of the glass any.

"Oh no, babe. You have to finish that thought. If you can take it, you can dish it out."

She pulled the glass away from her lips. "Isn't that supposed to be the other way around?"

"Sure, we can do that, too."

"The other way arou—?"

The look on her face was priceless when her mind went in whatever direction it'd just gone.

"Yeah. That." Because, seriously, he didn't care what it was she'd come up with; he was in.

The glass, once again, hit the tablecloth a little harder than was wise.

"Eat your appetizer, Dana. We have three more courses to get through."

"*This* is the appetizer? Then what was that in the limo?"

She picked up her fork and he was immensely proud to see her hand shake. It wasn't fear and it wasn't nerves. Dana was unsettled because he'd just made her come—and she wanted to come again.

"Just something to whet your appetite." He flexed his foot.

She hissed and dropped her fork with a clatter.

She slammed her hands onto the table and looked around. Then she glared at him. "Scott!" she whispered hoarsely.

"Just like that, babe. I want to hear you say my name just like that when I'm inside you."

"I don't think I'm going to have anything left in me if you keep doing… *that*."

"Oh you will. You'll have *me* in you and, trust me, I'll make it good."

He was thoroughly enjoying himself. Well, other than the fact that his dick was harder than it'd ever been, and he probably wouldn't be able to walk upright when they finished their meal, but he'd count on drive and anticipation to make him be able to. Might embarrass a few of the patrons—he hoped to hell he wouldn't embarrass Dana—but he wasn't about to stop flirting with her for the next two courses—not three. He was going to save dessert for later and have it sent to their room because nothing could be sweeter than Dana, and he really didn't want to wait that long.

"Eat your food, Dana. You're going to need it."

She stared at him for a few seconds longer—seconds in which he refused to listen to the little devil on his shoulder who was egging him on to touch her with his foot again—then she picked up her fork and slid a scallop into her mouth.

He ate one himself, but that was it. He should have had this served in their suite for all he was tasting the food. He'd wanted to wine and dine her, show her a good time, treat her like a princess, but he'd miscalculated. Neither one of them wanted to eat—well, not food anyway. He should have arranged for a post-midnight snack, Dana being the midnight one. *And* the—he looked at his Rolex—eight-thirty snack.

Eight-thirty? It was eight-thirty? Time was flying by and he didn't want to waste anymore of it.

He waved the waiter over. "We're ready for the next course."

The guy was to be commended for not raising even an eyebrow as he looked at the two artfully presented and completely wasted specialties. Big tip coming for that. And one for the chef so he wouldn't be insulted that they hadn't indulged.

Scott wanted to indulge in something else.

The next course appeared as silently and efficiently as the appetizers, and just as with the scallops, he and Dana only nibbled on the endive and black truffle salad.

Kobe beef with lobster tail was next. A cliché perhaps, but there was nothing cliché about the way the chef here prepared it. It was what Le Circlet was known for, with special glazes and a secret infused butter that had epicureans salivating within a hundred miles.

Two bites in, however, Scott was still salivating for something else. He could have been eating hotdogs for all he was tasting. He just wanted to taste Dana.

Again.

His cock jerked at the memory. Shit, his zipper. He had to be careful.

He reached under the table to put everything back where it ought to be.

"What are you doing?" Dana's foot was suddenly back in position.

"Closing up shop."

"Why?"

"Because I need to be able to get out from this table, and sitting here with my cock out isn't going to allow me to do that."

"We have another course to get through, right?"

"Well, yeah…"

"So leave everything just as it is."

He liked this bossy side of Dana.

"I need the pressure, sweetheart. Simple biology."

She pressed her foot against him. "There. I was a straight-A student in biology."

He chuckled. Okay, so she was right; there *was* a way to keep him under control.

Just the image of her being in control—on top, calling the shots—was enough to get his dick jerking again.

Dana raised an eyebrow with the piece of lobster. "I'd really like to know what you were thinking to get that reaction."

"Wrap your lips around that lobster and I just might tell you."

She did. God help him, she did. Slowly. Sensuously. With enough tongue to get him imagining what her tongue would feel like on him.

"You done eating yet?" He set his fork down. Who the fuck was he trying to kid? The only thing he wanted to eat was her. Food could wait.

"Actually…" She swallowed the lobster, then ran her tongue over her lips, catching every last lick of butter. "I'm finding that the limo ride worked up quite an appetite and I'm famished."

She sliced off another piece of lobster, dipped it into the butter, then repeated the torture all over again.

Thank God they weren't eating Maine lobsters; they'd be here all night.

"Aren't you hungry?" She nodded at his plate.

"Not for food," he growled, but picked up his fork and knife and took a bite—

Which he almost choked on when her foot stroked his dick again. "Dana!" He had to hack out the meat.

"Just like that, Scott. I want to hear you say my name just like that when you come."

"Which I'll be in serious danger of doing if you keep that up."

"What? It's my job to keep you up." She smiled slyly and did it again.

"Good lord, I've created a monster."

"No, just a grown woman who has been missing this for far too long."

"*This*? You've done this before?" Well, damn, he'd hoped to be original.

So why the fuck would her husband walk out if they did shit like this? Hell, if *he* were lucky enough to find a woman who'd do this, he'd never walk out. He'd sign over his fortune and his eternal love just to get to do this for the rest of his life.

"No, I've never done this before. I've also never had sex in a limo before."

"Technically, we didn't have sex."

"Okay, Mr. Semantics, I've never come in a limo before. Closest thing was the night my ex wanted to, but I got carsick."

"You get carsick?" Well, shit, he hadn't thought about that when renting the limo.

"Haven't before or after. It must have been the company."

He smiled. "Correct answer."

She cocked her head, her silky hair falling over her shoulder. "Do I get a sticker for that? A star by my name? Go to the head of the class?"

"Dana, you, baby, are in a class all by yourself. And if you'll hurry up and finish your dinner, I'll take you upstairs and give you your reward."

"And let all this food and ambiance go to waste?"

Dammit. He'd planned way too perfect of a seduction scene when he obviously hadn't needed to.

Not that that was why he'd done this. He'd never gone all out like this for a woman and he'd enjoyed planning it. He'd wanted Dana to have a night to remember. Unfortunately, he hadn't realized just how much torture it was going to be waiting to get her upstairs.

His hand drifted into his pocket where her panties were. Her satin-tied panties. He couldn't believe she'd actually gone out and bought some—he wasn't naïve enough to think she'd had those lying around her home. But she'd gone to the effort for him, as much as he'd gone to the effort for her.

He liked that they both wanted to please each other. He'd been on far too many dates where the woman had wanted something from him. The expensive meal, some jewelry, the cachet of being seen with him… If Dana knew who he was, or had heard of him, she didn't let on. And knowing Dana, he'd say she *didn't* know because she wasn't one to hide things.

For the first time in a long time, he could actually believe that a woman's interest in him was not based on his bank account or level of celebrity in the financial world.

That, alone, was heady. Given how Dana looked and how she responded to him, the entire package just worked for him.

Especially with her foot *on* his entire package.

He shifted—and her toes flexed.

"Feeling neglected?" She slid another piece of lobster off her fork.

She *had* to feel his cock jerk. "Neglected? No. Definitely *not* the word I'd use."

"Oh? What would you use?" Her tongue slicked away a teardrop of butter from the corner of her mouth.

He was going to have a carafe of that butter sent up to their room.

"I'd use horny. Or hard. Hot. Hurting. I'm aching, Dana, to get inside you."

It was her turn to cough up a piece of food. Good. She couldn't have all the control here.

He slid his foot back up her leg.

"No fair." She clamped her knees closed.

"I didn't know we were keeping score." He slid his foot to the outside of her leg and ran it up her calf to her knee, then along her thigh. Thankfully, he'd asked Henry for a smaller diameter table so his legs could reach her thigh.

And so hers could reach him.

He rubbed her leg where the stockings ended. "I'm going to peel these off of you. Then lick my way down your leg."

Her toes flexed.

"But that's after I fray them with my stubble when I eat you out in them."

Her toes curled around the side of his cock.

"And then I'm going to use them to tie your wrists to the headboard and make you come so many times you're not going to know what day it is."

"Big words."

He shifted his pelvis. "Not the only thing."

"Perfect, Scott." She ran her toes along the rim of his dick. "You're just perfect for me."

"You finished with your dinner yet?"

She smiled and speared a piece of steak. "Not yet."

He exhaled. "You're torturing me."

She took her sweet time slipping it off the fork and inching it into her mouth. "Good. Because you did the same thing to me in the limo."

"The limo was nothing. Just you wait."

"I can't."

"Then put your fork down and let's get going."

She chewed her food and speared another piece. "Hey, you're the one who said I need to make sure I get sustenance. I'm just doing what you ordered."

He practically growled. "Remember that. It'll come in handy later."

"Oh? Are you planning to boss me around?"

"And you'll like it."

She snapped the steak off her fork with a smile. "So now you think you know what I like?"

"I know you like when I suck on your clit."

He felt her thighs clench and her toes curl around him again.

The smile slid from her face.

"I know you like when I put two fingers inside you."

She bit her bottom lip.

"I know you like when I finger-fuck you while you're coming."

Shit. He was about to come himself.

He reached beneath the table and pressed her foot against him, trying to catch his breath and get himself under control.

She set her fork down, grabbed her napkin, and wiped the corner of her mouth. "Okay, let's go."

"Um…" He held up a finger. "Hold that thought."

"What? You're kidding me, right? You get me all hot and bothered—*and* make me come—and *now* you make me wait?"

"Sweetheart, I can't exactly get out from under this table."

She pressed her foot against him. "There. Does that help?"

"Some." He reached for the champagne and guzzled it.

"Want an ice cube?" She held out one from her water glass, a smile on her fact that looked as if it had a secret behind it.

He took it. "Something you want to share?"

"Later. Much later."

That sounded promising. He'd have to make sure they had ice in the room. Actually, there were quite a few things he could do with ice. Like melt it on her body and lick it off. Trail it over her body, down between her legs—

Shit, that wasn't helping either.

He stuck the ice on the head of his dick, sucking in a harsh breath at the sensation, trying not to like it. Which was damn hard with her still touching him.

Much as he hated to do it, he lifted her foot away. "I need some space so I don't embarrass us."

"Embarrass? I don't know who you've been talking to, but when the day comes that a man can't walk because of me, embarrassment is *not* the feeling I'm going to go with."

"Well good, because today is that day."

"You sure you don't want to get off here?"

That fucking almost did it. "Shit, Dana, I'm trying to get my mind *off* that. Say something not sexy."

She bit her lip.

"Without biting your lip. Or moving them."

"That's going to be kind of hard, hotshot."

"No, *I'm* kind of hard. Actually, I've very hard. And it's almost painful."

"Want me to kiss it and make it all better?"

He sucked in a deep breath. *Meadows and unicorns and puppies and kittens… Something so innocuous and innocent that he wouldn't keep thinking about her lips wrapped around his cock—*

Shit shit shit.

He squeezed his shaft, leaned it outward, the zipper biting into the base—and still that didn't take him all the way down. It did, however, buy him enough breathing room to be able to tuck it away, zip up, and stand.

He held out his hand. "You ready?"

She worked her foot into her pump and draped her napkin onto the table, then gave him her hand. "I've been ready."

He swallowed. "I know."

He swept his other hand for her to precede him toward the lobby.

Their walk was laden with anticipation, an almost palpable cloud of pheromones surrounding them, and he was surprised no one else was aware of it.

Then he got a look at Henry's eyes. Well, after Henry had stared at Dana for too long for Scott's liking.

"Shall I have your dessert brought up, Mr. Masters?"

"I'll call, Henry." No way was he waiting to touch Dana for some dessert, with the whole serving, tipping, "Have a good night, sir" thing. The time for foreplay was over.

He followed her out of the dining room—

Hell, maybe the pheromones *were* evident to everyone because they were all looking at her, men and women.

They were looking at *him*, too. Knowing looks. Some envious. Some… snickering?

Let them snicker. They didn't know. And he didn't care what anyone thought. Dana was the only one who mattered. She was the most beautiful woman in the room and they could all be jealous about it.

Still, the way the women were looking at her… He might have thought Dana had shown up with a gigolo if the guy weren't him.

"Dana? Dana Jenkins? Is that you?"

Dana slammed to a halt and he almost ran into her. But he didn't have to touch her to know she was shrinking away from him.

Shit. Real life intruded.

He gritted his teeth and as much as he hated to, he whispered, "Do you want me to leave?"

She looked at him, then at the woman who was striding across the hotel foyer.

The woman was probably Dana's age, though she looked it in ways Dana didn't. They'd probably been on the PTA together. Had had play dates for their kids. Went to back-to-school nights through the years—

Dana had this whole other life that he wasn't a part of and it bothered the hell out of him. Which also bothered the hell out of him. He had no right to lay claim to any part of her life other than the past week and this weekend.

But, dammit, this weekend was his. That woman had had Dana for the past however-many-years; she didn't get to infringe on his time.

And with the way Dana was worrying her bottom lip, the woman and all she represented *were* infringing on it.

Goddam it. All his efforts in making Dana feel comfortable with him were gone thanks to that woman's shrill voice.

"Dana?" He wanted her to turn to him with that sexy sly smile she had, grab his arm and tuck herself against his side, then face the woman head-on.

Actually, he'd be thrilled if she just ignored the broad and dragged him to the elevator.

But as much as he hated to do this, as much as he could end up regretting what he was about to do, he had to. Because beneath this insane attraction, beneath the hot sexting and R-rated limo rides, the teasing and the foreplay and the dirty-talk, he cared about Dana. He wanted her to care about him. He didn't want her to use him to forget her ex leaving, or get her groove on, or whatever the newly-divorced set were calling it these days… He wanted Dana to be with him because she was interested in him for who he was. Not just the sex. Not just a weekend out of time.

He let go of her hand. "Whatever you want, Dana. I don't want to make you uncomfortable."

Liar!

He gritted his teeth. This was her decision.

She looked at him, then at the woman, took a deep breath, and opened her mouth, about to either make or annihilate his weekend.

Chapter Fourteen

Cougar!

That word reverberated in my head as loudly as if Theresa had shouted it across the hotel foyer.

Not that she had to because I'd felt the stares; I knew what people were thinking as they looked at me and Scott.

I *was* a cougar.

And I wasn't comfortable with it.

"Hello, Theresa." I tried to put a smile on my face as my fellow homeroom mom flagged me down thirty seconds before I would have made it to the elevator scot-free.

Well, not *Scott*-free. Definitely didn't want to be that. And if that made me a cougar, I guess I had to own it.

"I thought that was you." Theresa Menotti sort of half-skipped, half-power-walked the fifty or so feet of marble between us. "That's a gorgeous dress."

That I'd already been out of once and couldn't wait to get out of again. "Thank you."

"It's been a while…"

The smile just stretched tighter across my face. "Two years."

"Uh, yes. I guess it has been."

Oh it was. I knew right to the minute when I'd gone into hibernation to regroup to try to get my life in order. The new order.

"You're looking well."

"Thank you."

Theresa was so trying not to stare at Scott.

But in the end, temptation won out.

Oh well. Guess I had to suck it up and deal with it—when I'd rather be sucking something else, but that wasn't going to happen until this did. I really hadn't planned on bringing Scott into my real world. As long as it'd been just the two of us—restaurant staff didn't count since they were trained to be unobtrusive and uninterested—I could pretend it was just a fantasy. *He* was just a fantasy.

But he wasn't. He was a living, breathing man who was standing a foot behind me, and the longer I *didn't* acknowledge him, the bigger a deal he became and the more awkward the situation would get.

But why did it have to be? I was fully within my rights to go out with whomever I wanted and Scott was definitely of legal age. It wasn't as if I was doing anything wrong.

Not yet, and here's hoping it'll be oh-so-wrong—

I reached back for his hand and tugged him forward. "Scott, this is Theresa. Our kids go to school together." I hoped he didn't mind that I was introducing him.

So make it up to him later if he does.

Now there was an idea…

"Very nice to meet you. Scott Masters." He shook Theresa's hand with such charm and sincerity that if I didn't know him any better, I might think it was genuine and he wasn't trying to hurry this along to get me alone.

Actually, I *didn't* really know him well enough to know that, but if that wasn't a boner in his pants, I'd leave now.

Oh hell. He had a boner going on in his pants. Theresa wasn't going to miss that.

I stepped in front of him just enough to hide the evidence. And if it looked a little proprietary, well… Good. Let Theresa tell all the girls that I had myself a hottie.

Actually… I was kind of liking that idea. Why *couldn't* I have a hottie? Why couldn't I be attractive enough for a younger man to find me interesting and want to be with me?

I inhaled and rolled my shoulders back slightly. Maybe even puffed out my chest a bit. Not peacocking, exactly, but maybe… proud? Happy? Confident and sure enough in my sexuality to admit to wanting this guy—and that he wanted me as well?

Okay, maybe more of the latter than the former, but I wasn't splitting hairs here—and Theresa Menotti and the rest of the PTA could eat their hearts out.

"Very nice to meet you. Is there a convention or something here at the hotel?" Theresa might be happily married, but the woman wasn't blind. She was definitely appreciating Scott.

"Convention?" Scott raised one eyebrow.

Jesus, that was such a sexy look on him. If we weren't in mixed company…

But we were. So I'd behave.

But the hand he put on my ass where Theresa couldn't see it wasn't helping matters.

"An author convention? I know Dana goes to those and has all those pictures with cover models…"

Theresa looked between us.

I had to bite my lip really really hard. It'd be *so* easy to take that as an out. Yes, sure; Scott was a cover model and we were discussing him being on the cover of my next book.

Not when I'd rather use what we were doing for the *inside* of my book.

"Thank you for the compliment, but no, I'm not one of the guys in Dana's books."

Not yet he wasn't. But I was already planning how he could be.

"Scott's not a cover model," I said, taking the leap. If I was going to own it, I might as well do it now. "There's no convention. We came for dinner." And dessert. Upstairs. If Theresa would only leave.

Scott's fingers curved onto my ass. "Have you tried Le Circlet?" he asked Theresa as if his index finger hadn't slowly started stroking between my cheeks.

Thank God the fabric of my dress wasn't very thick, and

that I wasn't wearing any panties. Not that the thong would have done anything, but still, to know but for a few millimeters of fabric, he might as well be caressing me indecently right here in this lobby—

Oh shit, I got wet. Well, wet *ter*. Moisture seeped onto my thighs and I could smell myself.

I glanced at Scott.

So could he.

"Oh. Well. I just assumed…" Theresa's eyes darted between us and I could see the realization crawl over her.

I should probably be offended. Why *couldn't* I have a hot date? Who said I had to date some paunchy bald guy who was ready to retire and piddle around in a backyard garden?

"I'm in finance, nothing to do with the writing world."

"Oh. You're her financial advisor."

Scott glanced at me.

I nodded at the question in his eyes.

"Actually, I'm not. I'm her date."

Surprisingly, my lip wasn't bloody with all the biting of it I was doing.

But I finally gave up that battle at the look on Theresa's face—first it was shock, then awe, and finally jealousy, cocking her head as she looked at me with an *atta girl* smile. "Want me to have Chuck thank your ex for you next time they go fishing?"

Chuck was Theresa's brother and he and my ex had been friends since childhood.

"Thanks, but I'd rather you didn't. He doesn't need to know anything about my life now." I squeezed Scott's hand and tossed my hair over my shoulder to look at him. "You ready?"

He swallowed. "Of course."

There was no *of course* about it. We were both chomping at the bit to be alone and I could tell by the way he'd moved closer—and the way his dick was poking me in the ass—that he wanted to get to our room as much as I did.

"It was nice seeing you, Theresa. I'll stop by bunco next

month if I have the time." The implication being, of course, that I wasn't planning to have the time because I'd be too busy boffing my hot young boyfriend.

Wait. He wasn't my boyfriend. Not yet. Right now he was my weekend fling and if we could make it to next month, *maybe* I'd consider calling him my lover, because *boyfriend* made him sound younger than he was.

"If you're ready, Scott…" I squeezed his fingers again.

His smile wanted to come out and play, but he managed to keep it hidden. The look he sent me, however, was enough to let me—and probably everyone else in the immediate vicinity—know that he was *definitely* ready.

He looked again at Theresa. "Very nice meeting you."

"Pleasure's all mine." Theresa glanced between the two of us, shook her head, and with a smile on her face, turned and walked away.

"Too much?" Scott asked as he curled my hand—still intertwined with his—to rest in the small of my back.

"Judging from the smile on her face, I don't think so. I think it was just enough."

"Enough to have tongues start wagging."

"As long as one of them is yours, I won't complain."

Scott jerked to a stop. "Jesus, Dana. You can't just say things like that out in the open."

I squeezed his fingers. "Well if you would keep moving, we won't *be* out in the open for much longer."

"I want to fuck you in the elevator."

Now it was my turn to stop moving—because my legs totally turned to jelly at that. "Do you hear yourself? Wasn't that what you just gave me hell for?"

"Yeah, but it's different when I say it."

"Care to explain how?"

He kissed my fingers—which wasn't helping the jelly-legs much. "More than happy to, but not here. I believe you were the one dragging me across the foyer to the elevator. Why are you stopping?"

"Because my legs are refusing to work."

"I could always carry you."

There went my damn legs again. This guy was hazardous to my health. "If I didn't think it'd cause a scene—"

"Who the fuck cares about a scene? Let them all be jealous."

And with that, he swung me up into his arms.

"Scott!" Normally, that would have come out as a shriek, but the butterflies in my stomach had lurched awake and sucked the breath out of my lungs, so it only came out a harsh whisper—even when his hand made contact with my bare ass beneath my dress.

"Yeah, baby, that's it. That's how I want to hear my name on your lips."

And then his lips were on mine and somehow, miraculously, he managed to not drop me or crash into anything as he strode to the elevator.

I held on for all I was worth, winding my arms around his neck so tightly, I hoped he could breathe. Then again, I couldn't breathe and it was all his fault. Because he was right, the hell with creating a scene. We didn't have to apologize for anything or to anyone, and as long as neither of us flashed a body part we shouldn't, no one should complain.

He was right… Let them all be jealous.

Chapter Fifteen

The elevator, thank God, was waiting for Scott to push the button—on the elevator, that was. Mine had been pushed hours ago.

Scott strode into the elevator, swung me around, hit another button with the forefinger of the hand that had palmed my ass, and the next thing I knew, I was feeling that *whoosh* of the elevator's acceleration.

At least, I thought it was from the acceleration, but it might be because the hand that'd been behind my back on my shoulder blade had slid around to my side, and his fingers found my nipple.

Scott trailed kisses along my jaw then to my neck, nuzzling beneath my ear as he stroked me. "I swear to God, I'd fuck you here, but I don't want our first time to be rushed. But know this, Dana. At some point, you *will* be riding me in this thing, and I'll make you come before we reach our destination."

Hell, I might do that now from his kiss alone. "I have no doubt you will, Scott."

He sucked my earlobe between his teeth, then nibbled on it. "There is so much I want to do to you, sweetheart. With you."

I arched my back at the sensation zinging from my ear to my stomach. And lower. "Tell me, Scott." I had to clench my thighs together to stop the ache.

His thumb slid up between them, however, pressing right against my opening. "Open for me, sweetheart, and I'll show you."

I relaxed and wiggled just enough—ah, yes. That. There. God.

I tried to say the words, but couldn't.

His thumb slipped inside me just as he swirled his tongue around the shell of my ear, and the sensations were so opposite—yet so not—that I wasn't sure which to react to first.

Then the elevator came to a halt with a slight bounce, and it was just like the limo ride when we'd hit that speed bump—I came. Again.

"Oh my God, Scott." I had to clamp my eyes and thighs shut, and my pussy clenched around his thumb all on its own, that pulse of muscles feeling so damn good as it just didn't stop—probably because he was circling his thumb inside me, finding every single fucking nerve ending I had.

The doors opened with a soft *whoosh*, but Scott didn't move. Good thing, because I couldn't either. I just hoped to God no one was on the other side of the elevator door, but right now, I couldn't care less. Scott's thumb was doing amazing things to my G-spot and if I could just catch my breath I'd only release it on a long moan.

"That's it, baby. Come for me. You are so fucking hot." Scott breathed it in my ear as he traced his tongue around the outer edge, sending even more tremors racing through me.

Jesus, this guy was talented. I didn't think I could feel any one individual part of my body; I was one big nerve ending, and I never wanted this feeling to go away. Thank God I'd answered his instant message.

Scott licked a path to my neck, nipping along the way. Little *zings* shot from each nibble.

"Come on, Dana. It's time I get to be inside you when you do that. You can't know how much I want to be inside you."

I managed to peel an eye open at that. "Wanna bet?"

That sexy-as-hell smile slid across his face. "I'd say, yes, but we both know what we'd bet, and we've spent too much time on foreplay already. I want to fuck you, Dana. Fuck you until you can't scream my name anymore. Fuck you until neither one of us can move… and then I'll fuck you again. Missionary, doggy, sixty-nine, and a few of my own private fantasies… I'm going to do every single one of them with you."

There was definitely something to be said for a younger man if he *could* actually keep it up for all the sexual gymnastics he was planning.

And I was more than ready to let him give it the old college try.

I wiggled against his palm—which made his thumb do a whole mess of good things to my pussy, but that wasn't why I wiggled. "I think we should probably get out of the elevator now, Scott. Before someone needs it."

He took his sweet time looking down my body—which just sent me into Tremorsville even more. "Just imagine what a show they'd get."

I didn't have to imagine; I was living it—and so was he. But, apparently, he wasn't as affected as I was.

Time to remind the guy what was going on here.

I flexed my feet, turning my ankles enough so Scott got a perfect shot of the heels. "I thought you were the one who wanted a show? Why don't you get us out of here?"

He buried his face beneath my hair and growled.

God, what that did to my insides…

"I'm kinda having a hard time doing that, Dana."

"A hard time is a good thing to have, Scott."

He licked my neck. "Tell me about it."

I really liked that he did that. I really liked *how* he did that.

What the hell, I was living my fantasy; I might as well make it be every single thing I wanted it to be. "Okay, Scott, first, you're going to march your sweet, tight ass out of this elevator, and over to that door, and get us inside as quickly as possible. Then you're going to carry me to the bed, toss me onto it, and crawl your way up my body, dragging my dress up with your abs as you slide against me."

His breathing got heavy. Heavi *er*. But he still didn't take one step out of the elevator. "And then?" He now sucked on the curve of my neck.

Oh, well, a hickey there wouldn't be obvious as long as I didn't wear a tank top or something strapless for a while. And I wouldn't because it was a small sacrifice to pay for that amazing feeling. "And then you'll remember that you actually *did* remove my thong with your teeth and I'm naked, so you're going to get inside of me so quick and so hard neither one of us is going to be able to make a sound because that first moment is going to steal our breath."

"Fuuuuuckkkkk."

He ground the word out harshly against my ear and the next thing I knew, he had us through the door and I was landing on the bed and Scott was crawling up me—yes, my dress was going with him, leaving me in only my stockings and heels— and then, thankyousweetJesus, he'd unzipped his pants and his dick was between my thighs—

But that was as far as he went.

"Scott?" He was *stopping*? Jesus. I raked my hands through his hair as his face was inches above mine where beads of perspiration dotted his forehead. "Why are you stopping?"

He closed his eyes as his cock jerked against me.

I relaxed my thighs just enough for his dick to slip between them.

He thrust between them—but not inside me. "What the—?"

"Condom," he ground out, his eyes clamping shut, a look of pain crossing his face.

Shit. Condoms. Modern medicine slicing into the moment of passion.

I would so love to tell him to forget it. To just go ahead and fuck me, but for all that this was a fantasy, there could be some very real repercussions and I was *not* a stupid woman. Horny, yes. Stupid, no. "Where are they? In your pants pocket?"

He nodded, his hips flexing so I could feel the very hard length of him *almost* where I wanted it.

I reached into his pockets, trying to ignore the angle of his hips against the backs of my hands so I wouldn't forget why they were there and flip them over to palm those sharp edges that would lead to someplace so very nice—

He had condoms in both pockets and I pulled out at least a dozen. I cocked my head. "I hope you can live up to all of these."

"Trust me, Dana, there are more in the bedside table. I plan to use every single one." He kissed me then, hard, his tongue thrusting between my lips as his cock thrust between my legs and melted my insides—only to have him pull away. Both his dick and his tongue.

"What—?"

"Ssshhhh." He kicked off his pants, yanked his shirt open, buttons going flying, then straddled me, his cock jutting above my belly. Truly a sight to behold.

Then he yanked a condom from my hand, sending the rest falling onto the mattress. He tore the foil with his teeth, all but shoved the thing onto himself, then was between my legs and inside me so quickly, I lost my breath on a gasp.

He thrust again.

No, that wasn't why I lost my breath. The man felt So. Incredibly. Amazing. There was no way I could breathe. No way I could ever hope to speak again. And that'd be okay if he'd only keep moving like this.

I arched up into him, my hands sliding along his waist, and I grabbed hold of those tight muscled cheeks and pulled him down into me.

"Wrap your legs around my waist, Dana. I want to feel those heels against my ass," he panted as he got his hands involved, shimmying my dress up over my chest, then over my head, dragging my hands off his ass long enough to get me naked. Well, from the waist up.

Which had its advantages when his fingers found my nipples just as his tongue slid over my lips.

I wrapped my legs around him, locking my ankles, heels clicking. I needed him in deeper. Harder. I swirled my hips, swallowed his groan. Hell, swallowed most of his tongue. The man was unbelievably sexy and I craved him more than any hot fudge sundae I'd ever wanted.

And yeah, just like that sundae, I wanted to lick him. Every single inch and twice on the six-pack.

He angled his head, his tongue thrusting deeper, and his cock mimicked the motion, two parts of him now fucking me at the same time and my hormones weren't sure which sensation to focus on, so I just grabbed hold and held on.

One of his hands curved along my waist then around to my backside, grabbing my cheek and stroking his fingers down the crack of my ass.

He—oh, God, no one had ever touched me there; my stupid ex had been too unadventurous to even *want* to try that.

Scott, apparently was all for it. And if truth be told—and I was going heavy with my truths these days—I wanted to try it as well.

I wiggled when he pressed against my opening, shifting.

He slid his finger in.

Holy mother of God. Stars exploded behind my eyes and I couldn't stop the long, keening moan at the back of my throat.

Scott sucked my tongue into his mouth when I tried to break the kiss to get some air going in. He wouldn't let me, his teeth scraping my tongue, the suction preventing me from going anywhere.

Yeah, well, two could play that game.

I clamped his cock with my inner muscles.

Scott moaned and sank onto me more, his weight no longer supported by his elbows.

Okay, that was a nice benefit I hadn't seen coming—but I wanted to see *him* coming, and while this was super nice and all, it was time Scott got a taste of what I'd enjoyed.

Hell, it was time Scott got a taste and *I'd* enjoy that.

"Fuck me harder, Scott," I whispered around his tongue.

His eyes shot open and he raised his head, his gaze searching mine. "Dana…"

"Do it. I want to feel you come inside me."

Sweat tracked down his forehead—he was holding back. That wouldn't do.

I dragged one of my hands off his ass and ran my fingertips across his hair line.

Then I licked my fingertips, tasting the saltiness.

I wouldn't mind tasting *another* saltiness.

That would've shocked me if I'd had that thought a month ago, but now, with Scott and all we'd done together… It turned me on.

"Come in me, Scott. Now. Do it."

I grabbed the hair at the back of his neck and dragged his head to my nipple. I needed him on me. Clamped onto me like I was clamping my legs around him.

His tongue raked over my nipple, not teasing, but hard and purposeful. Back and forth, he got it hard, then he sucked it in, his teeth scraping the sensitive peak, and more stars lit up behind my eyelids like firecrackers on the Fourth of July.

"Fuck me, Scott." I was able to get the words out but then he pulled his finger out and … *rammed* his dick back into me and I could only think them. *Dear God yes.*

I grabbed his ass—I needed to hold on. Do something. The feelings… I couldn't… Jesus... and—holy shit, he sucked my nipple into his mouth, then shook his head gently, the sensation of pain/pleasure almost too much to bear.

But then I could feel my orgasm start.

No. No way. I was not going to come first. I'd come so many times, I'd lost count. This was for him.

I slid my finger between his cheeks.

"Ahhhh, Danaaaaa," he hissed out, letting go of my nipple.

Just in time for me to slide my finger inside.

Scott bucked against me. Oh, yeah, that sent his dick into a motion I couldn't even begin to describe, but totally enjoyed.

I flexed my finger.

"Holy fuck." He bucked again, then ground himself against my pelvis, hitting my G-spot dead on. In any other situation, that'd be a good thing, but in this…

Fuck was right; I couldn't stop my orgasm. It roared through me, pulsing around him, clenching his dick, and I pulled my knees back, pressing down on his ass, my finger going deeper inside him as I tried to bring him inside me even more.

"That's it, baby. Fuck my ass." Scott pumped into me, his thighs hammering against *my* ass, his abs sliding against my stomach, sweat slicking the ride.

Jesus, he felt… amazing. *I* felt amazing.

I curled my fingers over his cheeks, my nails making indentations, my finger rubbing up against the gland inside him—I'd learned that trick researching my books and I was so very glad I did.

Scott's eyes shot open, his hips still pumping into me and the look of desire, lust, want in his eyes…

"Holy… Dana…Oh my fucking…I…" His head bobbed in time with his hips, his mouth falling open, and he raised himself up onto his palms, changing the angle of penetration, and I could see the ripples undulate over his abs as he kept the rhythm.

I pulled one hand off his ass to run it over those abs.

Dear God, every sculpted, muscled one of them… Skin stretched taught… Sweat slicking his skin so my fingers could glide over them…

I wanted to lick them. Wanted to run my tongue along all those grooves, take each perfectly formed muscle between my lips and taste him.

"Fuck my ass, Dana. Harder. Faster."

I shook off my haze of desire to be there for him, working my finger faster, as forcefully as I could from this angle, arching up, pulling my knees up even more to be able to slide down onto his cock so I could reach around there—it was a win-win for both of us.

His hips thrust harder and he grabbed my thighs. His fingers would leave bruises and I'd enjoy each one.

He pumped faster. On his knees now, dislodging my finger, his head falling back, the long column of his throat bared to me, making him look like a piece of sculpture in a museum.

And that was definitely marble between his legs.

I gripped his hip. "God, Scott, that's it. Make me come, honey."

He didn't answer—unless I counted a harsh hiss of air, and right this minute, yeah, I'd count it. It sure as hell said a lot about his state of mind.

I smiled at that. His mind was blown and I was the one who'd blown it. Talk about a rush of pleasure. I'd done this to him.

I spread my thighs wider, my ankles still locked, and I clenched my pussy around him.

"Dana! Fuck!" He fell forward over me and began pounding into me. No finesse, no thought to my pleasure, and it was *that* that gave me pleasure. Scott who'd been so considerate, so giving, so generous, was taking. Because he wanted to. Wanted me. *Had* to.

I wrapped my arms and my legs tighter around him, taking every hard, fast stroke. I turned my head and found his ear, sucked in the lobe, and bit down on it. He tasted so fucking good. Felt even better. I was a fool to have doubted this for a minute. Hell, I should have said yes that first night.

He shuddered against me, his mouth buried in my neck, his teeth scoring my collar bone. Fuck my no-hickey rule; I wanted him to mark me.

The bed banged against the wall when he sped up, his thrusting shifting the mattress.

I tried to breathe, but the sensations… Yes, I wanted him

to come, but he was stroking me in just the right way, at just the right place…

"God, yes, Dana. Fuck me, baby. Grab my cock."

I concentrated on my inner muscles—and if *he* didn't fucking come soon, I was going to.

"Hurry, Scott. Come for me."

"Want… To… Hold… Out…"

Oh fuck no. I couldn't hold out and he didn't get to. Later perhaps, but not now.

I twisted a little to my left, giving him more access to my throat, and I slid a hand along my ass to his sac. His heavy, cum-filled sac.

I stroked it.

"Oh. My—" Scott groaned as he thrust inside me and stayed there, determination etched into every line of his face, his lips stretched taut, the muscles in his arms quivering as I felt his sac empty into me.

"Oh God." He adjusted his palms beside me, grimacing at a fresh round of sensation—that I just had to help along by clenching him again.

His body went rigid—a good thing—all but for the pulsing of his sac as he came. Sweat slid down his throat and I wanted to lick it off, but I didn't dare move and interrupt his orgasm.

"Jesus." He said on an indrawn breath, then fell on top of me, catching his weight at the last second on his elbows.

I smiled at him. "No, *Dana*."

I got a half-smile out of him at that.

"Funny."

"Got you to smile." As I was doing.

"Oh I've been smiling. On the inside. Where it counts."

He kissed me and rolled onto the bed beside me while I tossed those last three words around in my brain.

Counts? What exactly did he mean by that?

Chapter Sixteen

"Penny for them." Scott ran his forefinger from my collarbone down between my breasts once our breathing had returned to normal.

Well, relatively normal.

"They're worth more than a penny. People pay good money for my thoughts." I shivered when he circled my nipple.

"Ah, so we *are* going to make it into a book."

I got up on my elbows. "I thought you said you wanted to? I don't have to, you know. I have a good enough imagination without using what we've done together."

"How about you use that imagination on me *and* put it in a book?" He flicked his tongue over my nipple then looked up at me. "It'll probably be a best-seller." He sucked that incredibly sensitive part of me into his mouth.

My head dropped back. "It will if you keep doing things like that."

He tugged one last time then let go, but kept his lips there, just touching. "Baby, I got a whole repertoire you haven't seen yet." He shifted and trailed kisses back to the middle of my chest. "Starting with this."

His lips headed south.

Oh good God… He was going to… I couldn't even think as he dipped his tongue into my navel. I had to suck massive amounts of air into my lungs.

He chuckled against my skin, his warm breath making my shiver. "Liked that, did you?"

"Hmm mmm." I couldn't form words because I had to bite my lip to keep from begging him to hurry up and get to my clit. I was aching and wanted him there. Fuck foreplay; get on with it already. He was right, we'd done enough. Now I wanted the real stuff. The stuff I couldn't do on my own—not that it'd be like this even if I could. There was just something about watching a hot guy go down on me that couldn't be replicated no matter how many batteries it needed.

He slid his lips to my hip.

Ran his tongue along it.

Nuzzled the hollow beside it.

Then went lower.

"I like this," Scott whispered against my landing strip.

I'd felt so decadent having that done a few months ago. Back when I hadn't had anyone to use it with, but oh how glad I was I'd decided to change things up. It'd made me feel sexy to my own self, but now…

"Open for me, babe."

Gladly. I slid my legs apart.

"I can smell you."

I nodded, still not trusting myself to speak. I could smell myself, too, and it turned me on.

"You want me to eat you, don't you?"

I nodded again. That turned me on, too. Hell, there wasn't anything about Scott that *didn't* turn me on.

"Good." Scott kissed just above where I wanted him to.

Then he sat back. "Hold that thought."

"Hold—" I propped myself back up on my elbows, my chest heaving. "What do you mean, 'hold that thought'? Are you trying to kill me?"

Scott ran his finger over my nipple. "What a way to go, though, right?"

Between the sexy look on his face, the ache in my pussy, my poor neglected clit, and the sensation in my nipple, I wasn't sure which to react to first. My elbows gave out and I flopped back on the bed. "I can't take anymore."

"Bullshit." Scott worked himself up beside me on his knees and bent over to kiss me. "You'll take everything I dish out, babe, and you'll like it." He kissed me again, all tongue and hard lips, his stubble rubbing against my cheek and I wanted it against my thigh. "You'll even thank me."

I would, I knew that, but getting to that point was testing my patience.

Especially when he pulled away to lean over me to grab the phone.

"You're making a call *now*?" I couldn't imagine what in the world was more important to him at this moment than finishing what he'd started.

Scott grinned that wicked grin at me and pressed a button. "Room service, please."

Oh. Well that made sense. Sort of. I could see where he'd have worked up an appetite, but I wasn't hungry.

Although… Scott had made one miscalculation. When he'd leaned over me, he'd put his dick in *just* the right position for me to take a taste.

"…bottle of champagne—uhhhhh."

I smiled as I slid my lips over the head of his cock.

He cleared his throat. "A selection of fresh fruit."

His voice was lower… which could be because his dick was down my throat.

"Uh, yeah. Hot… fudge sauce."

I swirled my tongue under the rim.

"Iccccccccccccccccce." He'd hissed that very well. Maybe the guy on the other end of the phone didn't have any idea I was blowing Scott while he ordered our dessert.

I raked my teeth over his head.

"Fuck."

Then again, maybe the guy *did* have some idea…

I ran my tongue along the throbbing vein.

"Hundred buck tip if it gets here in five minutes." Scott slammed the phone down and flexed his hips forward. "Suck me, baby."

Wanting to do that, I tried not to smile while I deep-throated him, but it was hard not to.

I stroked my hands up his hamstrings and palmed his ass. He had *the* best ass. Firm and tight. I could feel the strength in the muscles as he pumped into my mouth.

I slid one finger between his cheeks and found his anus again.

"Fu…ck, yeah, Dana."

I loved the hard, raspy tone, the fact that he couldn't quite get the words out. His hips shook the next time he pumped in, and his cock swelled against my tongue.

Five minutes, huh?

I flicked the tip of my tongue under the rim of his dick, my finger flicking his other rim. Then I changed the angle of my head and tilted his hips with my hands on his ass so I could rub his head along the roof of my mouth.

He moved, then, straddling me, and the rhythm changed. He fucked my mouth as if he were fucking my pussy, banging against the back of my throat so that I had to relax my muscles to make this perfect for him.

But time was ticking away.

I nudged his ass with another finger.

That did it.

"Danaaaaaa!" Scott's glutes tightened as he thrust deep into my mouth and cum shot out of him, coating the back of my throat.

I breathed heavily—not that I wasn't already, but that'd been from being utterly turned on by what I was doing; this was to keep from coughing because I didn't want to ruin this.

Round after round of cum filled my mouth and, Jesus, he tasted good. My ex and I hadn't done this much, but when we had, I'd never enjoyed it like I did now. I'd never liked the taste.

Oh how different this was with Scott.

I sucked him harder, felt him shudder with the last of his cum, then held him in my mouth as the tremors slowed.

He exhaled and leaned his head against the large padded headboard. It took him a few seconds to open his eyes. "God, that is one beautiful view."

This time I couldn't stop my smile around his dick. But I didn't want to release him, so I licked him instead.

"Ummmm." His eyes closed.

"Room service!" A knock sounded on their door.

Scott's eyes shot open. "Fuck."

I pulled my mouth off him slowly, giving his head one last circle with my tongue. "I—"I had to swallow—"guess one of us has to get up."

His cock jerked in front of me. "Since I already am, I guess that's me."

"You mean you can still move?"

He swung one leg over me. "Barely."

"That's true; you are." I ran my hand along his abs, then down his thigh.

"Room service, Dana. Don't distract me."

"Food's more important than this?"

"Food's important *to* this. Just wait." He got off the bed and headed toward the door, grabbing his pants and stepping into them along the way.

Scott bending over to pick them up was a hell of a nice view; it a sincere shame to cover that ass.

Then he looked around.

"Your shirt's over there." I pointed with a lethargic, sated hand.

The server knocked on their door again.

"Fuck it. The guy's gonna have to live with it." He dragged his wallet from the back of his pants. "Two bills ought to negate any embarrassment." He looked at me. "You, however, might want to cover up. The bed's a straight shot from the door."

"I remember."

I had to get up. The sheet wasn't going to hide what we'd been doing, and while I hadn't minded people in the lobby guessing what we were going to be doing, I didn't want to be on display for the waiter.

I scrambled off the bed and headed to the bathroom, dragging the sheet with me and trying to get my legs to work in the heels before Scott made it to the door. Let the waiter wonder at the absence of sheets; I wasn't going to supply the evidence. The idea of exhibitionism was hard enough to wrap my brain around; *doing* it… I didn't think even Scott would be able to talk me into something like that.

I heard them talking while I finished up in the bathroom, then peeked my head out to see if it was safe.

"Care to join me?" Scott was sitting naked in the middle of the bed, two glasses of champagne in his hands.

Couldn't get any safer than that.

So I decided to play it a little risky.

I dropped the sheet.

Chapter Seventeen

Scott sucked in a breath and just stared at me.

I had never felt sexier in my life.

"You're still in the heels and stockings."

Okay, *now* I'd never felt sexier in my life. "I thought you liked them." Though they had fallen to my ankles in all our, um, excitement, but I'd worked them back into place.

"Oh I do. Trust me, baby, I do. I just wasn't expecting you to walk back in here like that."

"What's wrong with this?"

"Not a damn thing. And considering all we did online, I guess I should've expected it from you."

The blush blazed up my body, pooling in my cheeks. It was one thing to have done what we'd done online in the heat of the moment, but to talk about it…

"You're blushing?" Scott got up on his knees, set the flutes on the bedside table, then held out his hands. "Jesus, Dana, you shouldn't be shy about any of this. It's all good. We're consenting adults who are enjoying each other. Nothing to be embarrassed about at all."

I took his hands. When I was touching him, I agreed with him. "I know, but this is all so new for me. I'm just not used to it when I start thinking about it."

He tugged and I fell, twisting so that I ended up in his arms.

"Then don't think." He kissed me. Tenderly. Softly. As if… well, as if this were a big emotional moment.

But I wasn't naïve enough to go there. This was sex, pure and simple. Okay, not so pure, and definitely not so simple, but definitely sex. All about giving each other pleasure and enjoying the experimentation.

He nuzzled my nose when he finished the kiss… probably the least carnal kiss he'd given me, but still sexy enough to turn me on.

"So you want that champagne before the bubbles fizzle out?" He leaned over me to get a glass.

Don't lick his nipple, don't lick his nipple, don't lick his nipple…

Of course I licked his nipple.

He let out a sound that was half-laugh, half- *whoosh,* and rocked back onto his knees, some of the champagne sloshing over the edge and falling between my breasts.

It was my turn to *whoosh.*

"Hey, that's what you get when you don't play fair."

"There are rules?" The champagne slid down my breastbone and curved under my breast before sliding down my side.

"Of course there are rules." Scott got an impish look on his face. Then he shook the champagne glass again. More droplets fell onto me. "You have to make the other person feel good." He bent down and licked the champagne off. "And you have to make yourself feel good, too."

I had to force myself not to shift and put my nipple in his tongue's path. Scott obviously had some very definitive plans for us and I was going to be a good girl and try to let him call the shots.

Or I'd be a very bad girl and *still* let him call the shots.

"So what all did you order for us?" I tried to keep the huskiness out of my voice, but I really liked the way his stubble rasped across my skin—and, yeah, it did make it to my nipple. Thank God something did.

"Oh, this," he licked the underside of my breast, "and that." He trailed his tongue up to my areola and circled it, but he wouldn't touch my nipple, dammit.

"Scott?"

"Mmmm?"

He softly blew on me and, yeah, my nipple reacted, tightening so that I felt it in my pussy, too.

"Can I have some more of this?" I ran my hand down his side to his thigh, but had to stop since I couldn't reach the part of him I wanted to with him bent over me like he was.

He smiled against my ribcage. "Don't you want some champagne first?"

"That's what I was talking about."

"I meant to drink."

"Is there a law against drinking out of anything other than a glass?"

He raised his head. "What were you thinking?"

I pointed to my navel. "This could be interesting."

"I like the way your mind works, woman." He tilted the flute so a thin stream splashed into my navel. When I sucked in a breath at the sudden coldness, the champagne overflowed and pooled in the hollow between my hips.

"Hmmm, yes, this could be very interesting." Scott's lips tickled my tummy when he sucked the champagne from my navel, swirling his tongue around so that I felt that movement in my core. Then he mouthed my belly, sucking in the rest of the drink.

He brushed his mouth on my hip. "Yup, you were right. That was interesting. Tasty, too." He tilted the glass again. "You know what else might be interesting?"

I had an idea but shook my head so he'd show me.

"This."

He poured the champagne over my pussy.

"Oh my God." I couldn't stop the words. Just like I couldn't stop writhing when he bent over to lick it off.

I also couldn't stop myself from reaching for his dick. Well, I probably could have, but why?

"Ah, Dana, you have to give me some time, sweetheart."

"We have all night, Scott. And tomorrow. But I want to

touch you." I stroked my thumb over the head, feeling some moisture at his slit. "And it might not be as long as you think." I swirled it on him.

"Then I'm going to have to hurry." He shifted so he was between my legs.

"No, you really don't have to. Feel free to take your time."

He lifted one of my legs, running his palm up my calf then my thigh, stroking the silk covering my skin.

"These are so fucking hot. And the heels…" He groaned and mouthed my instep above the shoe, sending shivers racing up my spine. Damn, the man knew just how to touch a woman.

I wasn't going to think about Scott and other women. He knew how to touch *me*. That was the important part. He knew just how to touch me, and I was going to put it down to us being in tune with each other, not any kind of experience he had.

Though—man!—that experience was definitely coming into play when he mouthed his way over my ankle, then up my calf. He did some swirly-tongue thing to the back of my knee that, if I hadn't already been on my back, would've put my there.

And then he was pressing hot, wet, open-mouth kisses to the inside of my thigh, one slow inch at a time. The anticipation was just about killing me.

I gripped the sheets, trying not to arch off the bed, but that wasn't helping much. I just wanted his tongue on my clit.

And then it was.

For a second.

"Scott—"

"Sssh…"

Damn, the breath from his *sssshhhh* wafted right over my swollen flesh. I. Needed. Him. There.

"Please, Scott."

"Oh yeah, baby. I like when you beg."

I groaned. I'd beg. I would. I had no pride at this moment. Pride was overrated anyway. "Lick me, Scott. Dear God, please just put your tongue on me and lick."

The man could follow directions.

Exceed them, actually.

The first touch arched my back—because I wanted more. I wanted it harder. Faster.

He slid a hand under my ass, and held me against his mouth, and his tongue—dear God, his tongue—flicked against my clit so fast and so hard and so perfect that I couldn't take it. My head thrashed from side-to-side, my breathing went manic, and my hips… My hips flared out as much as possible, my knees hitting the bed and my heels going somewhere in the middle of his back, and if Scott weren't holding me right where he was, I'd be writhing off the bed.

The fact that I couldn't move from the spot was a turn-on in itself.

He thrust his tongue into me, fucking me, then he moved back to my clit. The guy was like a human jackhammer and, man, was he jacking me. I couldn't catch my breath, the sheets were probably going to be shredded from my fingernails, and the stars behind my eyelids were exploding with every stroke of his tongue.

Somewhere along the line, he got a finger inside me, pumping in time with the rhythm of what he was doing to my clit, and then I felt… Oh dear God… he worked his other thumb into my ass and the two digits were working opposite each other, so it was as if he was conducting a symphony of sensation, all building to a crescendo that came crashing over me in wave after wave of pleasure so intense it was almost painful.

Almost.

I felt my juices flow out of me, unendingly so. The orgasm went on and on and on and Scott kept licking and licking and—oh, yeah—that tongue thing again, driving me insane. One, two orgasms… possibly a third, but I could barely remember where I was let alone count how many times he took me to paradise.

All I knew was that when Scott finally eased off, I couldn't stop shuddering with the aftershocks.

It didn't help that he crawled up my body, placing soft kisses followed by the stubbly rasp of his chin, a sort of hot-then-cold approach that made me burn.

"How was that?" he whispered when he nuzzled my neck.

"You know exactly how amazing that was." I was surprised I had the energy to not only smile at his silly question but to even answer him back. "And if it hadn't almost killed me, I'd ask you to do it again."

"You never have to ask. The only reason I'm not still down there is because you need to catch your breath. But rest assured, Dana, that was only the opening act."

"Your opening act just might close the show, maestro."

He smiled and those damn dimples had almost the same effect as his tongue did. "I can go with *maestro*."

"Well it *was* a virtuoso performance."

"And you want an encore."

I smiled at him and managed to stretch one hand over my head, since he was laying on the other one. "Yeah, I do."

"Damn, woman. You're insatiable."

"Only for you, Scott. Only for you."

"I like the sound of that."

He planted a big ol' wet kiss on my lips and I tasted myself. Not something I'd ever really enjoyed, but, just like everything else I'd done with this man, I found I liked it.

"However..." He sat up. "Your healthy appetite needs something besides sex."

"Says who?"

"Says me. I can't have you passing out from hunger on me."

"It won't be from hunger."

His dimples came back into play. "Okay, then. How about *I* need some sustenance to keep up with you? I've heard women reach their sexual prime in their forties, and I'm not twenty anymore."

True. He was thirty-three. And I'd think about that

tomorrow. Right now, he was here, I was here, and I was going to enjoy. "Are you saying you can't keep up with me?"

"I'm saying I don't want to test my endurance, so let's eat up. Just think how much fun we'll have working off the calories."

"True. But I honestly don't think I can move." I didn't even bother trying because I was feeling so lethargic I just didn't want to. I wasn't hungry and the only reason I'd eat anything was if he held it to my lips.

Especially a certain part of him.

I glanced between his legs. Yes, he was definitely *up* for that, but for some reason, he wanted food.

I laughed at myself as he got off the bed. I'd been so worried about the age thing. About being a cougar, when, really, what I was, was a woman. A woman attracted to a guy who was just so hot that nothing else mattered. And I didn't mean that in just the physical sense, because a guy could be physically gorgeous, well-endowed even, but if he didn't know what to do with any of it, it was a waste.

Nothing was wasted on Scott. Every inch of him, inside and out, was designed to give me pleasure, and I'd be an idiot not to take what the universe had so graciously dropped into my lap.

Which was where his hand landed just then.

"Come on, babe." He stroked me.

Yeah, I'd come…

"We can't be all about the sex."

"We can't?"

He gave me that half-cocked smile. "Are you just using me for my body?"

"Of course not." I did struggle to sit up, and if the movement caused his fingers to slip a little lower, well, hey, we were both winners. "There are other parts, too, like your lips, your tongue, your fingers."

He slicked the last through my folds, fluttering against my clit before withdrawing them, leaving me aching. "Well, these fingers are good for holding food, too. Let me show you how well I do that."

"If you insist." Look at me; Ms. Horny. I giggled. I'd never been so decadent in my life. And I had a feeling life was never going to be the same from this moment on.

"I insist." He held out his hand, and tugged me onto my feet when I clasped it.

And if that had me stumbling against him, well... it wasn't as if that was any big hardship.

Though there was a very big hard *ship* against my belly. I giggled again. I ought to write this stuff down for my books.

"Wanna share the joke?"

"No joke. Just a delicious irony."

"Well something's delicious all right." He licked my lips. "So come on, give. What were you smiling about just now?"

"This. Us. How uninhibited I feel."

This time he planted a hard kiss on my lips. "Good," he said when he let me come up for air. "Keep that in mind. I've got plans for you. Starting with... this."

Chapter Eighteen

Scott uncovered the fruit tray. Grapes, melon balls, pineapple, strawberries, watermelon, bananas. All good stuff, but nothing to whet my appetite. Well, for food.

Until he picked up two of the melon balls and rolled them around on his palm. "Know what I want to do with these?"

"I can't imagine."

"Seriously? You can't?"

Actually, I was starting to. But was he really going to…

He popped them into his mouth and rolled them around with his tongue.

I could almost imagine them doing that inside me.

He put them back onto his palm. "On your back, Dana."

Apparently, I didn't need to imagine.

I sat on the bottom of the bed, propped myself on my elbows, rested my heels on the edge, and let my knees fall open.

He sucked in a breath, his fingers tightening around the melon. "God, that's so pretty."

"You like the stockings and heels."

"Those, too."

He knelt in front of me and I bit my lip to stop groaning. Seeing him there, between my thighs, was such a turn-on—and knowing what he was about to do…

He tucked one, then the other melon ball inside me.

"Keep them in."

"Uh huh." I couldn't manage words. Sounds were about all I could get out because this was so sexy that I could come right now without much stimulation at all. Well, stimulation other than what was happening inside me.

I'd tried Ben Wa balls before and they were interesting, but the melon balls… the idea itself was more erotic than the actual fruit, but this entire scenario worked for me.

Then he took a banana from the serving tray.

Slowly he peeled it, one flap, two, a third… The fourth fell away and Scott ran the tip of the banana along my clit.

I sucked in a breath. It felt… I couldn't describe it. Firm, like the head of his dick, but not silky, though the texture seemed to touch more nerve endings, if that was possible.

Then he slid it along my folds.

"Scott…"

"Feel good?"

I dropped my head back when he placed the length of it between my labia, my inner muscles clamping on the melon balls. "Yeah."

"Want me to fuck you with it?"

My breath *whooshed* out and I fell back onto the bed, all strength gone from my arms at the thought. I'd never done anything this decadent in my life and I wanted to. Had never *thought* of anything this decadent, and in my industry, that was saying something. "God, yes, Scott. Fuck me with it."

He ran his stubbled cheek along my inner thigh, mouthing a few kisses as he slowly dragged the tip of the banana down to my opening, my muscles clenching in anticipation. With the melon inside me, I was already feeling sexy, but then the banana slid in and I couldn't help it; I started to pant. It was… it felt… there were no words.

He pulled it out. Not all the way, but just enough to have me clenching again to draw it back in.

"Greedy, aren't you? How many orgasms do you need, Dana?"

I heard the teasing in his voice, but this wasn't funny. It

was so incredibly hot that I wanted him to push it inside me again.

"Fuck me, Scott." I tugged my knees back, opening myself to him. Hell, there was another banana on that tray; he ought to use both.

Instead, he shifted away from me.

"Where are you going?" I struggled back onto my elbows.

Scott smiled at me from a few feet away where he was on his knees beside the room service cart. "Don't worry, babe. I'm not going anywhere." He dragged the cart back to the bed. "I wanted to have everything handy." He picked up a cluster of grapes. "Like these."

I couldn't imagine what he was going to do with the grapes. My pussy was already full.

My ass, however, wasn't.

He rimmed me with his finger, his gaze never leaving mine. "Feel good?"

I bit my lip and nodded.

He slipped one of the grapes inside.

Jesus. The sensation… The stem was still attached, and the rest of the cluster was on the bed, a slight weight that made it more intense.

"Now, where was I?" He got that wicked smile on his face and dragged the banana along my pussy lips again. "Ah, yes. Here."

He nudged it into me again.

My arm strength gave out once more, and I fell back onto the bed, my ass and my pussy clenching the fruit. The banana sliding in and out of me, the slight tug on the grape cluster, the rasp of Scott's stubble against my silk-clad thigh…

He pulled away. "Wait a second."

" *Wait?*" I shot back up onto my elbows. "I can't wait, Scott. Please don't stop."

"Ah, babe. You know me. This is all about making it better for you." He picked up an ice cube and sucked on it.

Seeing his lips around it as they'd been when he'd sucked my nipples sent my imagination on a tangent I really hoped he would follow.

But… no. He pulled the ice cube out and moved *it* to my nipple. The sensation was shocking. Cold, yes, but it also started a delicious burning sensation that I didn't think could get any better.

Then he put his mouth on me.

It was too much. His cold lips on my hot clit, the banana filling me, the other fruit rubbing against each other… Scott licked my clit hard, then soft, drawing it between his cold lips, and my legs started to tremble.

I pulled back on my knees again, opening wider, and the pressure became intense.

Especially when Scott left the ice cube, letting it slide between my breasts then head down toward my navel, the cold etching a trail in its wake, and he tugged out the grape, releasing my orgasm, all the while still fucking me with the banana.

"Oh… My… God… Scott…" I moaned as my orgasm spiraled through me. I thought the melon balls came out at one point, but I couldn't tell because the waves of intense pleasure wouldn't stop.

I heard a clatter but couldn't focus enough to open my eyes to see what Scott was doing.

I didn't have long to wonder when I felt something warm and thick flow onto my belly, then Scott was nuzzling his way up to it.

"My very own banana split sundae," he said, his open-mouth kisses sucking what I guessed was chocolate syrup off me.

The banana dipped into my navel, followed by the remnants of the ice cube and what was probably one of the melon balls. I was going by touch alone and that really wasn't a bad way to go.

"Look at me, Dana." Scott whispered hoarsely.

Still trembling at the ending of my orgasm, I slid my head to the side and opened one eye.

Scott was leaning over me, the fruit resting on my stomach, his chin coated in chocolate. "You taste so good, woman." He licked a line from my pussy to my navel, then slipped one of the melon balls into his mouth, smiling to show me it between his teeth.

Then he shifted, his hands now beside my waist on the bed, and he leaned over me.

Then he kissed me.

The melon ball changed mouths and I wrapped my legs around him when I tasted the sweetness beneath the saltiness that was me.

The rest of the fruit was forgotten as I tucked the melon into the pocket of my cheek and kissed Scott with all the strength I had left inside me, somehow managing to get my hands in his hair and pull him down onto me.

Mashed banana slid between us, the sweet scent of it and the chocolate perfuming the air along with the scent of our arousal.

Scott scooped the melon ball out with his tongue, never breaking the kiss. God, that was so erotic.

So I did it back.

Scott groaned into my mouth and thrust his hands into my hair, devouring my lips as his tongue tried to take the melon back, but I wasn't letting him have it. I tucked it into my cheek again and swept my tongue into his mouth, forcing his back, dueling with it until Scott, smart man, sucked my tongue into his mouth so much it hurt a little. But the burn was a turn on—as was everything with this guy—so it just made me hot all over again.

I groaned, arching beneath him, wanting him inside me again.

Scott pushed up, breaking the kiss."Jesus, Dana. How is it that you take all my good intentions and turn them into a heat-seeking missile? No finesse, no consideration, all I want to do is bury my dick inside you and fuck you until the end of time."

"I'm not stopping you." I wriggled my hips and chewed the melon. No way did I want to choke on it and miss one minute of what he had planned. "Matter of fact, you might even say, I'm begging you."

"And I'll let you beg me." He was off me in a flash, yanking open the bedside table drawer, then working another condom on himself.

He was back in place—and back inside me—in under a minute.

"I swear to God, Dana, sex has never been like this." He arched his back, thrusting deep inside me, the smudge of chocolate down his chest making him good enough to eat.

So I leaned up and licked it.

"Fuck, yes." It was his turn to pant.

I flicked his nipple with my tongue. It'd probably taste really good with chocolate on it, though, in all honesty, I liked the taste of him. And with the chocolate too far away for me to reach, that was a good thing.

Not that Scott seemed to care. He pumped into me, then kissed me, thrusting his tongue into my mouth in rhythm with his dick, the mashed fruit making the slide between us an interesting experience.

Especially when it warmed up. Jesus, the scents alone were erotic enough, but then Scott twisted his hips and it took me to a whole new level.

"God, Dana. You feel so fucking amazing." He licked the corner of my mouth and I could still taste the chocolate.

"I do, thanks to you."

He smiled as he sucked my bottom lip between his teeth for a quick nibble. "You're going to give me a big head if you keep saying things like that."

I clenched him and swirled my hips. "Too late."

He chuckled and nudged my nose with his, all the while his hard dick still pumped inside my, stroking every nerve ending, sending that spiraling feeling deep into my core, unraveling the beginnings of yet another orgasm.

I didn't know how I could keep having orgasm after orgasm. At some point my body *had* to reach saturation.

Something's saturated all right…

Yeah, the sheets weren't going to be salvageable after tonight. And I didn't care.

However, there was a way to preserve them a little longer. A very pleasurable way.

"Scott," I said when he went to kiss me again.

He pulled back, and every movement stopped. "What's wrong?" His eyebrows veed and a worried look came into his eyes.

"Nothing's wrong." I smoothed his hair back from his face. "But I want to be on top."

Damn, his dimples were sexy as hell—and he flipped over so fast, dragging me with him, that he somehow managed to stay inside of me. And *that* was even sexier than his dimples.

"I'm all yours, baby."

I liked the sound of that. Even if it was just for this weekend.

I wiggled my butt and sat back on him, tracing a finger down his chest through the mashed chocolate banana, right to the base of his dick.

Then I clenched my muscles around him.

"Ah, jeez, Dana. That's incredible." His eyes closed and he tilted his chin, his back arching just enough to stuff his dick up a little more inside of me.

I ground down on him, my finger now swirling the chocolate around his nipple.

His mouth fell open and he let out a groan. "God, yes, baby."

I lifted myself off him, only to slam back down, earning another groan—and his fingers now clamping onto my hips.

"Do that again," he panted.

I did.

This time, we both groaned.

"Again."

His voice was a hoarse whisper, but I heard him. Every sense I had was tuned in to him.

I lifted myself then fell back down. Then again. And again.

His fingers helped maintain the rhythm, though I had to plant my palms on his chest to keep up.

That was okay; I made sure my fingers were on his nipples so I could play with them while I fucked him.

"Harder, babe." His fingers bit into bone and I liked it. I didn't care that I'd have bruises; Scott was about to lose control, and with the tight rein he'd kept on his reactions, I wanted to see him lose it. Wanted to know I could make him lose it.

And then he did.

I grabbed him with my pussy muscles and tried to release, then re-clench as he pumped me onto himself. Harder, faster, it became a frenzy of movement and sensation and I just tried to keep up with him.

He planted his heels on the mattress, arching up, lifting my knees off the bed beside him, the vein in his neck pulsing with the rush of sensation, his jaw clenched, chest heaving.

I pinched his nipples and tried to clench him harder.

"Don't move, babe. Don't move." He rasped it out between his gritted teeth as his body fluttered under mine, swift, sharp strokes, as he ground me against him.

I tugged his nipples and Scott let out a long groan then, every muscle—and I did mean *every*—going rigid as his orgasm overtook him.

I could feel his dick pulsing inside me as it sent cum shooting into the condom. I so wished we didn't need a condom—and maybe at some point, we'd be together long enough, and monogamously enough, to be able to do that. Because I sure as hell wanted to get to that point.

And I'd deal with the ramifications of that thought—of an actual *relationship*—with Scott later. Right now, I just wanted to enjoy his orgasm.

Actually, I wanted to make sure *he* enjoyed it.

I swirled my hips. Not a lot because he still had a tight clamp on them, but there was enough movement for me to get another harsh groan out of him and a whole new round of pulsing in his dick.

He adjusted his hold on my hips as he sank back onto the bed, then his grip went slack. "Fuck meeeee," he whispered on a long groan.

"Already did that, Scott," I said, enjoying the final orgasmic spasms of his dick inside me.

"Yeah, you did."

I'd also done something else; I'd worn him out. I, a forty-nine year old mother of four, had worn out a hot guy in his prime. Hell, that realization might just get me off, too.

"You're looking like the cat that swallowed the canary."

"Canary?" I shook my head, enjoying the swish of my hair against my bare back—every sensation heightened by the sexual haze. "Interesting euphemism."

He smiled a lazy, sated smile and reached for my hand, then tugging it. "Come here, woman."

Chapter Nineteen

I braced my fall with my hands and shook my hair back when it fell forward.

"Nah, don't do that. I love your hair." He threaded his fingers into it and dragged my mouth to his, giving me an open-mouthed, carnal kiss I hadn't been expecting.

My arms trembled at the rush of sensation that came with it. How was this possible? How could this guy, whom I hadn't known for very long, do this to me?

Don't question the gift.

True. I was just thankful he could and did and wanted to.

"I'm so very glad you IM'd me, Scott," I murmured between some sexy wet kisses.

"I'm glad to hear it. I was really hoping you wouldn't shy away."

I straightened my arms, putting some space between them so I could look him in the eyes. His gorgeous blue eyes that I could get lost in. "I guess we can put shy on the shelf, huh?"

Scott lifted his head and looked between them. "Yeah, mashed bananas kinda puts the kibosh on shy."

I looked, too, and smiled. "It sure is fun mashing the banana."

"I guess that's what we're going to call it, huh?" He slid a hand to the back of my neck and tugged my back down onto him. "Come here, Dana, and mash my banana."

"Do you *not* get tired?"

"Oh I'm tired. But I'm figuring sleep can wait until Sunday night. I only have a limited time with you and I don't want to miss a moment."

I kissed him, then propped my arms on his chest and my chin in my fist. "Here's where the age difference is going to come into play. I'm exhausted and really need some sleep."

"Age has nothing to do with it, babe. Don't sell yourself short. You're exhausted from the half-dozen or so orgasms." His dimples came into view again with a sexy-as-hell smile. "My work here is done."

"Done?" I grabbed hold of his chin. "That's it? Can't we say it's on hold for a few hours instead?"

"I like the way you think, woman." He kissed me quickly, then slid out from under me, to lay beside me. "Sure, I'm up for round two. Or is it four?"

I laughed and flicked his chin. "Who's keeping count?"

"I would've if I could've thought straight, but thinking doesn't seem to happen around you. All I do is feel." He ran his hand down my back and curved it over my backside. "I guess I can wait a few hours. But…" He snaked his arm around my waist and rolled me into him so my backside was cushioned against him. "I'm not letting you go."

I was fine with that. Especially since he was *still* hard. Hell, there was definitely something to be said for sex with a thirty-three-year-old.

"Comfy?" He cupped my breast.

"I was until you did that."

He withdrew his hand. "I'm sorry. You don't like it?"

I pressed his hand back to where it'd been. "Oh I like it. But it doesn't make me feel comfy. It makes me horny."

I felt him smile against my shoulder.

"Ah, well then." He flexed his fingers and one *just happened* to brush my nipple. "I think I'll leave my hand right where it is."

"You do that."

"I will." He kissed the curve of my neck. "I'm so glad you said yes, Dana."

"Me, too."

He shifted, spooning around me, and tugged me even more tightly into him—where his dick twitched against me. "No, I mean, I'm *really* glad."

I arched my back, pressing against his erection with my ass and thrusting my tit into his hand. "Right there with you."

He exhaled and nibbled on my shoulder blade. "Get some sleep, lady, before I forget my good intentions and keep you up the rest of the night."

"Just a nap. To replenish the well." Though, if his fingers kept doing that to my nipple, I might get a second wind.

Then those fingers drifted downward.

"The well, huh?"

He slid one between my thighs, and damn, there was no refilling necessary. I flooded with arousal and couldn't help but open my legs.

"I thought you wanted to sleep," he said, chuckling.

"Nah, you were right. We can sleep on Sunday."

***

There was very little sleeping that night. Or the next morning.

I figured we'd gotten about an hour all combined between rounds of lovemaking, but I'd never felt more alert or alive when room service delivered our breakfast at nine a.m.

"I'm assuming you actually plan on eating all of that?" I joked when Scott lifted the serving lids. Bacon, eggs, hash browns, toast, more fruit…

"*This* we will eat. Definitely need to replenish our energy."

"Why? What more could you possibly have in store for me?"

"Wouldn't you like to know?" He dropped a kiss on my nose and popped a tangerine slice into my mouth—then kissed

200

me, biting the slice in half and letting the juice dribble on my lips. Which, of course, he licked off. "Baby, I have the coup de grâce planned for you. Guaranteed you're never going to want to have sex with anyone else any other way ever again."

I didn't want to have sex with anyone else period.

The realization shocked me and I choked on my half of the tangerine slice.

"Dana? You okay?" Scott patted me on the back then cupped my cheek when I stopped choking.

I forced a smile and swallowed the fruit. I was just caught up in the moment. I didn't mean it. Scott was just temporary. A fling. A jump-start to my after-marriage sex life. There'd be other guys and there'd be other experimentations and other fun sexcapades. I wasn't falling for the first guy to make me feel this way and think he was It. He couldn't be It. I had kids; what would they think if Mom dated someone so much younger?

"I'm fine." I planted a kiss on his palm. "Matter of fact, I'm better than fine. And I'm ravenous."

"For food?"

"For now."

"It's a deal."

One that Scott modified as the mood struck him. And the mood did, indeed, strike him.

We got through the bacon and eggs just fine. But once he started on the fruit… all bets were off. The grapes had to be fed to me as I lay on my back and he dangled them above me. The orange juice had to be sucked from my navel. The jelly for the toast got the body-shot treatment, and the bananas… Well, he decided to save the bananas for later.

But the pineapple rings… *I* got creative with those and Scott got his first pineapple-ring blow job, which had him deciding to check the market for pineapple futures. He was going to invest. Heavily.

At last, exhausted but exhilarated, we flopped back onto the sheets. The sticky sheets. "We have to burn these," I said as a dollop of jelly slid off my thigh onto the bed.

"I'm keeping them as a souvenir. Maybe I'll frame them and hang them on my wall. Avant garde artwork."

"And will you tell people where you got them?"

"Nah. Our little secret."

I stroked him. "Not so little."

"Gets the job done."

"So very well."

He covered my hand with his. "Not that I won't appreciate another round, but I actually hadn't planned on keeping you in bed the entire weekend."

News to me. "You didn't?"

"Nope. I mean, yeah, we do need to get some shut-eye. But I want to go out with you. Do things with you. At the very least, take a walk and get some air. Life gets complicated at home with your kids, but right now, you're all mine. I want to enjoy our time together."

"And being in bed isn't enjoyable?"

"Stop. You know what I mean. Or… are you worried who's going to see us?"

The thought hadn't even crossed my mind. But obviously it had his. And I couldn't blame him. I could, however, reassure him.

"Actually, I don't care who sees us. Theresa will have spread the word by now and I'm completely fine with that. Otherwise, I wouldn't have introduced you last night. I'm not doing anything wrong."

"That depends on who's defining *wrong*." He waggled his eyebrows, eliciting a giggle from me.

"And that. See that? I haven't giggled in I can't tell you how long. You make me giggle, Scott. In addition to making me moan and groan and scream and lose my breath."

"And come. Don't forget that. I make you come."

"No way am I going to forget that. For as long as I live. Which, if we *do* stay in this room, might not be for very long because many more orgasms like that and you just might kill me."

"So, we're agreed then? Quick shower and then we head out?"

"Sounds like a plan."

***

Of course, there was nothing *quick* about the shower because there was just something about hot steam, silky soap, and warm water cascading all over our bodies that led to some very imaginative shower sex. Scott was obviously warming up for the elevator sex he said we'd be having as he'd wrapped my legs around his waist and fucked me up against the tile wall.

I'd never had had shower sex before, so I was both terrified that he'd slip, and turned on beyond belief.

In the end, the orgasms had beat out the fear, and I was very sure Scott had created a monster. The problem with that was for the guy who followed Scott in my bed. I had a feeling no one else would ever be able to live up.

"That's a pretty serious expression on the face of a woman who's just had two orgasms in the past twenty minutes. What are you thinking?"

I tried to put a smile on my face, but the ramifications of how wonderful my time with Scott was were hitting me.

"Dana, honey. What is it?"

"You."

"Me? Well, shit. What's wrong with me?"

"Nothing. That's the problem. You're perfect, Scott. Too perfect. No mere mortal can ever compare. How am I supposed to move on with my life once I've had perfection?" My voice got a bit shrill at the end. Lack of sleep. That's what this was. I was exhausted and just blurting out the first silly thought that came into my head. "Forget it. Forget I said anything. I'm acting crazy."

He gripped my shoulders. "I don't think you're crazy. I think you're very right to be worried. Don't you think I am, too?"

"You?"

"Yeah, me. I'm with you, Dana. And I know you're still hung up on our ages. You have kids, a family, friends. A whole life that'll look at me—us—funny because of our ages. I get it. But I don't care. I am so lucky to have found you and I don't *want* to give us up."

It was nice to know I wasn't alone in this, but how the hell had we gotten to the next phase? I wanted to enjoy *this* phase. For however long it lasted.

"Look, I'm sorry. Just forget I said anything. Let's go enjoy ourselves and the time we have together now. The rest will take care of itself."

He stared at me a bit too long. Long enough to make me fidget, wondering what he was thinking. He'd revealed a lot more than I'd expected he would—that I expected he'd feel—and I wasn't sure what to do with that knowledge. I also wasn't sure what to do about the future, but if there was one thing my divorce had taught me was that I could plan my life all I wanted; it didn't mean it'd turn out that way. So, for now—today, tomorrow—I was just going to live the life I had in front of me and consequences be dammed.

Chapter Twenty

"Scott, put it down."

"I don't want to."

"I want you to."

"No way. Come on, Dana. Let me do this."

"I've let you do a lot of things; this is not one of them."

"Please?"

"No."

"With a banana on top?"

Damn it. When he said that with such an impish yet sexy look on his face, how the hell was I supposed to turn him down? And he knew it, too.

I exhaled. "Why?"

"Because I want to."

"That's not a good reason. Do you do everything you want to?" As soon as I said the words, I wished I could take them back.

Especially when he waggled his eyebrows. "Not yet I haven't."

Okay, so maybe I was glad I'd said them because that look in his eyes told me there was a lot left he wanted to do. And if it was anything like what he'd already done—and I had every reason to suspect it would be—I would enjoy every minute.

I shook my head, unable to keep the smile off my face. I was a fool for telling him no when I really wanted to say yes.

And since he really wasn't giving me the opportunity to say *no*, why fight it? "Okay. Fine."

"Thank you."

He planted a quick kiss on my cheek and dropped the sexy nightgown on the countertop of the lingerie shop he'd dragged me into. So much for a simple walk to get some air. I should have known he'd have an ulterior motive— *not* that I was complaining.

"I can't wait to see you in this."

I cocked my head. "Really? Because I have a feeling I'm not going to be in it very long." And I didn't even care that the woman behind the counter was enjoying this conversation. So was I.

Scott leaned over to whisper in my ear—which he also licked, sending delicious shivers all over my body. Not that it needed any help—and he didn't even know I was commando under this dress. That was my little sexy secret and had been putting a smile on my mouth since we'd left the hotel. I planned to tell him at just the right time.

"Nightgowns are easy access—don't even need to take it off. All this silk sliding against me… Nah, we're definitely keeping it on. Matter of fact…" He tapped my butt and walked past me, back to the rack where he'd gotten this one, pulled an assortment of colors from the rack, and flourished them onto the countertop. "We'll take these as well."

"Scott! You can't buy all of those." I grabbed his arm when he pulled out his wallet.

"Says who?"

"Well… me. We only have one more night left."

He cocked his head with those dimples that just made my melt. "*This* weekend we only have one night left. There are three hundred and sixty-four more nights left this year. We'll get to them."

I couldn't stop the shiver that raced over me at that statement. So, apparently, this weekend wasn't a one-time deal.

Had I really wanted it to be?

While Scott paid the cashier, I walked to the front

window and stared out at the people in the shopping center. They all looked so normal. Every day. But it wasn't *every* day that I had a hot young guy buying my lingerie with the sole purpose of fucking me in it.

Was this really my life?

"Hey. You okay?" He slid an arm around my waist.

I looked at him. *Really* looked at him. He was just a guy, asking me a question. Not some life-altering god to whisk me to Mount Olympus. So why couldn't I just accept this as my new reality and go with it?

"Dana?"

"I'm fine." I smiled at him. Wanted to reach out and plant a kiss on those amazing lips that tasted and felt—and could kiss all over my body—perfectly.

So do it.

Right. I did. Because I could.

"What was that for?" he asked when I pulled back. "Not that I'm complaining, mind you, but it came out of nowhere."

"I'm not allowed to kiss you outside of a hotel room?"

"Baby, you can kiss me whenever and wherever you want. I'm just glad you wanted to."

"Oh I want to, Scott. There's no doubt about that." Exactly. So I shouldn't be doubting anything. No more questions. Scott was the guy I was with and if anyone else had a problem with his age, well, they could just deal with it. Right now, I just wanted him. "Do you have more things planned for our excursion or can we go back and put one of those nightgowns to use? Maybe a few?"

Scott's arm dropped from around my waist as his mouth fell open. A smile curled my lips. I liked the way I affected him.

"Why, Ms. Jenkins. Are you asking me to skip all these wonderful plans I have for us and run back to our hotel room so you can jump my bones?"

The mock outrage made me laugh, but it didn't kill the mood. If anything, it enhanced it. I could be so free with Scott. In a way I'd never been with my ex.

And that was the last time I was going to think about my ex ever again.

"Yes, that's exactly what I'm saying, Mr. Masters. What're you gonna do about it?"

Scott dragged me out of the store, shot his hand into the air, and let out a shrill whistle. "Taxi!"

***

We barely made it back to the hotel.

I even took my shoes off in the cab so I could run to the elevator.

The minute the doors closed, Scott punched the floor button, undid his zipper, pulled a condom from his pocket and put it on in record time, then backed me up against the wall, hiked me onto the railing that ringed the walls, wrapped my legs around him, and thrust inside me.

"How did you know I was commando?"

He smiled that devastating smile. "Baby, I knew the minute I stood behind you in that dress. How do you think I got this hard?"

Jesus, he could turn me on. "I can't believe we're doing this—"

"Oh believe it, woman. I couldn't wait to get inside you." Scott thrust again. Forcefully—enough that my head banged against the mirrored wall.

"Oh, shit. Sorry." Scott started to pull away.

I grabbed the back of his hair and pulled his mouth to mine. "Don't worry about it," I managed to get out between some of the hottest, wettest, open-mouthed kisses we'd shared.

Scott thrust into me again.

"Hurry," I said before burying my nose into the crook of his neck where I could smell the male scent of him. "Fuck me."

"Oh, baby, I'm going to fuck you so hard and so long tonight, you're not going to be able to walk tomorrow."

"Good. Then I'll just have to stay in bed."

"That's my plan."

He changed the angle of his hips, and—shit!—I could feel my orgasm roar through me.

"Scott...." I breathed out as I came, a quick, hard, pounding wave of pleasure that was almost painful, so I clamped my legs and my pussy muscles, trying to keep from coming apart.

"Yeah, Dana, that's it, baby." Scott fucked me harder, rattling the railing beneath my backside.

"More... More..." I tried to catch my breath, but then Scott stole it on a long kiss, his tongue fucking my mouth like his dick was doing to my pussy.

I rode him like that as the elevator ascended, the chimes of the floors we passed marking the amount of time left before we reached our floor. I wanted to get him off before then. He'd gotten me off so magnificently that turnabout was only fair.

I clenched my inner muscles again and slipped my palm beneath the waistband of his pants, sliding my finger down the crack of his ass as I tongued his ear. I found his anus at the same time I took his lobe between my teeth and slid my finger in one, my tongue in the other, and I felt him shudder.

The elevator dinged again. Four more floors.

I swirled my finger and that was it. His orgasm happened so fast and hard he turned and sagged against the control panel when it was over, trapping my hand in his ass.

He'd probably done that on purpose.

I smiled, clenching his dick with all the strength I had left, trying to wring the last bit of cum out of him, cringing when the bell dinged again. Three floors to go and I still had to put myself to rights.

"Goddamn, woman. I think I need to install an elevator in my house." He shuddered again, then lifted me off his dick. "Only I'm going to need about seventy stories." He exhaled, then tucked his gleaming dick back into his pants.

The bell dinged again.

"Better get ready, sweetheart. If we run into one of the housekeeping staff, reality is going to come crashing back."

He wasn't kidding because no sooner had I smoothed my dress down and tried to get my hair somewhat back in place when the elevator stopped on the floor below ours and the doors opened.

There stood reality all right.

"Hello, Dana."

In the form of my ex-husband.

Chapter Twenty-One

"Jonathan." My fucking ass of an ex-husband. Just when I'd sworn I'd never think about him again. Of *course* he'd show up here, the prick. "What are you doing here?"

"Obviously not what you are." He looked Scott over from head to toe—and he had to look *up*. I liked that. Jonathan was vain, so for Scott to be taller—not to mention, younger, better looking, in better shape, among many other "er"s that Scott had over Jonathan—was my slap in *his* face.

Not that that had a single reason to do with why I'd said yes to Scott. But it was a nice bonus.

"Who's the boy toy?"

"What the—"

"Scott Masters." Scott slid his arm around my waist. "And I'll give you those two remarks because you're obviously upset at finding your ex-wife with someone else. But the snide comments stop now or I *will* take the matter further."

For once, Jonathan thought before opening his mouth because Scott meant it. And with his financial resources, not to mention his build and his age, he could make things very tough for the prick. Not that Jonathan would go down that path. He might have been stupid enough to leave me, but he didn't have a death wish.

"So you're with him, are you?" But he just couldn't keep the sneer off his face. "One of Rick's friends?"

Scott's arm slid from around my waist, but I grabbed it. "Don't, Scott. He's not worth it."

The rigidity in his arm surprised me. They were only words.

But as a writer, I knew the power of words. And as Jonathan's ex, I knew the best way to get to him.

"Besides, I don't want you to break any of your... fingers."

Jonathan exhaled and Scott grinned as he tugged me closer. "Yeah, that'd be a shame, wouldn't it?" His hand slid a little lower to rest on my hip. "So, you getting on, Jon? Dana and I are about to get off. Um, on the next floor."

Shit, I giggled. Couldn't help it. And at the look on Jonathan's face, I giggled again. I didn't know which he was more annoyed at; the thought of me getting off with Scott or Scott calling him *John*. That was a sore subject.

I was loving Jonathan's indecision. Usually he had all the answers—especially when he was walking out. Told me I was a washed-up, middle-aged woman who could only write my fantasies since I couldn't live them.

Wrong.

And I'd actually refrained from pointing out that *he* would have been the beneficiary of my so-called fantasies if he'd taken the time to actually learn what I liked, but I hadn't. I hadn't wanted to sling mud at him because he'd twist it to think I wanted him back. It hadn't been worth the energy to engage. I'd had other things to think about, namely getting my kids through our breakup.

I purposely hadn't talked poorly about him to the kids for just that reason. They had to come first. Funny thing, though, I hadn't needed to; the moment the word "girlfriend" came out—thought I think Matt had actually said *bimbo*—I hadn't needed to. They were smart enough to figure things out. By being the bigger person, I'd come out ahead.

And gotten Scott as my reward.

"In or out, John?" Scott's finger—that oh-so-talented finger—hovered over the Close button on the panel, that dimple-wink smile of his telling me he'd chosen that phrase on purpose.

"In." Jonathan barked the word and stepped into the elevator.

"You're bad," I whispered, when Scott stabbed the Close button.

"Not yet I'm not. And then you're going to have to watch out," he whispered back, but who were we kidding? Jonathan could hear every word.

Good.

I was especially enjoying the way his lips thinned. Lips that I'd once liked kissing when we'd gotten together sophomore year in college.

I looked at Scott. How could I have been so blind?

Then again, Scott would have been in kindergarten. Which only made me giggle again.

"Are you on drugs, Dana?" Jonathan sniffed his not-quite-so-superior nose at me. "That's taking this midlife crisis a bit too far, don't you think?"

"Look, *John*." Scott stepped in front of me before I could respond, obviously getting that the nickname irked my ex. "Back the fuck off. You were the jackass who walked out; you don't get to say what you want to her anymore." The elevator dinged as we reached our floor. "Here, babe. Let me help you out."

It wasn't an affectation on Scott's part. I was so angry, my knees had locked. If he hadn't nudged me, I might have been stuck there until I'd unloaded on Jonathan. Something I didn't want to do. He *still* wasn't worth my energy.

No, my energy was better spent with Scott.

It was that that got me moving.

But when I stepped onto our floor, it hit me—Jonathan had summoned the elevator to go *Up*. To this floor; there weren't any more above us. And there were only two penthouse suites.

Oh hell. He had the bimbo here, too.

Question was, was she the same bimbo he'd left me for?

"Tell Kiki I say hi." The woman's name was Nicki but the kids had come up with that nickname.

"Her name is Marcia."

Oops, Kiki/Nicki was gone already. Didn't really say much for her staying power. Or maybe… Jonathan's.

I looked between the two men I'd slept with in the last three years. Man, I'd been an idiot to keep Scott waiting.

"Coming, babe?" Scott tugged on my arm.

I looked at him and smiled, mouthing the words, "Not yet."

He grinned—and then we saw Jonathan's frown in the mirror on the wall facing the elevator. He'd seen exactly what I'd said.

Oh well, his loss. And my gain.

Jonathan, still in the elevator, looked at the floor number on the inside of the door. Touched it as if he couldn't believe it said *P* for *penthouse*. "I'd thought we were going down," he muttered almost to himself, but just loudly enough for Scott and me to break out in giggles because we both planned for at least *one* of us to be doing that in the next few minutes.

"Bye, John," Scott managed to toss back as we stumbled in laughter toward our door.

He had to swipe the key twice, the opening *click* coming just before the *ding* of the elevator as the doors closed on Jonathan's disgruntled look.

"You were married to *that*?"

"Don't go there." I shoved Scott into the room. I wanted as much distance from my ex as possible. "I was young and stupid."

"How young?"

"Twenty-one."

"Thirty-three is older than that. More mature. Has more life experience. Makes better decisions."

"Touché." I chuckled and reached for his waist.

He held me at arms' length. "No, no. I want to hear it. I want to hear you say, 'Scott, you were right. Thirty-three isn't too young.' Come on, Dana. Let me hear it."

I rolled my eyes. "Fine, Scott. You were right. Thirty-three isn't too young."

"And it ain't old either." He waggled his eyebrows then grabbed *my* waist and tugged me toward the bed. "Let me prove it."

"You're on!" I went for his shirt, but he stopped me.

"Hang on. Aren't you forgetting something?"

I cocked my head. "I'm not that old, mister, that my memory's going."

"Never said you were, babe." He held up the bag from the lingerie store, then yanked one out. "Here. Put this on."

It was teal. I looked good in teal. Though from the look in his eyes, he thought I'd look good in any color.

There was something to be said for a man's appreciation. Jonathan had been all about getting naked under the covers, climbing on, getting off, then climbing off. Even back in the early days, sex with him hadn't been what it was with Scott. And Scott was older than Jonathan had been—

And that was the absolute *last* time I was thinking of Jonathan.

"Uh, babe?" Scott had his t-shirt halfway up his chest. "You're not getting undressed."

"Oh. Right." I looked at the gown in my hands. Seemed kind of pointless to strip down and toss this over my head…

I chucked the gown onto the bed and walked over to Scott, flattening my palms against those tight abs.

"Hey." His head poked out of the neckline of the shirt. "That's not what—"

"Shut up."

Those gorgeous blue eyes widened. "What?"

"I said, Shut. Up." I pushed him backwards.

He raised his hands over his head. "Yes, ma'am."

"You're talking again." Another couple of steps and he'd be just where I wanted him to be.

He exhaled when the backs of his knees hit the chair behind him.

"Good boy." I gave those abs a little pat. Because I could. "Actually, it's *man.*"

I wagged a finger in his face. "Hey, you're talking. I said no talking."

He nipped the end of my finger.

Fire shot to my pussy.

Dammit.

I wasn't ready to go there yet. I was having too much fun bossing him around.

And if his half-cocked smile was any indication, so was he. "It's worth risking your wrath to clarify that distinction. Make no mistake, Dana, I'm a man."

"Trust *me*, Scott. I know it." I shoved and he fell back into the chair. "Now, no more talking."

He sat back and spread his arms, palms out. Man, what that did to his abs. And probably his chest, too, but his shirt was in the way.

I hiked the toe of my shoe onto the chair, next to his knee, and leaned in. "Arms up."

His grin grew wider as he did what I asked. "Got a gray tie on you?"

"No talking. Or I might have to put one in your mouth."

"Go ahead." He jerked his head toward the bedside table. "Second drawer down."

Now it was my turn to be speechless. He'd packed ties…?

"Don't move." I wagged my finger in his face again.

He, smart-ass, tried to nip it once more. "Not planning on it."

"You're talking again." I looked over my shoulder as I headed toward the table.

"And I will until you gag me."

"That's what she said." I couldn't resist. Gave him a little shake of my tush, too.

He laughed. "Damn, woman. You're good."

"Still talking."

I heard his sigh as I opened the drawer.

Oh my.

Scott had planned well.

Silk men's ties, silk scarf-like things, some chiffon ones, and—um… was that a crop?

Wasn't so sure about that. Never had the fantasy; wasn't into pain.

Still, as I'd learned from being with him, my preconceived ideas had been proven wrong on several occasions.

"Like what you see?" Smart-ass just couldn't keep quiet.

That was reason enough to pick up the crop. I spun around, slapping it against my palm. Ouch. Actually, that *did* hurt. "Do you *want* me to use this?"

"Do you really need to ask?"

Oh hell. I wasn't *quite* that adventurous.

Yet.

I ran the end of it down my throat, then down between my breasts. "I'm… not… sure… about… that…"

"Babe, don't bring that thing over here unless you mean to use it. Otherwise it's cruel and unusual punishment to tease me with it. Or without it. Whatever." He gulped as he was saying this, his eyes focused on the crop.

Wow. He was really enjoying this.

I slid it over one of my breasts. "I bet this would hurt."

"Exquisitely so."

There was something decadent about that word. Something so… I chuckled. *Exquisite.*

"Yes, well, if you're a good boy—I mean, *man*—we'll see about it, but for now…" I set it back in the drawer. Like I said, I wasn't that adventurous. Yet.

I pulled out one of the ties. Gray, of course. Had to go with the obvious, but it was still sexy.

I slid it through my hands ever so slowly as I sauntered toward him, putting as much sultry in that walk as I could.

Not half bad for a not-old broad.

I put my toe back up on the chair and stretched the tie tight between my hands in front of his face, then leaned in and whispered, "Open wide."

I loved that he had to gulp and lick his lips before he could.

I also loved that the tent in his pants jerked.

That made *me* lick my lips.

I slid the tie between his lips. And I swear Scott shuddered when I did so.

He bent his head, giving me access to the back to secure it, then he looked up, fire burning in his eyes.

Oh he was going to enjoy this.

I ran my finger down his nose. "Not another word. You hear me?"

He nodded, his gaze never breaking from mine.

Holy crap, this was fun. Sexy. Empowering. I'd never played like this before.

I would definitely be doing it in the future.

I grabbed the teal gown off the bed and twirled with it, using it as a harem scarf. "You want me to put this on, don't you? You want to see me in it. See the way it hangs off my nipples." I shimmied it across them, dancing to an inaudible tune that I somehow knew the rhythm of.

I raised the gown over my head, my hands holding it as they'd held the tie, the fabric draping over my head, then I slowly lowered it onto my shoulders, then slipped it down to slide between my breasts, until it pooled on the floor, a slash of teal from my hand across my jeans.

Showtime.

Chapter Twenty-Two

Scott smiled behind the tie, shifted in his chair, and pulled his phone out of his back pocket.

"You're making another phone call? *Now?*"

He held up one finger, then held out the phone.

As I took it, he tapped the button.

You Can Leave Your Hat On by Joe Cocker. Holy hell, that was *perfect*. Too bad I didn't have a hat, but I did have the stockings.

I smiled and set the phone on the dresser, then flicked the gown so it draped over my shoulder, propped my hand on my hip, getting ready for the beat to start.

I'd seen this movie a few times. Kim Basinger had totally rocked this song and I was determined to do it justice.

The beat started and a smile curved my lips as I flicked the gown in time with it, the silk flowing against my silk stockings. I understood his fascination with the stockings now.

I drew the gown up my body, so easily imagining his hands following it, my hips catching the beat. God, the rhythm was hot.

And so was I.

I wanted out of my dress.

I slid the gown across my mouth, imagining Scott's mouth on it as he nuzzled it up my body. How long was this song because I didn't think I was going to be able to finish it.

I flung the gown onto the bed. Right now, I wanted to be naked. If I got the gown on, I'd consider it a plus.

I swayed to the sultry beat, sliding my hands up my body to my face, tracing my lips then licking one before I slid them into my hair, my hips seeming to have a mind of their own.

I honestly don't think I'd ever felt this sexy.

Slowly turning, I gave Scott a view of my backside shifting beneath the dress, and looked over my shoulder. Oh yeah, he was watching.

I bent over, slowly. Verrrry slowly, the music infusing every muscle. It was like having sex by myself. Standing up. Really really good sex

I undulated up then down again a few times, clenching my ass, feeling the tension in my pussy as I did so, spiking my heels a couple of times with the horn blast.

I shimmied, my ass getting a good sway going with the dress, then came back upright, doing a slow hip-turn back to the front, my hands going from my hips to my hair and back again, singly, together, whatever the music moved me to do.

I couldn't stop moving. Couldn't stop my hands from messing up my hair and bunching up my dress over my ass, teasing him… until I slid them behind my neck and down to the zipper.

Started it, then did another slow hip-turn so he could watch me slide it down.

Dragged my hands down my body again in the front, touching myself. He couldn't see it, but he knew; I could feel his stare through the dress.

My nipples were tight, wanting pressure, my breasts heavy, and my thighs… Let's just say there was a lot of heat there.

My hands slid down my sides, curving over my hips and down to my cheeks, caressing them in time with the beat, then back up over them, swishing my dress as I did so. I curved my arms then, one hand gripping the bottom of the zipper, the other reaching for the tab.

My hips kept the rhythm, shifting beneath the dress, the fabric sliding against my skin so incredibly erotically as I lowered the zipper slowwwwwwly.

I looked at Scott over my shoulder through my messy hair, a couple strands stuck to my lips, and I wasn't about to move them. Gave me that just-fucked feel and I was enjoying the anticipation.

Scott was leaning forward in his chair, his eyes glued to my ass, his foot tapping in time to the music.

The zipper reached the bottom, the dress gaping enough that I felt the air on my heated skin. I curved my palms over my ass again, squeezing.

His eyes widened and he shifted in his chair. Then he put his hand on his crotch and rubbed himself through the jeans.

I spun quickly in one beat, slamming my toe into the rug to stop in time with a break in the music, the dress swishing around my thighs.

I turned my knee out. Flexed my heel down, then back up with the music, my shoulders shimmying with the rhythm, and I kept doing it, leaning forward so the dress slipped down my right shoulder.

Then I tossed my head back, flipping my hair over my shoulders, another jumbled mess, and switched sides.

My breasts slid against the fabric, tightening my nipples—not that they needed the help because the sexiness of this dance had me strung tighter than the piano strings in the background.

Marking the downbeat with my left heel, I shimmied again, this time the dress sliding down my left arm.

Then I shimmied upright, tilting my head back and leaning back, hips thrust forward. He was looking at my thighs, I could feel it.

Wanted to be there.

And I wanted him there.

I slowly turned again, my hips tapping each beat. This song was just sex personified. How could anyone not feel sexy with this beat? I'd surely never think of it without connecting it to this moment ever again.

With my back to him, I slid the dress down my arms, raising each arm above my head as it slipped free. I undulated like a harem girl, letting the dress fall to my hips, feeling my hair sway against my back and over my shoulders, down to my nipples. It felt better even than the dress on them, stroking so softly, so tantalizingly, making me want more.

Threading my fingers through my hair, I punctuated the tempo with my right hip, swaying my knee out, and I turned my head that way, looking at Scott. I was pretty sure I could hear his heavy breathing over the music.

Good. Because I was panting.

I winked then flipped my head back and shook my hair down to the small of my back. It felt so good caressing the curve of my waist.

Gliding my palms down my sides, I slid them under the dress, working it over each hip on a downbeat, then letting it drop to the floor.

I was naked but for my stockings and heels.

I glanced back.

Scott had fallen back in his chair, legs splayed, and was rubbing himself through his jeans faster, the curl that'd fallen on his forehead damp.

Marking the downbeat with one hip, I turned enough to give him a profile shot, then undulated my pelvis, clenching my ass as I did, feeling almost as if we were horizontal on the bed together.

I drew my hand along the top of my thigh.

Then up over my hip.

Up my torso, making sure to run it over my nipple—swirled it around it actually, just because—then up my breast to my neck. I tilted my head back, running my palm up my throat and curling my fingers over my chin, sucking on one, then sliding my hand into my hair. Tits thrust out, my heel banging the floor, my hips thrusting… I wish he'd jump out of that chair and tackle me onto the bed and take me.

My breath shuddered, moisture pooling between my thighs. Scott wanted to do that, too, I knew that, but I also knew he wouldn't. Both of us wanted to play this out.

And then, by God, and then we'd…

My stomach fluttered in anticipation and I missed a beat, but I got back on track pretty quickly. Couldn't not do that; the music was in my blood. My heated blood.

I planted my right foot on the floor and raised my left onto the toe, switching sides to give him this view. Propping my right hand on my ass, I drew the left along my thigh and repeated the slide up to my breast, this time cupping it.

Turned slightly.

Swirled my nipple between my fingers.

Tossed my head back, my mouth open.

Licked my lips.

Left my tongue in the corner of my mouth as I tossed my hair over my shoulders again.

Scott raised his free hand and beckoned me with one finger.

I stepped out of the dress in time with the music and took my sweet time doing a sexy catwalk over to the chair—close enough that if I bent forward I'd be able to reach him, but right now, he couldn't touch.

That's how I wanted it.

For now.

My hips were marking the downbeats, my breasts jiggling with the motion.

I bent forward, ran my hands from my knees up to my belly. Fluttered them towards my pussy but changed direction and moved up to my breasts. I slid my fingers over them, catching the nipples for a few seconds between them, but kept grazing my skin up to my neck, my pelvis keeping the beat.

Scott was panting.

I sucked my little finger into my mouth on my left hand, my right threading through my hair, messing it up even more.

He reached for my hip.

I let him get a quick touch in, but then I spun and sauntered back to where I'd been, making sure to keep my hips rolling. I felt unbelievably sexy. Better than Kim had been. Every cell I possessed was owning this music.

A few more pelvic thrusts—because my pelvis wanted to thrust—and I did a sexy side-ways undulation as I grabbed the nightgown he'd bought me, sliding it around my waist and up between my breasts, the cool silk feeling so good against my damp skin.

I worked my arms into the gown and raised them straight, turning slowly as the straps slid down my arms, the dress enveloping me a silk slide of pure sensation.

My blood roared through my veins, the music pounded in my heartbeat, my hips were hitting every hard sultry beat as I lowered the gown onto my body.

It bunched at my waist and before I pulled it into place, I decided to be a little daring.

Well, a lot given that I'd never done a striptease before.

I bent over slowwwwwly. Dragged my fingertips down my thighs to my knees, then around to my calves, tracing the seam of my stockings.

Grabbed my ankles and looked at him like that for about two seconds, before I undulated my way back upright, and when I turned around—

Scott was there.

The tie was off his mouth and hanging around his neck, and his t-shirt was gone.

I waited for him to touch me, my body still moving with the rhythm, but he stood still. Stone cold still.

"Scott? What's wrong?"

He opened his mouth to say something, then closed it.

He tried again, this time sucking in a big breath and exhaling first. "I want you, woman. I want you so badly, I'm shaking with it."

I put my palm against his chest. He was.

Good.

I couldn't stop the Cheshire cat smile as I leaned in, only my palm touching him as my hips still kept the beat, and whispered, "You can have me."

His hand clamped onto my waist and he dragged me up

against him, his hips finding the rhythm to the song, and ohmygod, it was the hottest dance I'd ever done.

I turned my face to his neck, nibbling my way up to his jaw. His hands didn't move. His head didn't move. His lips… his sexy-as-hell lips didn't move other than to set in a tight line.

"Scott?" I wasn't getting his reaction. Below the belt, he was all swivel and jutting hardness, above… He was a still as stone. "What's going on?"

"I'm going to fuck you, Dana."

"Well I certainly hope so."

"I'm going to give it to you in a way you've never done."

"So you keep saying."

"Now."

I skipped a beat. A couple of them. There was something about his "now" that let me know I had no idea what he'd come up with but I was going to love it.

The music faded away, but it was still in the air. All around us. That sultry sexy beat that was the perfect rhythm for making love and I was now shaking with the need to have him take me in his arms.

The anticipation was going to kill me because Scott *still* didn't move.

"Scott?"

He exhaled and cleared his throat. "Give me a sec."

"I'd rather give you *sex*." I leaned in, whispering that into his ear. I liked that I could get to him. That I could do to him what he did to me.

His had clamped onto the back of my neck and he brought my face to his, our lips within in inches of each other's. "I'm going to give it to you, sweetheart, like you've never even imagined."

"Oh I don't know. You know what I do for a living. I have a pretty good imagination."

"Yeah, but now we're going to give you some reality."

I shivered. The determination in his voice, the way he wasn't letting me go—the intensity in his eyes that told me I was the only woman for him. Whether it was just for this moment, this weekend, or not, I didn't want to explore. Right now, this was everything I could have ever wanted.

Well, except for the fact that I was still not wrapped around him.

His tug in the small of my back put an end to that.

"Jesus, woman, you are so fucking hot," he whispered right before he ran his lips all over the curve of my neck.

My head dropped back as every touch of his lips sent fire burning along my nerves and my already aching pussy ached some more. This guy was sex personified and I was inhaling his scent as if it were the elixir of life.

I wrapped my leg around him and rubbed my pelvis on his hip.

His hand cupped my ass as he nipped—and I do mean nipped, there was some teeth involved—his way over my collarbone and down my chest.

My nipples swelled—ached—in anticipation and I arched back, wanting him to suck me in. Wanting his talented wet tongue on them.

And then it was and I saw stars.

My other leg gave out and if Scott hadn't been holding me, I would have slid to the floor in a puddle of pheromones. "Scottttttttttt…"

"God, I love hearing you say my name."

"Get on the bed with me and I'll say it as many times as you want."

"We're not using the bed."

Chapter Twenty-Three

"We're… *not*?"

He cocked his head with that sexy smile, his dimples wanting in on the action and he kissed my fingers.

Then dropped them. "No. We're not."

He unwrapped my leg from his hip and left me there, none too steady on my feet.

I reached for the bed. My legs weren't capable of keeping me upright as I tried to process what was happening.

Especially when he walked over to the desk, picked up the chair, then carried it toward the dressing area.

"We're going to have sex in the chair?" He thought a chair was better than a bed? I'd never had sex in a chair, but I couldn't see why I'd want to with a perfectly good, very large, comfortable bed to roll around on right in front of us.

"Technically, *I'm* going to be in the chair. You…" He set the chair down in front of the full length mirror, rested his hand on the back of it, cocked his hip, and beckoned me with that finger again. "Are going to be in my lap."

His lap. Oh I could do this. Just straddle him and fuck him until we couldn't see. It was a great idea, but still, I'm not sure how he'd thought that'd make me want to give up sex in a bed, but he hadn't proved to be wrong yet.

I willed some strength into my legs and stood. Flattened the nightgown against my thighs——which got his eyes going there. Good. Just because he was all about this big new sex position didn't mean he got to call *all* the shots.

I walked up to him and ran my fingertips down his chest.

Then I walked around him, dragging my nails across his abdomen. "So why aren't you sitting already?" I whispered in my most husky voice.

Not that I had to work on it—the sexual tension in the air did it for me. I was so turned on, I could probably think myself into orgasm, but where would be the fun in that? I'd been alone for far too many orgasms to want to do that now with a living, breathing, unbelievably hot guy in front of me who was more than *up* for the task.

"Aren't you going to sit, Scott?" I cocked my hip and rested a hand there. The other one… well, the other one still had the music thrumming through it and was sliding from my shoulder down to my breast—just lightly over my nipple— along my torso to my hip. I brushed the backs of my fingertips over it, then slipped it to my thigh, bunching the fabric so I could get it out of the way when I straddled him.

Which damn well better be soon. "Scott?"

"Uh. Right." He shook his head and scooted around to the front of the chair.

He dropped trou.

Jesus, the guy had an amazing ass. Tight and firm, he had a runner's butt. Or maybe it was a soccer player's. I didn't care; all I knew was that for the rest of today, his ass was *mine*.

My hands itched to feel it. "Sit."

He sat.

I managed to make my legs work to get me in front of him while he put a condom on.

Both hands on my thighs, I gathered the rest of the gown and lifted it as I started to straddle him—

Until he stopped me. "Not like that."

"What?" I let the gown slide back down.

It was Scott's turn to raise it, his hands gliding up my thighs to my ass.

Okay, this could work.

Then he turned me around.

There we were, in the mirror. Scott's naked legs nudging my stocking-ed ones apart, his hands visible as they slid beneath the gown to grip my hips.

Then he tugged me back until the backs of my knees hit the chair.

"Open your legs, Dana." His voice was soft, but very firm.

As I knew something else would be, so I opened my legs.

His fingers tightened on my hip bones. "Sit down."

I sat.

Yes, there was definitely something else very firm on him. And it was gliding against the seam of my ass.

I tried not to moan.

And failed.

My head dropped back, my eyes closed, and I wiggled against him.

He gripped my hips tighter and whispered in my ear, his hot breath making me shiver again. "Watch."

I opened my eyes and he opened his legs.

Which stretched the hem of the nightgown across my hips, baring my—

Oh.

"And now—"his fingers left my hip and slid oh-so-tantalizingly downward—"you can watch yourself come as I touch you."

And then he did.

Holy hell—! I gripped my thighs, watching in the mirror as his finger stroked me. Just one, the pressure just right, the sight… It was so incredibly erotic, almost like it was happening to someone else but I could feel it.

And, man, did I feel it.

"Like that?"

I could only nod.

He slid another finger along the next time he stroked down, and the pressure was so intense, I throbbed against them, feeling my juices flowing out of me. Could smell myself as he stroked again.

He opened his legs wider.

There I was, perched atop his thighs, gown bunched between the arm he had wrapped around me and his six-pack as I watched his fingers give me incredible pleasure, my clit throbbing and my toes actually curling.

"Bring your arms over your head and run your fingers through my hair," he whispered, his other hand slipping beneath the neckline of the gown to cup my breast, his thumb stroking my nipple in time with the way his fingers were stroking my clit.

"God, you're so pretty, Dana." His voice was harsh as his eyes met mine in the mirror.

I didn't have enough breath left in me to respond; it was all I could do to lift my arms. It was so utterly erotic to be sitting here, spread open, his hands on me, unable to do anything but let him do whatever he wanted—whatever *I* wanted. Because this was for me as much as for him. By now, Scott knew my body. Knew how to get me to respond, and he was playing me as well as any musician played his instrument.

He pinched my nipple then palmed it, and I shuddered against him.

"You like that."

It wasn't a question, but still, I nodded, still unable to make a sound.

Then he ran his nail along my clit gently and a moan managed to escape.

"Ah, there's that throaty sound I love. The one that means you're going to come."

"Not… yet…" I had to get *those* words out. One more stroke and I *would* come and I didn't want to. Not yet. I wanted to see how far we could go with this. How far Scott could take me.

"True. I want you to enjoy this." He slid his finger down and teased my opening.

Then he pulled away.

No no no. That wasn't what I'd had in mind. "Scott… please…"

"Please, what?" He teased me again, so close to what I wanted him to do yet way too far away.

"Please." I swallowed, trying to get some moisture in my mouth so I could ask for what I wanted. "Fuck me with your fingers."

"Yes, ma'am." He pushed one finger in.

Jesus, it felt amazing. He felt amazing. *I* felt amazing.

I arched back and bore down on his fingers. He was right; this was something I'd never done, couldn't have conceived. And it *would* probably spoil me for anything else ever again— well, aside from actually having him inside me. That, I'd never want to give up.

Though with his dick hard against my back, I was beginning to imagine that that could be possible in this position.

The idea got me even wetter. The idea of him taking me like this, of him being inside me while I was spread-eagled on his lap, his fingers rubbing my clit—

Shit. I could feel my orgasm begin. I didn't want to come. Not yet.

"That's it, baby. Thrust those tits out for me."

I was nothing if not amenable to his every desire.

I smiled as I arched even more, loving the feel of his free hand caressing them. The way he palmed my nipple, circling… It wound a spiral all the way to my pussy.

But it wasn't enough.

I was really thinking about him fucking me this way. The image wouldn't get out of my head.

Scott grazed my neck with his teeth, all the time murmuring hot sexy things that I tried hard to concentrate on, but, really, wasn't having much luck with. The way he was touching me— the way I was sitting—the mirror in front of us—

Oh right. The mirror.

I opened my eyes again, not wanting to miss one moment.

The sight was incredibly erotic. One breast bared, my pussy in full view, his dick rubbing along my ass…

"I… want… you… in… me…, Scott."

He slid his fingers out, skimming them along my clit, sending shivers racing through me, then he gripped my hips and closed his legs.

"Fine." He set my feet on the floor, and, with one hand on the small of my back, he tilted me forward. "Bend over."

I couldn't oblige fast enough.

"Watch in the mirror."

I lifted her head. Through my tits, I saw his hand on his dick between my legs—such an amazing view.

"Come back a little."

Didn't have to ask me twice.

I moved back then bent my knees, putting my pussy—my hot, aching, *wet* pussy—right on the head of his dick. I shifted, swirling my hips just enough to coat it with my juices.

Then I lowered myself some more, watching him guide his dick inside me.

He was so fucking thick, he filled every part of me.

"Sit back down, Dana." This time his voice was as tight as mine had been and almost as inaudible.

I sat, taking him to the hilt. Holy Jesus, this was incredible.

Then he opened his knees again.

Incredible just got ratcheted up to breathtaking. Amazing. Unbelievable.

My knees opened with his and now I was once more spread open on top of him, filled so fully with his throbbing cock that I couldn't believe it was possible to feel what I was feeling and survive it.

And then his fingers slid over my thigh, right to my clit and I realized I could survive anything if he'd only keep touching me like this.

"I'm going to make you see stars, Dana."

"I… mmmm…. already have." Oh, shit, this was good. Incredible. Amazing. There weren't any words appropriate enough for how amazing this felt, so I gave up trying to find them and just rode him.

I clenched my butt, raising myself a little that way, pressing down on his thighs with mine.

"Yeah, baby, that's it. Work me." He grazed my shoulder, then licked it, his other hand stealing around again to cup my breast. Then he took my nipple between his thumb and forefinger and rolled it and the sensation went straight to my core.

"Jesus, Scott." I panted. "I can't… take… much… more."

"Yes, you can, baby. Just enjoy it."

"I… am."

He rubbed me fast, then slow. His dick pulsed inside me, his hips shifting slightly as he rocked in the chair. Damn, he could—and did—hit my G-spot like that.

I rocked with him, clenching my muscles around him, watching us in the mirror. "Fuck me, Scott. I need you to fuck me."

I didn't care if it sounded like I was begging. I was. I needed this.

I needed him.

And I'd think about that later.

Right now, he just needed to fuck me. To end this tension. To give me the pleasure I knew he could.

His dick jerked inside me and he tore his hands from where he was touching to grab hold of my hips and pump me onto him.

"Oh my God, yes!" I swirled my hips a bit and felt him tense behind me.

So I did it again. I wasn't the only one enjoying this.

"Fuck, yes, Dana." Scott shoved me down, arched his back so his abs were pressing against me, and thrust his dick higher into me.

And then he was fucking me, impaling me, and I had to reach back to grab hold of his arms to keep up with him.

"Yeah, baby, that's it. Dig your nails into me."

He asked…

I dug them in some more, enjoying his moan that meant

he was enjoying what I was doing. Not that there wasn't much Scott wouldn't like, I was coming to realize.

Actually… I was just coming.

I met his eyes met in the mirror. "Scott… I'm going…"

"Yeah, baby. Come for me." He ground me against him again, and slid his fingers back to my clit.

One touch. Just one.

He was right; I saw stars.

And rockets. And meteors. Nothing so banal as fireworks; Scott was beyond the mundane.

"Look at you, Dana." Scott kept stroking me while I shuddered and writhed against him, his fingers biting into my hips only prolonging the pleasure.

I couldn't take my eyes off the mirror. I'd never seen myself like this—so uninhibited so… so… primal.

I moved on him—bounced even—trying to keep up the intense pressure and get him to lose his control. "Come… Scott…"

"Right behind you, baby." He smiled as he nipped my shoulder blade *right* behind me, the smart ass. Then he did one more swirl of his hips and—

He came. Every muscle went rigid— *every* muscle—and his teeth closed onto the cord in my neck. Not enough to hurt, but he was definitely going to leave a mark. And I liked that he would.

His gaze never left mine. It was as if he was willing me to feel what he was feeling, and with the way he was looking at me—all burning fire drilling into me in the mirror—I could.

This wasn't just sex between us. Not this connection.

And I couldn't not deal with it.

But not now. Later.

After.

Chapter Twenty-Four

After came way too soon.

It didn't take Scott as long as I would've hoped to come back to himself and loosen his grip on my hips. And my shoulder.

He kissed the spot and I shuddered.

But not from pain. And not from his touch.

I had to deal with this. *We* had to deal with this.

I had no idea how.

"I'm sorry." He kissed the spot again. "I didn't mean to do that."

"What? Make me scream in pleasure?" I smiled. Humor was good to break the tension.

"Oh no. *That* I meant to do." He ran his fingers over the spot on my shoulder. "No. This. I didn't mean to put a mark there. It's probably going to bruise."

"Probably." I smiled. "It's okay. I like that you did. That you weren't able to control yourself."

"Hell, sweetheart, I can't be held accountable for my actions around you because the minute I'm with you, all I want to do is touch you, taste you, feel you, be with you. I don't know what it is about you, Dana, but I can't get enough."

He was saying all the right things as he mouthed kisses up the curve of my neck to my ear, but I was trying to figure this out. Figure out where we went next.

"I don't *want* to get enough of you." He sucked my earlobe into his mouth and, man, I wanted him all over again.

"You do something amazing to me, too." I clenched and unclenched my muscles again. The guy could get me going. And if I *did* get going, I wouldn't have to deal with my big, heavy issue.

Reason enough to lean against him when he wrapped his arms around my waist and tugged me back, his gaze still on me.

"Look at you. You're gorgeous."

I had to smile. "I don't know about gorgeous, but I'll go with sated."

"Not for long, I hope." He nipped my ear.

"Keep doing that and I won't be." And that wasn't a bad thing.

"Is that a challenge?"

I should say yes. Let him take me away to where I only *felt*. Where I didn't think. Thinking would get me into trouble. Thinking could end this… whatever-we-were-doing. Because the reality was, while this was great, and I'd loved every minute of it, it wasn't practical. A weekend of sex with a hot young guy wasn't something I could sustain. I had kids, obligations, a career. I couldn't just chuck it all for a weekend fling. My kids were hardly ever away all at the same time for more than a day anyway, so chances of a repeat with Scott were few and far between.

Which was why I should focus on finding someone I could spend time with. Spend my life with. Someone I could come home to. Bring to my house to hang around. Someone who could blend in with my family.

I could just see me walking in with Scott and telling the kids he was going to move in. Or that I was going on vacation with him. They'd think I'd lost my mind. Was I going to bring *them* on vacation with us? Scott would have to keep his hands and his lips and his looks to himself if so. As would I. And, frankly, I didn't think that was possible. Having sampled what Scott had to offer—hell, having had a smorgasbord of it—I wouldn't be able to slow it down. Tame it. Keep myself respectable in front of my kids. What kind of example would I be setting for them?

"Hey. Where'd you go?" He propped his chin on my shoulder and his hands splayed across my abdomen.

Oh, crud. I'd zoned out. Not good. Not good at all.

I re-focused on him. On us. In the mirror.

"Ah, there you are."

He smiled at me and I wanted to turn around and crawl into his embrace. Why couldn't he be older? Have a family? Be more relatable to mine? Because what I was feeling for him was definitely starting to go beyond sex—or at least, I was wanting it to. But that was the problem. I'd adjusted to being able to handle the boy-toy thing, but as for feeling more for Scott… That just wouldn't work in my life.

"Penny for them." He nipped my shoulder again, playful.

I had to summon playful up from somewhere inside me. I'd gotten too serious. In many ways.

I worked another smile to my face. "I was just thinking I should probably be embarrassed by this. But—"

"Why?" He dropped his arms to my thighs, and I could hear the exasperation in his voice. So much for being playful. "And if you make one comment about your age, I'm never going to fuck you again."

I clamped my lips shut. Anything I'd say now would be wrong.

"That's better. But why, Dana? I thought you liked what we were doing."

Duh… "I did, but—"

"Then there's nothing to be embarrassed about. We're two people who are enjoying each other."

One more than the other? No, that wasn't true. I wasn't doubting Scott felt something for me; I was doubting that this could ever work, regardless of what we felt for each other.

"Hello?" He tapped my hip. "You're zoning out on me again. What gives?" He shifted then, sliding out of me and I clenched to keep him in, but that wasn't happening.

No, apparently real life was.

"Dana, talk to me."

Talking was the last thing I wanted to do.

But, hell, I was an adult—as I'd proved over the last thirty-six hours; I had to tackle the big issues.

I inhaled and climbed off his lap, smoothing the hem of the nightgown back into place and tucking my breast back into the bodice. Damn shame, that.

"Where are you going?" He leaned forward.

I brushed the mussed hair out of my face as I walked toward the bedroom. "I need some clarity."

He stood up and stepped into his pants, pulling them on as he walked after me. "Clarity? You need clarity? What, exactly, do you need clarity about?"

He grabbed my arm and tugged so I'd turn around.

I didn't want to, but I did. Because I should.

He stood there, hands on hips and his breathing doing mighty fine things to his bare chest.

A chest I wanted to lean against and forget the real world existed beyond our room.

"Dana?"

"It's…" I gnawed on my bottom lip.

"Hey, let me do that." He leaned in and ran his tongue over my lips, then sucked the bottom one into his mouth and nibbled on it.

Heat streaked through me.

"You're thinking too much." He tapped the end of my nose when he let go of my lip. "Stop. I forbid you to worry about what's out there." He swept his hand toward the window. "That's what you're doing, isn't it?"

I puffed out a breath, blowing some of the hair off my face. Damp hair. That was damp because of what we'd been doing together. "I can't help it."

He cupped the back of my neck and put our foreheads together. "I know. I'm trying not to think about it, too."

"You are?" Which meant that he realized the futility of trying to keep this going beyond this room.

Our eyes met. "Yeah, I am. Because I know you are. The

thing is, sweetheart…" He reached for my hands and brought them to his chest.

I wanted to flatten my palms against it, but didn't. For the first time since Friday night, I reined in my impulse because I was going to have to start doing that anyway.

"The thing is, Dana…" He shifted, tugging me closer, and he took both of my hands in his and wrapped his other arm around my waist.

I wasn't going anywhere.

"You're making problems where none exist. I thought we'd gotten past our age difference."

"We have—I have, Scott. But the reality is, others won't."

"And by others, you mean your kids."

"I can't show up with a guy closer to my son's age than mine." Oh, God, I hadn't done the math until right now, but it was true.

"I can see that, but it's not like we're going to walk in and say, 'Hey, we've spent the weekend at a hotel doing the nasty.' I mean, come on. We can start out slow. Let the kids get used to the idea of you going out with someone on a consistent basis. Then, when they're used to that, we'll take another small step."

"Another one?"

"Yeah. You know, like maybe I meet them when I pick you up for a date."

"Meet them? You want to meet them?" Why would he want to meet them?

"Well, yeah. That's part of having a relationship, getting to know the people you care about."

"Relationship?" Okay, he was talking a lot of stuff I hadn't expected. Dating was one thing, but relationship?

"Yes, Dana. Relationship. What'd you think? That I just want you for your body?"

"Don't you?"

"Babe." He put his hands on my hips. "As delectable as your body is, there is more to you than tits and ass."

Well, yeah, there was another very important part…

"I *like* you, Dana. You, not just the boobs and other parts. I like what's in here." He tapped my head. "And here." He tapped my heart.

"You haven't known me long enough to know what's in there."

"I have, actually. You're not that hard to read. Every move you make is who you are. Everything you say, what you've said about your life and your kids—and what you *haven't* said. I get that you're not someone who jumps into bed with the first guy she meets. I get that our age difference is a hurdle for you. I get that the idea of continuing this in the 'real world' is tough, but I'm not going to let you slip through my fingers because of a number, or other people's perceptions. You introduced me to Theresa. To your ex. You didn't have to, so somewhere inside of you, you're wondering. You're wondering if something between us could work outside of these four walls. I'm saying I want to try. And I think you do, too."

I did. But I was scared.

And not scared of other people's opinions. Not really scared of what the kids would think either.

I was scared of getting hurt.

Of him leaving once I'd grown attached.

Yeah, there it was. The truth. My ex had walked out—a midlife crisis that I'd had to pick up the pieces from. Scott hadn't had his midlife crisis yet. He had a good fifteen years to go before that happened. Did I want to hang around waiting for it? Again? Once in a lifetime was more than enough and getting involved with a younger guy was just opening myself up to the possibility again.

"Hey, let's sit down." He tugged me over to the bed.

I let him.

"There's something I should tell you."

The tone of his voice…

Oh God, something was wrong. I immediately flashed

back to him saying at the very beginning that I had no idea what he'd gone through in his life and that life was short—

Something was very wrong.

I started to shake. Got cold. Took in a deep, shuddering breath, trying not to panic.

How long did he have? He'd been talking about a relationship, so it couldn't be imminent, or maybe—

"Can I speak before you go imagining all sorts of bad things?" He stuck that dimpled smile on the end of that question and it allowed me take a breath.

"Sorry. Yes. Go ahead."

"Okay." He took my hands in his and rested them on his thigh. "First of all, this isn't bad. It's good. But hopefully you'll understand where I'm coming from and it'll alleviate some of your issues."

"You're really fifty but you have a very good doctor?" I asked hopefully... Not really. But I needed to break the tension because a writer's imagination is not a place anyone wants to get lost in. Especially not me, because I knew what my mind was capable of. And right now, it was all over the place.

"So... this. Us." He punctuated those last two words with a little pound of our clasped hands on his thigh. "Why I was— and am—so persistent with you."

"Persistence isn't a bad thing."

"I know. It's what's gotten me to where I am in my life."

I didn't like how he said that.

"See, Dana, fifteen years ago, I was in a car accident with my dad in a bad snowstorm. He didn't make it, and I..." He sniffed and cleared his throat. "I was in a coma for long time. No one thought I'd pull out of it."

My heart thudded. I could see it. Him. There. In a hospital bed. God, what his mother must have gone through. The rest of his family... "But you did. You're here."

"I am. But it wasn't easy. I woke up and had to relearn everything. From how to tie my shoes, to how to hold a fork, to what day it was. Lots and lots of rehab."

I refrained from running my hands all over him. I'd done that already and hadn't suspected a thing. "You don't show any signs of, well, anything."

"That's because I worked my ass off not to. I wasn't going to be *that guy* for the rest of my life. My mother had to deal with my eight brothers and sisters, my father's death, the house, the bills… And then an invalid son on top of it? I've never worked so hard in my life before or since. I *had* to get better. I had to be a hundred percent. My mother needed me. So did my siblings. Not to mention the cost. Dad's life insurance went to pay my medical bills. I had to give that back to her. To all of them. I had to make sure we didn't have one more loss.

"I wasn't going to allow some random weather event to change the course of my life. So I learned to push forward. To find ways around obstacles the professionals said were in my path. I wouldn't take *No* for an answer even from myself. Which means that I'm not taking it from a woman I want to get to know just because of some obstacles society says are in our path. Your kids will come around if you're happy. And I want to make you happy. I want to be that guy who puts that secret smile on your face that you get when you're excited but think you shouldn't be. I want to be the guy who's there—and allowed—to kiss you awake. The one who can put his arm around your waist in public and draw you in for a perfectly acceptable kiss when we're out and about and then a decadently wicked one when we're alone. I want to be a part of your life, Dana. I want to know what you had for breakfast and if the dog ran through the mud, and whose homework is due. I want to be the one you share these things with because you like to share all of your life with me, not just the sex. Though, don't get me wrong, the sex is good. Beyond good. Better than I've ever had before."

I was still trying to get over the image of him lying in a hospital bed as his mother waited for him to wake up. Of him standing between parallel bars, trying to get his legs to move.

Of him learning to poke a button through a buttonhole. Of teaching himself to eat… The man who'd made love to me this weekend had no residual effects from that accident. Except maybe… psychological ones.

"*That's* why you said life is too short. That if you saw something you wanted, you were going to go after it."

"Yeah. My father died too young. Too many people still needed him. And I was faced with the possibility of living a life less than what I'd wanted. I could have died in that accident just as easily. The car was totaled. The tree we hit… shattered. One slick road and an oil spot and my life could have been over. Dad's was. I don't want to leave this world with any regrets, whether it's things I don't say to people or things I don't do. I saw you and I wanted to get to know you. And now that I do, I'm not willing to walk away. If you didn't like me, if you weren't attracted to me, fine, I would. But you do like me, you are attracted to me, and it's only your worry about what other people will think that's holding us back. What if I'd listened to what those other people had thought? I'd be in a wheelchair with an aid feeding me. I would have given up and accepted the status quo years ago. But I didn't. I focused. I fought. And I saw the life I wanted and went after it. I've seen what my life could have been and knew I didn't want that. So I made it what I wanted. Do you have that drive, Dana? Do you see something you want and go after it?"

I wanted him. And not just physically. Because he was right; this was my life. My only life. One shot. Scott had gotten lucky and had a second chance; not everyone did.

Though… actually, it could be argued that *I* had that chance. That Jonathan's leaving was *my* second chance. I'd played by the rules during my marriage and where did it get me? Left with a mountain of bills, the kids—whom I adored, but let's get real here; four kids are a lot of work day in and day out and it only got worse as they got older. I'd done what was expected of me. I buckled down and wrote more books per year. I locked myself away from dating until the loneliness got the better of me. I even used a pen name so what I wrote wouldn't impact my daily life.

But now I was ready to step out of that mold. Out of everyone's preconceived ideas and perceptions of how I should be. This was my second chance and I wasn't going to *not* take it.

"You know something, Scott?"

"I know lots of things."

He smiled that smile that could make my knees melt and, yeah, they wanted to. But I straightened them. Like Scott, I was going to learn to walk this walk.

I cupped his cheek, loving the rasp of his stubble—on my palms, on my thighs, on my breasts… everywhere. And I wasn't ready to give it up.

"I do have that drive. I do know what I want."

"And?"

"And?"

He was already slipping the straps from my shoulders.

"I want you."

***

And I had him.

And he had me.

In the most basic, missionary position, in the middle of the bed, without fruit or syrup or gymnastics of any kind, Scott and I came together as two people who wanted each other *beyond* the physical.

And it was amazing.

For all that this weekend had been a fantasy, this time, this instance, it was so much more than sex. I was hesitant to say we made love because I was, after all, an adult and had been around the block a few times. It was going to take a lot more than really great sex and an intense conversation to say I was in love with him, but I wasn't shying away. Which spoke volumes.

He brushed the hair off my face, his weight on my hips and his elbows as he lay on top of me. "So. Was this weekend what you'd hoped?"

"You have to ask me that?"

"I wouldn't have asked if I didn't have to. I don't make empty promises or insincere gestures, Dana. The accident, losing my dad… I learned then what's important in life and all this serial dating, or using people for a short time… That's not me. Not what I'm about. I told you that I saw you and I wanted you. I didn't mean just for one night. And now that I know you…"

He kissed me and it said more than any words could. More than any words **should** at this point in our relationship, but what it did show me was that Scott was serious. That he was in this to take it somewhere and he wasn't running away.

"I'm so very glad you IM'd me," I said on a sigh when he took a break from kissing me.

"I'm so very glad you answered." He nudged my nose with his. "And I'm really glad you weren't too shy to keep coming back for more."

I shifted under him, flexing my pelvis. "Coming back for more isn't the problem."

"There's a problem?"

"Yeah." I gave him a come-hither from beneath my lashes. "Getting out of bed is a problem."

He laughed and rolled off of me. Damn, not what I'd intended

"Not to fear, my lady. We can get out of the bed, but as long as there's the promise of getting back into it."

"Play your cards right, mister, and you'll have an open invitation."

He kissed the back of my hand. And even that sent shivers down my spine. I was amazed at the physical effect his touch had on me after all the times he'd touched me. But I wasn't about to complain.

"So, much as I hate to say this, check-out time is fast approaching."

"I'm shocked you didn't get us a late check out."

"I did."

"This is late?"

"I know. Obviously no one on the executive team has had a weekend like ours or they'd make check out at midnight. And while I am more than ready to stay another night, you have to get home."

Home.

Back to reality.

One I was somehow going to have to find a way to bring Scott into.

Chapter Twenty-Five

"Hey, Mom."

"Hey. Kate." I stopped abruptly in the middle of the foyer, surprised to be caught by my youngest sneaking into my own home from my decadent weekend. Thank God I'd insisted Scott not walk me to the door—and that I'd left my suitcases by the garage to sneak in when the kids wouldn't see.

Katy cocked her head. "Did you do something to your hair?"

No, but Scott did. I almost said it, but didn't. Much as I wanted to thrust him into my family, my kids were going to need longer than a weekend for this. "No. Just washed it."

She looked at me, her lips skewing sideways. Then she shrugged. "Oh. Well, you look different somehow."

"Good different, or bad different?" *Or well-fucked different?*

Again, kept that little tidbit to myself.

"Oh, good. You always look good."

I did? That was news. Usually I didn't know anything. Especially about the latest fashions, but then, I worked in my yoga pants; how trendy did I have to be on a daily basis?

"Oh, hey. I was wondering…" She nibbled her bottom lip.

Wonder where she got that from.

"Yes?"

"My friend Charli? She's new? She lives with her dad and he's single and pretty hot. For an old guy, I mean."

Oh jeez. Old. And trying to set me up with him?

Before this weekend, I would have bet Katy would have found a conversation like this uncomfortable, but that just proved that I didn't really know how my kids felt about my single status. And now, she was actually talking about me dating someone she knew. As in, having some guy around.

"Thanks, Kate, but, um…"

Jeez, this had sounded so much better in my head.

"What, Mom?" She stared at me then her mouth dropped open. "Oh my God, you're dating someone, aren't you? You found some guy and you can't date Charli's dad because there's some other guy? Who is he? Tell me!" She bounced over to the sofa and hopped into it, crossing her legs lotus style as she landed on the cushion. She patted the cushion next to her. "Tell me."

I sat down. "Who are you and what have you done with my daughter?"

"What are you talking about? I know you've gone on dates. Have I ever given you a hard time about it?"

"No. You've never even spoken to me about it."

"That's 'cause I thought you were embarrassed."

She was looking out for *me*. When had the parental tables turned?

And when had my baby grown up?

I took a deep breath before I responded. One of the things the therapist had said after Jonathan had left was to keep the lines of communication open with the kids. If they gave me an opening, I was to take it.

Hadn't thought this would be one of those openings. "Um, I didn't say anything because I thought you'd think it was too weird. I didn't want to make you uncomfortable."

"Uncomfortable?" She readjusted her legs, tugging them tighter to her hips. God, if I could do that—

Okay, inappropriate thought. But, man, I wouldn't mind being that flexible—something that'd never even crossed my mind before.

Scott had a lot to answer for, and if Katy hadn't initiated this conversation, I might just think he'd put her up to it. Then again, he wouldn't do something like that. Scott had been open and honest from the first moment he IM'd me. He'd wanted me and let me know it.

And now he had me.

"… I'm glad you're going out," Katy was saying. "I've felt bad for you that you're stuck at home while we're all out having a good time. That's why I came back early today. I didn't want you to be here all alone."

If she only knew…

"So tell me about this guy. What's he like? Where'd you meet him? What's he do?"

"He's younger than I am." Great. Brilliant. I was supposed to build Scott up in my kids' minds so the age thing wasn't a factor and what do I do? Blurt out the biggest negative there is between us.

"So? So's Charli's dad. I don't have a problem with it, do you?"

"He's fifteen years younger."

I winced, waiting for her reaction.

"Go, you! Nice!" She knuckle-bumped me. "So when do we get to meet him?"

My head was spinning. I had *not* anticipated this reaction. "Just like that? You're okay with this?"

"Oh, Mom," she said in that *my parent is such a dork* mode teenagers mastered like nobody else. "Who cares about age? As long as you're happy and using protection, I'm happy for you."

"Using protect—" Seriously, the surprises just kept coming.

"Well, yeah. Don't want to be stupid. Isn't that what you're always telling us?"

Yeah, but it was one thing for a mom to remind her kids to use condoms; it was a whole other level of inappropriateness for them to return the favor.

And what the hell did my almost-sixteen-year-old daughter know about condoms anyway?

That was a thought for another day. I could only take so many surprises at once and I'd reached my limit.

"So tell me about him."

Or maybe I hadn't. Never would I have expected to be having *this* conversation with my daughter.

Well you wanted the chance to talk to the kids. Here you go.

I took a deep breath then gave her the bare bones. The very bare bones. We'd met online, we'd been to dinner, he'd never been married and we were going forward to see where this took us. And he wanted to meet them if they were amenable.

"Sure. Invite him to dinner. You should cook. You're a good cook. They say the way to a man's heart is through his stomach. You should work with that."

She was giving *me* dating pointers. Seriously, since meeting Scott my life had been tossed around as if I were Dorothy in that tornado. I was starting to think I should look for some munchkins and a rainbow.

"Well, I'm happy for you, Mom. Now we won't have to feel guilty when we go out with our friends." Katy unfurled her long legs. "Speaking of which… Is it okay if Carrie comes over tonight? We took a bunch of pics and want to edit them for a video of the weekend."

"Sure, honey. That's fine."

She gave me a quick peck on the cheek and a quick squeeze on my arm before walking away while I sat there, dumbfounded.

Everything I'd been worried about… for nothing.

The hell with what the rest of the world thought; if my kids were okay with it, I was okay with it.

The kids were all about telling me about their weekend, a fact for which I was glad. With them growing up, they didn't need me as much as they used to. Didn't want to be around me as much as they had when they were younger. I got that, but still, it made me treasure these times together.

Even if it meant that I couldn't talk to Scott.

"Guess what, guys." Katy flounced onto the sofa again with her usual lotus-cross.

"What runt?"

"Don't call me runt." She tossed a pillow at Luke.

"Why not? You are."

"Go stick it in your—"

"That's enough." I tossed my own pillow into the ring. Hey, if the kids could, why not me?

It did get them all to shut up and stare at me.

"Stop calling your sister names."

"Aw, Mom—"

"Do you want to hear what I have to say or not?" Katy now crossed her arms. Give her a harem outfit and she could be a genie.

On second thought, I shouldn't be thinking about giving my teenage daughter a harem outfit.

Me on the other hand...

Hmmm. Scott and I hadn't had much time to role-play. Maybe that'd be another weekend. If he was into that sort of thing.

I got a flash of myself in that costume. Who was I kidding? The guy would do whatever I was willing to.

I shivered at the thought—which was completely inappropriate considering my daughter had the floor. "Go ahead, Katy."

"Thanks, Mom." She sat up a little straighter, a Cheshire grin on her face. "So… Mom's got a boy-toy."

"Katy!" Oh my God. That's what I got for sharing Scott's age with her. Damn it.

"Way to go, Mom." Matt gave me a high-five sign from across the room.

"You cougar!" Luke actually punched me on the bicep. Damn kid didn't know his own strength.

"Who is he?' Finally, a voice of reason. Unfortunately, it came from my twenty-one-year-old son who was closer in age to Scott than I was.

I gave them the watered-down version of who Scott was and how we met and I had to say, I was pleasantly surprised at how open they all were to the idea of me dating. And the age thing didn't freak them out at all. In fact, I got the impression it was something of a badge of honor for them.

Man, if I'd have known that, I wouldn't have had to have that big discussion with Scott.

Which I told him later that night as we were Facetiming once more.

"See? I told you that you were the one with the issue."

"How was I supposed to know my kids would be okay with this?"

"So that's one hurdle down. Now on to your friends."

I smiled as I remembered the thumbs-up Sheila had given me when I'd driven home today. Word had spread fast.

"I don't think that's going to be a problem."

"Good. Because I have something I want to ask you."

For a second, my heart stuttered. Something he wanted to ask me… he didn't mean… He wasn't going to—Not on the phone…

"What?"

"Are you wearing those satin tied panties ?"

The look in his eyes… The heat in my cheeks—both sets and all parts in between—got me to smile.

And wet. All of it got me wet.

Because, yeah, I did have the panties on.

I shifted the iPad so he had a full view—of me in just the panties.

"You read my mind," he said.

"Not really hard to do. I knew you'd be thinking about them since they're what started this between us."

"But wait a minute." Scott moved around on the bed and I got a nice shot of his ass as he got off of it and walked over to the dresser in his bedroom.

He crawled back onto the bed, hiding the money shot, but that was okay since I knew what that looked like. Intimately.

He held up a scrap of red satin fabric. "How do you have those on when I have them here?"

I tilted the iPad back to my face.

Then I tugged my lower lip between my teeth. Just to hear him groan.

Which he did.

"You didn't think I bought just one pair, now, did you, Scott?"

"Jesus, baby." He dropped his head onto his forearm then looked up at me with that hungry look in his eye. "I think we need another weekend."

I ran my finger on the screen, imagining I could feel his skin under my fingers, that rasp of his stubble that would feel so good between my thighs. "No we don't, Scott."

"Aw, man, Dana. You're killing me. I need more than one night with you. I mean, I know we said we'd date and all, but damn, woman, I can't do to you what I want if we're out to dinner or in a movie theater."

"Oh really? I seem to remember some very clever and imaginative footwork at Le Circlet. I'm sure you can think of something."

"Yeah, I guess." He exhaled. "But I want to get naked with you. All the way. Not some fumbling under our clothes in public. Honest-to-God, skin-to-skin, naked with you and that's just not possible on a date night."

"Then I think we ought to make it an entire week."

The look on his face was priceless.

As was our relationship.

I couldn't wait for that week to start.

ABOUT RAVEN MORRIS

Raven Morris writes spicy romance novellas as a break from her writing contemporary RomComs as Judi Fennell. She has several series under both names, so you're sure to find something to tickle your fancy. (Hmmm, might have to put some tickling in one of Raven's books…)

Check out her books at:

www.JudiFennell.com

Other Books by Raven Morris

TIED WITH A BOW series

Aren't birthdays fun? Especially when there are
presents involved.
And what presents they are...
See if you've ever gotten a present as, um, exciting as
these women get.
After all, the best gifts are always tied with a bow...

JACKED
JACKED AGAIN
MAXED
ROCKED
MARKED
DICKED
TYED

*Available individually or in 2 anthologies

Other Books by Judi Fennell

Beefcake, Inc.

Girls' Night Out never tasted so good! Magic Mike has nothing on these guys. Sit back, relax, and enjoy the show as Gage, Bryan, Tanner, Dare and all the guys show you how it's done...

Manley Maids

What happens when three sexy brothers and their friends lose a poker bet to their sister who owns a cleaning service? It's the Manley Maids at your service! Satisfaction guaranteed...

Bottled Magic

Careful what you wish for... it just might come true! As these humans come to find out when a magical genie ends up their laps... literally before they're whisked off to the most magical adventure of all... falling in love.

Royally Sunk

Mermen and mermaids are just mythology, right?
Try telling that to the unsuspecting humans who fall head-over-heels for those who don't always have heels...

Once-Upon-A-Romance

Once Upon A Time sounds good in a fairy tale, but real life isn't like that. Or... is it? With the help of a guardian-angel-in-training, these lucky couples will find that falling in love is the greatest tale of all!